thN Lng folk 2go

thN Lng folk 2go

Investigating Future Premoderns™

The Confraternity of Neoflagellants

punctum books ✳ brooklyn, ny

thN Lng folk 2go: Investigating Future Premoderns™
© The Confraternity of Neoflagellants [Norman Hogg and Neil Mulholland], 2013.

First published in 2013 by
punctum books
Brooklyn, New York
http://punctumbooks.com

punctum books is an independent, open-access publisher dedicated to radically creative modes of intellectual inquiry and writing across a whimsical para-humanities assemblage. We solicit and pimp quixotic, sagely mad engagements with textual thought-bodies. We provide shelters for intellectual vaga-bonds.

ISBN-13: 978-0615890258
ISBN-10: 0615890253

All images on cover and inside of book by The Confraternity of Neoflagellants (2013), except for image on p. 125, by Fergus Moore (2013).

This book is supported by the Carnegie Trust for the Universities of Scotland.

TABLE OF CONTENTS

The Seven Courts of the Mall
(or, We Have Always Been Medieval)

Simon O'Sullivan

PREAMBLE

The Brothers had asked me for a preface (as if there is really
anything left of the faciality-machine in our contemporary
scene!) and I am happy to oblige . . . me, whom they did
formerly cast out on the basis of misuse (oh, the irony) of
Confraternity Technology, i.e. phee-loss-so-phee, and, in
general, speculative thinking (and, in turn, the positing of a
diagrammatics for the production of new selves at odds to
their own strictures). A Free School did I set up, away from
the aforementioned Confraternity, nay Church, for it is my
belief that the technologies in question—including the grasping of
our own age as neomedieval (in both its geopolitical and ethico-aesthetic character) has much to offer those who refuse
the Church (however this be articulated) and its scriptures.
Be that as it may. What could I do? Perhaps the invite were
also a sign of sorts that my long days of exile are at an end
and that once more I will be embraced by the joys of collab-

orative Neoflagellant writing and art-werke. Avalon once more! Certainly it has been testing to ruminate alone on questions of art, the subject and ontology in a time of Capital that is so late that it loops around—like Ouroboros— to its own beginning, nay, pre-beginning. This fact being, in fact, not tangential to the matters here under dispute.

So, how to understand the following thesis that masquerades as print-on-demand, para-academic and post-USB art? If this tome is a space-time-capsule, then what are the operating protocols hidden within its arcane coding? It seems to me that there are seven logics—or, more specifically, courts—that might operate as guidance system for any reader.

1. FICTIONING

What follows is a schizo-comic fictioning that lays bare the connections between our hyper-modernity and a medievalism that is its appropriate accompaniment and frame of reference (this being precisely, neomedievalism, or, in short, the laying out of a "Medieval-Tech®" as the only adequate frame of reference for these Troubled Times). Old World meets New World in an untimely assemblage (or, "Mall") in which, in fact, all temporalities—futures, pasts, future-pasts, past-futures—are deployed, mashed up and then realigned so as to open, at last, a space for something different (this most cramped court allows us, at last, to breathe!).

2. ACCELERATION

In this speculative venture avatars and scenarios proliferate and spin out as redundant probe-heads from the central processing machine that is Capital. Indeed, such a book as this accelerates the process. Here one finds characters composed of advertising refrains and slogans, cruising the mediascape, guided by a telematic standardization that manifests itself in brands and slogans, fast-food outlets and jousting tournaments. This book speaks of consumers and commodities that move at a pace which outruns the regulative speeds of the market, but that also move slower. Is this the future of Capital? If it is, then it is also its past. A court *sub specie aeterni*.

3. GEOPOLITICS

Contained within these pages is a further treatise—and prophesy—on a "new" geo-political order that harks back to a pre-modern landscape. Apparently contemporary global relations (and their attendant intra/supra-national citizenships) become evidence for a neomedievalism that has run underneath—and against—the stories of the achievements and advancements of our so-called Western civilization. For, let it be known: We Have Always Been Medieval. This book lays bare these often-conflicting logics—the causes beneath the surface effects of what we witness in our age as chaos and confusion. The medieval grid is revealed! Modernity? A ruse, a veil . . . an attempt at spinning an alternate narrative pitched against what has always been a Dark Age.

4. THE SPECTACLE

A meta-comment on this commentary: what follows is an account of the "Spek-taa-kal" in its most advanced phase . . . so advanced that it starts to mutate, producing experimental and only half-operational assemblages. In this grey zone, agents and counter-agents slip and slide, double one another in a game of "this-and-that", waiting for the dust to settle so that they (and we) can see, finally, "who-is-who". Indeed, who is this book written for? Certainly for those few intent on producing a New World Order out of the ruins of this one, but also for those even fewer intent on bringing all such New World Orders down! In particular, an online hyperstitional economics becomes the stage set on which a number of strange currencies and transactions are played out: a groundless-ground of a virtual gaming terrain. Forsooth, all becomes increasingly psychotic as the book in your hand involves the Symbolik (including the Economik) bending back on itself and generating new combinations. Has the sinthome ever meant anything else?

5. SCENES

Herein is the telling of the tail of the contemporary scene of art—from a future-past perspective that is at once learned and partisan. In this account art scenes operate as, and across, fiefdoms in a world in which vassals, overlords, and the omnipresent mercenary (all had already recognized this figure!) determine the relational aesthetics of practice. At certain key junctures alchemical workshops and laboratories attempt something transformative (this book is nothing less than this). This account is a looking for signs and sigils within the present: of the past; of the future (all around us, patchwork like); and of pasts that are yet to come about. In other, more strictly speaking, mathematical terms: a looking for the Universal in the local and the local in the Universal. This is then a specialist meditation and manifesto on a certain kind of neomedieval 'contemporary art' when the latter is understood as post-post-internet, or, indeed, specifically pre-internet, and when the socalled "world-wide-web" is itself the violent and bloody dream of Modernity (Q.E.D.).

6. GIFTS

In this adventure and survey numerous allies are ushered in to play their part: Gilles Deleuze, Georges Bataille, a host of other players . . . all, it is shown, having a neomedieval aspect to their thought (the "general economy" of the sun; a "rhizosphere" of man/animal/plant relations). Within this dense web of references, gifting and relic-ing become the signifiers for an alternate cartography of a capitalism that has outrun the uses of its previous protocols (shedding these as a viper sheds its many skins . . . SSSSSS). At last! A market set free! Here entrepreneurs as storytellers are the nodal points of far-fetched conspiracy theories. Is this something anti-capitalist then? Only if anti- is read as a platform for the launching of that which it appears to be against.

7. THINGS

Finally, clarity emerges from obscurity, a clear zone is drawn: this is a Magikal and ritualistic account of the possibility of a different kind of subject. A statement of the self-as-thing— and the associated practices of such a production. At last, the rival Confraternity of SpeculativeRealism® has its missing subject! Here, the human-object/thing sits still-as-stone, disconnected from one regime in order to connect to another. As such, this book is a contribution to Thing Theory, but of a very queer and wonky kind. An object-oriented ontology© on amphetamines and psilocybin. This conjured figure is not a simple return to a pre-modern assemblage composed of animist object-subjects and a close infinite-finite weave, but nor is it the imposition of a transcendent enunciator that reduces and standardizes the aforementioned heterogeneity (under the single eye of a single £, and a curtain drawn against the infinite). Indeed, it is a return to pre-modernity, but one that is indelibly marked—branded—by its passage through an increasingly moribund modernity. Good news! There is a third way! Neomedievalism as the autopoietic nuclei (the strange attractor, the partial object, the Z-point) around which something else might, finally, begin to constellate and cohere . . . .

How to Rede this Boke

Iz thri riwles:

Die earste riwle speketh ov *journie*—iz al outward, ant riwles de body. Schulen ov swucche thinges az flk bear thmselvs outward; eat, drunch ant werke.

Dis riwle speketh ov *anchorit*. Schulen ov ascetic.

Die thridde riwle speketh ov *host*. Schulen ov embody ant transfigure.

thN lng flk 2go iz an boke in fif bokes:

1. L'AMÉRIQUE SOUTERRAINE

Dis earste dale speketh *iter pro peregrinis ad* metro. Dis boc iz todealet in fif leasse bokes ov journie-men Gambini's *2 doze hu Lng 2 g0*. Iz earste riwle ant ov swucche thinges az duble homo-feaste, drunch ant werke, ant iz ov othre (*dug-heids*) ant quazi-thinges.

2. IMPERIUM ET SACERDOTIUM

Dis other dale speketh ov nuncii ant procuratores, ov assemblies ant *crusades*.

3. THE JOURNEYMAN'S GUIDE TO ANCHORITISM

Dis thridde dale iz'ov *translatione corporis*. Dis dale iz ov customz, liturgica, blak noiz, ant *self-discipline* ov d post-homo man-thinge. Dis boc iz todealet in thri leasse bokes ov ancre's wittes.

4. xyzzy: CONTEMPORARY ART BEFORE AND AFTER BRITAIN

Dis feorthe dale iz'ov beatific ant ov swucche thinges az doth *come from the eye's arrows. Ad te levavi*.

5. WHEN TRANSFIGURATION BECAME COMMONPLACE

Dis fifte dale speketh ov host. Dis dale is al of the thridde riwle, wen *translatione* bcAM hyper-economicus.

The Confraternity of Neoflagellants
Montréal, Québec et Édinbourg, Écosse

The Confraternity of Neoflagellants was founded in 2009 by Serjeant-At-Law Norman Hogg and joined by Keeper of the Wardrobe Neil Mulholland. It is a secular and equal opportunities confraternity bound by chirograph.

∽

Chapter 1

L'Amérique Souterraine

Antonio Gambini

The crucial importance of the five sagas in securing our sovereignty, our outrageous wealth, our sense of moral superiority, exceptionalism and entitlement absolutely cannot be disputed. The recent work of Université du Monde du Sport scholar, honorary member of the Cascades Historical Society and foreigner Professor Mike McManus, suggests that there may be more to the glorious story of L'Amérique Souterraine than the sagas imply. It's now almost certain that L'Amérique Souterraine's prime no longer exists on flash memory and so will never been seen for what it was. However, from a combination of fashionable hermeneutic readings of the sagas, nationalist revisionism and newly declassified archeological research on Antonio Gambini's teeth, Professor McManus is starting to develop some fresh aggrandisement regarding our transcontinental labyrinth's miraculous life and times.

> Jack Cade, Editor, Journal of the Cascades
> Historical Society

Prologue

We think, from the Matter of Trudeau, that the lieutenancy of L'Amérique Souterraine began in the Kingdoms of RÉSO, stretching from the Shanghai Tunnels, a damp network of *maison des compagnons* in Westside with fast and frequent dragonship links to China, to the sacred commercial halls on the St. Lawrence. A densely populated subterranean frontier of Francophones, heathens and artisans, the Kingdoms of RÉSO did not organise itself according to the corrupt conventions of the terrestrial world. It was a series of autonomous manufacturing nodes and passageways that did not respect state, provincial, or even national borders. Kingdoms comprised smaller chapters known as *galeries*. Most activities in the Kingdoms of RÉSO were organised by the *maison des compagnons* of the *galeries*. The houses were advised by the Compagnon du L'Amérique Souterraine, the master artisans of Les Cours Mont-Royal, home of the awe-inspiring chandelier of the Monte Carlo Casino and RÉSO's most exclusive boutiques. RÉSO's Grandmasters had achieved Outremont by embarking upon la tour across every centimeter of the tunnels and *galeries* of continental L'Amérique Souterraine, a 4,500 km journey to the West. On the way, they worked with the great master artisans of the Kingdoms of RÉSO, acquiring skills and smurfberries. Having attained enlightenment, they finally rested as Sedantaire bestowing their wisdom from Les Cours Mont-Royal's Spa Diva, RÉSO's largest and most luxurious spa, providing them with finest treatments and bespoke services designed, ultimately, to make them feel better than they had felt in a long time.

As any playgroup student will tell you, Bob Sacamano's anchorhold lay just beneath the former Red Light vintage store, directly opposite the historical site of the Waffle Window. In Sacamano's days, the National Waffle Window & Vintage Store Memorial Museum was an infotainment experience and gift shop that doubled as the waiting lobby of Westside's monorail station. Thankfully, the old monorail is long gone, replaced by a popular monorail heritage centre situated just over a fathom away. What remains of the National Waffle Window & Vintage Store Memorial Museum today is evident today only in a small polycarbon 3D print of a waffle embedded in the lobby of the SE Powells *galerie*. This marks the historical location of Sacamano's anchorhold, and of L'Amérique Souterraine's no.1 site of pilgrimage.

For his billions of followers around his great nation, Gambini's quest to honour The Sacamano is one of sacrifice and fortitude, good negotiating skills, pain and gain. The Sacamano, in his anchorhold, was kept up most nights by the bibble-babble of local spods on Cat Chat and the pitter-patter of bare feet falling from SE Hawthorne's young hippies. Some nights he'd lie on a plank of the knarr and tuck into the Liège, Blueberry Tillamook and Kvikk waffle scraps, biscuits and gravy and Peppermint Lattes that dropped down the cracks in the walls under the gift shop trashcans. He would while away the midnight hours engrossed by his ancestors, the heroic old terranean diaspora, concocting vivid legends valourising the brave diggers who had perished in establishing the arrondissement's early Shanghai Tunnels. Gambini has left us a rich literature of the Westside underground filled with ghost stories, volunteer archaeology, steampunkery and forced conscription into the merchant navy, all obscured by the unrelenting karaoke emanating from Hobo's Restaurant upstairs. Gambini's "this is my story and I don't care if you believe me or not attitude" has certainly helped to secure the credibility of his scripture. Those legends, the five sagas, have formed the basis of L'Amérique Souterraine's identity, but to what extent are they reliable witnesses of life lived in early RÉSO?

By the time Sacamano entombed himself in his anchorhold, Gambini's persistent yet vain attempts to publish counterfactual podcasts in the PDX Guide had already attracted the attention of the local cops. Then, one Sunday, Gambini's unfounded recensions were overheard by a hungover journalist from Willamette Week who had been enjoying Fried Chicken and Waffles while awaiting the monorail. Week 16 was a no news week. The rest is history. Or is it? By day, Gambini lived his real life as a respected journeyman, a pillar of the local community, denizen of local physical theatre directors, homeopaths, bookbinders, canvas workers and vintage curators. By evening, he would shape-shift, moonlighting as a mercenary for Westside's sworn terranean enemies using the hyper-nationalistic belligerence of his pod-casts as cover. All the evidence to be discovered suggests that Gambini was a double agent.

In Gambini's prime, L'Amérique Souterraine boasted but a 400-year history, the political union of the Kingdoms of RÉSO had been achieved for more than 300 years. And yet, it was unthinkable that our glorious nation could have im-bued anything other than the most unshakable loyalty and passion in its subjects. The five sagas concur that Gambini adored the Westside arrondissement with every last drop of his blood. More recent dental evidence nevertheless sug-gests, controversially, that Gambini had, in fact, spent most of his professional life outsourcing his services to contending overlords in the PATH Confederacy that lay beneath the icy streets of downtown Toronto. PATH followed the allemande traditions of Wandergesellen, a network of tunnels exclusive-ly designed to facilitate the Wanderjahre of MBA students. In contrast, "La Tour", facilitated by the Kingdoms of RÉSO, could take both ecclesiastical and commercial forms, the merchant and the compagnon itinérant rubbing shoulders with the pilgrim.

Any proud patriot knows of the jingoistic skirmishes with Anglo settlers under the Coach Terminal at Dundas and Bay, the guerrilla napalm attack on the paper and card recycling bin close to the Ryerson School of Business[1], the top un-screwed from a salt-cellar in The Merry Kettle Tea Shoppe, the 'dog donut' left in the counter of Tim Horton's—all blamed on one or more of RÉSO's chief infotainment com-petitors within the PATH Confederacy. Gambini's molars suggest that these infamous acts of terror, while legendary, were infrequent and ineffective. RÉSO, PATH and the terra-nean states and provinces held a steady military truce, pre-ferring to fight it out symbolically in the wrestling ring rather than on the killing fields of the continent's paintball grounds.

---

[1] In retaliation, a PATH pensioner was tarred by an angry mob in Les Promenades Cathedral.

Gambini's pivotal role in these neomedieval power games is only now coming to light.

Following the saga podcasts, it is commonly thought that, by Gambini's prime, the competing *galeries* of RÉSO and PATH had little in common and were increasingly set on their own courses. Wrestling, of course, remained one of the few things that bound them; it was the foundation not only of their culture, but of their legal and infotainment systems. RÉSO Law, for example, was based on the two-thousand-year-old judiciary established by the pan-European Monde du Sport empire. Following the fall of the Monde du Sport, trials continued to be conducted in public rings over three-minute rounds (the number of rounds varied from trial to trial). Of course there were important differences nevertheless. RÉSO's lawyers usually won a case based on two out of three falls instead of the sudden death single fall favoured in PATH. RÉSO's Sheriffs had greater authority too as they could issue "public warnings"—a third public warning meant disqualification and exile from RÉSO followed by tough infotainment sanctions such as de-authorising viewing cards. Such differences were worth fighting for.

"By the prime [of Gambini]", the Matter of Trudeau argues, "increasing incidents of inter-ethnic violence and local relic manufacture were compromised by social denationalisation, the erosion of sovereign loyalties and their replacement by conflicting and overlapping authority aided by a transnational wrestling-based ethics". This was a bout-based system that could be manipulated by ambitious journeymen such as Gambini.

As evidence that plurilateral defection was commonplace in the prime, I draw your attention to the double meaning of the motto emblazoned on official RÉSO national t-shirts, fridge magnets and key rings—*"Durable Disorder"*—and to Gambini's own motto, *Astutia non Animo* ('By craft not by courage'). I speculate that Gambini's nocturnal calling was to perpetuate RÉSO's "new security dilemma", to ensure that the nation was bound together by being on a constant high alert status.

According to the sagas, the DEFCON 2 footing that stood against PATH in Gambini's prime was partly thanks to some inspired sectarian chanting at the back of the monorail terminal in the Westside's Greenhorn Dock. This led to the arrest and trial of Muller Ltd., a visiting dignitary from PATH, for the crime of "discriminatory singing". Ltd.'s attempts to flee the scene of his barking led to his near lynching. To save his skin, the sheriff moved quickly to ensure Muller Ltd. of his third public warning and swift repatriation to the PATH Confederacy. The enumerators of the Gambinian Prime Census show that Gambini might have been in the Shanghai Tunnel underneath Turk's House for Sailors Tourist Information Centre on a team-building exercise around then.

Could he have visited the monorail terminus during his lunch break? He certainly would have had ample time to grab a voodoo doughnut and incite religious hatred. He would have been rewarded handsomely by RÉSO's Sedantaire and the Chief Risk Officer of PATH for his clandestine involvement in a plot aimed at making Muller Ltd. a folk devil and national hero respectively. But, the question remains, would Gambini have attempted such a heroic heist during daylight? Of course he would.

Prof Mike McManus (Université du Monde du Sport, EU) delivered this year's annual Gambinitacht Podcast "Plurilaterialism and the Gambiniian Recensions" from the booth in the window of the coffee shop of The Merry Kettle Atrocity Relic and International Monorail Heritage Centre, PATH.

PODCAST I — DANS LES COURS MONT-ROYAL

At around 7:00am,[2] I squatted atop the colossal chandelier, larger by far than the world's largest, in the grand forecourt of Les Cours Mont-Royal.[3] Gazing through the twinkling prisms of the world's largest gross leasable space, I observed two Customer Service Attendants locking the facilitator washrooms and heading towards the world's fastest and longest escalators. Months of careful observation of this unparalleled vista through the world's most avant-garde, highest powered, telescopes told me they were heading down to the Foire Alimentaire on level one for breakfast at Tikki Mings in Les Promenades Cathedrale.[4] Enjoying the experience of taking a closer look at the sweeping terrace below, I knew they would need some time to make their choice from over 1,430 food and beverage options. At night, the mood

[2] Gambini: Hi.

[3] Muller Ltd.: Hey. This is our commentary.

[4] Gambini: It's specifically developed for those of you who wanted to be able to read the commentary in your head at the same time as reading it out loud. Since it's not perfectly synchronised, we're going to start and we'll sometimes describe what's, um, happening as it's goin' on, but if it's a little bit out of sync, that's kinda okay.

shifts. I'd had plenty of time to complete my preparations for the long journey ahead.

Organising my transport in a timely and professional manner had been a major consideration.[5] If you are traveling to the mall there is no direct bus. There is a roundabout not far from this retail experience. At the north side of the roundabout, there is a bus stop. This was designed, at great expense, to allow passengers to pass close to the mall's fully retractable roof without having the hassle of getting off the bus. If you bus through early enough, you get a swell view of the latest store displays and over 31,400 price markdowns and merchandise transfers. Laid end to end, these would extend over 63 times around the world. You could board if the bus stopped there. Well, it does stop, but not for passengers. The stop just means that you have to pay the fare again. So, if you are traveling to the mall, there is no direct bus. That's why I came in by metro.

As the guttural joual of the Customer Service Attendants faded, I dropped my Willard satchel to the floor, leapt across the foyer and clung to a pillar outside Spa Diva.[6] I paused for a moment to adjust my grip, control my breathing and take another bite of the Bacon Maple Doughnut that I'd invested in earlier that morning. High in sugar and carbohydrates and low in protein, it sure was super! I could feel the sugar rush as I shimmied down, rolled across the marbled floor collecting my Willard satchel, and completed the movement by executing a controlled fall over the east balustrade. As I landed with a quiet splash in level three's Fountain Court—the hub of my mission here—a shard of crispy bacon jostled itself loose from the raised yeast and maple frosting and melted delicately on my tongue. As I turned, licking my

---

[5] Muller Ltd.: Nope, in fact we only decided to work with each other pretty late in the day, mainly since we worked together on our previous commentary—so it's a co-write. It's coming out a critical juncture in history, so it was important to get the right people involved.

[6] Gambini: Yeah. It's as if you're walking in our shoes, through the world as we see it.

teeth, I came face to face with the most striking symbol of modernity.[7]

Shivering slightly, I waded through the bamboo-lined lagoon and plunged my head inside the murky lamprey tanks at the foot of the stepped waterfall that lay between the Discovery Center and the University of the Mall of America. It was a replica of waterfall I saw in a photo on the Internet while visiting the Niagara-On-The-Lake Outlet Village; nice view. The most picturesque scene I have yet come across this side of Nova Scotia, ideal for model railroad set or wargaming terrain. It seemed to have that kind of commitment to providing a diverse environment that turns static items into dynamic ones.[8] A signature spa, it made me realise, you really can use just about any kinds of rocks you want, including large rocks, round stones, river rocks and pebbles. I thought of it as sandbox that continues to define waterfall experience, flowing with a wonderful and seamless effect. And the rocks? Have fun smashing! Well, how was I to know that was illegal in some *galeries*?

Under the cover of parties of schoolchildren up from the provinces to view the *galerie*'s revolutionary monuments I was able to make my way through the lagoon unnoticed. Guddling on all fours through the invigorating waters, my fingers soon settled upon an object, one that was familiar even through my Otter Ultimate 4/5mm compressed neoprene suit. I gave a firm tug and my one-piece Samsung day-sleeve floated to the surface.[9] I let it scan my retina, pulled it

---

[7] Muller Ltd.: So, we started writing this commentary at, um, the beginning of this year when we were asked to write something. So this bit ended up being a very last minute addition to this commentary, I don't think it was in the version that we first proposed.

[8] Gambini: Yeah. The team will always have ramifications, which we, of course, know is inevitable.

[9] Muller Ltd.: We wanted to be clear about who was facilitating and who was actually writing. I asked my ghost-writer and former assistant to play me since I wanted to actually appear as myself in the

over my head, and within seconds I stood fully clothed as a respectable Québecker power buyer. Before leaving the water, I scooped some coins from the fountain bed and used the end of my Hermès tie to dry them off. Three loonies, a toonie, a few slime encrusted US quarters and an unvalidated parking token. I threw a quarter back for luck. Hey, I guess I was the kinda guy who makes random objects return in a variety of new scenarios.

I sat down on a bench amongst the indigenous faux birch across from the 3 Monkeys boutique and opened my old satchel. The label momentarily caught my eye: Object size: Height: 0, Length: 0, Breadth: 0. Machine wash only. (C) Willard 2011. Rummaging through I gathered my supply of sacred ampullae and slotted them into the holster inside my jacket. Next, I withdrew a Tim Horton's coffee cup, removed the lid and placed it on the bench beside me to admire it. Horton was a hero of mine, a guy who paired sublimely, a guy with a rewarding career and an engaging manner who always supported the goals of the team, a guy struggling to survive in an age of robotic demons. Horton's was one of the world's most extraordinary experiences. Double-double Vanille Francais and nothing else matters but you.

Checking quickly that the retail staff of the Simply Botox beauty bar were yet to arrive, I fished out the cool-bag containing the ceremonial merkin of Kateri Tekakwitha (Lily of the Mohawks) and extracted a few hairs. These I placed in Horton's cup—I could later brew up a powerful energy drink from this second-class relic—and replaced the lid. The remaining items I placed in various pockets about my suit included a fine tooth electric comb and a Brandeum pendant cellphone pre-programmed by CIA artisans with bespoke weaponry, gastronomic apps and holographic cartogram generators. You can relieve some of your stress by punching the hell out of some cars and your enemies.

---

commentary rather than as just a character. And he was gracious enough to agree. I think I got it just about right.

Finally, I leaned back through the foliage behind me and extracted a small black monogrammed attaché case from the misty waters. I waited till the remaining water droplets evaporated from its touch sensitive surface before scrunching it into a ball and placing it inside my Willard satchel. I then rose and strode toward the locked entrance beside the washrooms that the Customer Service Attendants had left only minutes ago. Bypassing the washrooms—for I felt no need to further acquaint myself of their unique tailoring to withstand multiple activities in a safe environment[10]—I proceeded up the adjacent stairwell. I swiped the code into the keypad and entered into the beating heart of the premier lifestyle and entertainment destination: *galerie* Carrefour Industrielle Alliance.

---

[10] Muller Ltd.: "Be sure to be involved, and take this information back to your local communities. This has to get out". I remember that one in particular. I think it's valid. Yeah?

PODCAST II — THE CENTRE OF MOTION, TIME, AND PEOPLE

One of the oldest *galeries*, Carrefour Industrielle Alliance, mainly focused on the manufacture and trade of cellphone accessories and horse-class Brandeum pendants. It was home to the telecompagnons and its Compagnon siège. True to its motto, "The Centre of Motion, Time and People", CIA was hosting a large dinner in preparation for the tele-compagnons adoption ceremony the following day. Jour-neymen feasted on potatoes sautéed with marjoram, shallot, and ham fat, and bathed in a drop of mountain olive oil from the Cailletier of Sospel (Nice A.O.C.) combined with Barolo and Xérès vinegars.[11] Master telecompagnons enjoyed a traditional tomato stew with red and yellow peppers, seasoned with Espelette pimento and mixed with Niçois sausage. Three thick slices of poached stockfish were placed on the top.[12] This dish was very smooth and creamy, served with crispy lettuce, coated with lemon-flavored cream and well-seasoned with pepper.

Taking in the aromatic air, I strolled past the siège's bustling Avant-Garde Meetings and Events facility towards the street-view gallery in that looked out from CIA's underground food court into the 13 auditorium IMAX Cinéma Banque Scotia above. I imagined cooling myself with the food court's wide choice of frappes and quick-served, freshly-squeezed juices, smoothies and frozen yogurts, as I gazed into the narrow two-story breezeway where homeless terrestrials huddled cinematically around the steel ventilation grilles in winter, a unique blend of traditional and modern vagrancy just minutes away from where warmth and style meets sophistication. There, pacing out a quadrangled pilgrimage through the steam rising from the authentic homemade crepes, delicious waffles and reasonably priced pancakes bathing under reheat lamps below, was my principle contact and mentor Muller Ltd., an immigrant from PATH.

---

[11] Gambini: Kinda reminds me of the geeky one from Scooby Doo. Yeah, but I can see already that there's a tendency to draw out the strengths of the last commentary rather than get on with this one. This is starting to develop all the hallmarks of a clunky bit of prose—the introduction of the second character's health problems is always something that I'd wanted to happen earlier on.

[12] Muller Ltd.: Stockfish was the name of the cod or haddock caught and dried on the Lofoten Islands in Norway. The Perugina was a round peppery sausage that came from the area around Perugia in Umbria; many people in Nice originated from this town. The cod was caught with a rod, the old-fashioned way, by fishermen from the Faeroe Islands. Mmmmmmmmmmmmm.

Red-faced, his great doghead sweating vigorously, Muller Ltd. emerged from the fog and pressed a bloody sheet of butcher paper up onto the reinforced glass that separated him from RÉSO's fresh fruit salads. He leaned in pressing his black wet nose close against the window, licking the glass, his long snout mouthing out the rich blend of coffee and Devil's Pastries of Café Dépôt: "like a deadly assassin . . . chilli comes creeping into your palate . . . Ah yea. I'd quite happily put my face in it. . . ". "Cor, that is bang on the money", I mouthed back. "Vision, passion and resources? A comprehensive inventory of all tastes?" He nodded his canine head sagely and held up an Android smartphone inside a pastry bag. "Food is a peep-hole on a man", he appeared to say. We'd built and maintained a strong vendor relationship—I wasn't about to let that go! "Let's just simmer down and share a bucket of chicken", I concluded firmly, gesturing as if delving greedily into a boneless box. " . . . nicely seasoned he mouthed", playing air pepper grinder, then confidently slapping an imaginary spatula onto his open palm. He continued in his reverie. "Mmmmmmmmmmmmm, I would quite happily bathe in that . . .I'll have a plate of that!" he exclaimed, eyes bulging.[13] Sighing heavily I retrieved my Brandeum from my pocket. We launched apps and synced.

CIA was famous for the deal-busting berserker boutique of Dollarama. It was run by three tele-masters, crypto-anarchists hell bent on one thing, obtaining unbelievable wealth and power. Fueled by the late 20th-century dream of reviving pre-modern tribalism, their prophets crowd-funded a multiplicity of anger-channeling cerebral sex collectives, re-seeding the human race through rhizomic privation autonomous from the centralizing forces of familial birthing actions. It was surrounded by a massive wall of malicite that reeked tremendously of decaying stem cells and other unpleasant-

---

[13] Gambini: It's sad, this bit here; one of those Tiny Tim moments. We were always going to edit this sentence, but we never did. Now it's really grown on me.

ries. "Now, I'm not going to criticise until I actually stick it in my mouth", growled the ever-adventurous alchenomicor Muller Ltd. I placed lavender incense burners at the four corners of our collapsible Faraday Cage and we began our navigation of Dollarama's obligatory snack maze. A volcano of food emotion, Muller Ltd plunged in snout first. "God you've got some bold flavours Dollarama!"

Immediately inside Dollorama, I scooped up some unbeatable deals (including Beaver-brand Whole Smoked Scallops in Oil, Cadbury Crunchie Twin Fondue Gift Set, Cheezy Pizza Cheeto Puffs and ten Plastic Solar Driveway Stakes), throwing them all in the air to create distraction. Before the Dollar-a-men arrived to investigate, I rolled under the shelving unit to the Shenzhen Dianman Macguffin aisle and dived head first into a colossal box of assorted choking hazards. Then, after rearranging myself so that my head poked free of the surface, I tore open a Cover Girl Mascara set and celebrity death-masked my face in the Hanna Montana stage-melt fashion. To complete the disguise I glued a nine-piece, life-size, KFC Play Meal to various strategic locations about my neoprene suit. After some final adjustments to the plastic bucket, which kept slipping over my eyes, I settled down to wait for my contact to appear.

After a brief spell of napping, I was startled to apprehend, just millimeters before my eyes, a tiny action figure standing with arms akimbo atop a battered carton of John Frieda Root Awakening. At such close proximity I had to close one eye to bring it into focus. It was about four centimeters tall, undersized as action figures go, and garbed in a Canadian Spirit onesie and matching red and grey Lonsdale boxer boots. It sported an ill-proportioned cell phone slung awkwardly over one shoulder like an AK-47. Its head, bald and grey, bore an unflinching expression of utter astonishment. Finding the figure's bug-eyed stare somewhat disconcerting, I pursed my lips and unleashed a mighty gust of European "dental apocalypse" seasoned breath in its direction causing it to swoon backwards off its cardboard plinth and disappear from view. As I moved to correct the collateral damage of an unhinged chicken wing sideburn, the tiny figure clambered back defiantly, wearing the same wondrously gaping expression. Recognition finally dawned.

This was my obviously my mark, an outrider dispatched by the Fraternity of Tiny Ontologists [FTO]. I had yet to meet these onto-tribesmen and had been momentarily taken aback by just how tiny they are in the flesh. The FTO, so legend has it, are the sworn enemy of the deodanthropologists who terrorize the dismal thoroughfares of PATH. In marked opposition to the Dedodanths, the FTO have no time at all for the species narcissism of the "new evolutionists" and express their outright disdain for the human subject by reversing the former's practice of corporeal up-scaling. The exact process by which the FTO achieve such diminutive proportions is a closely guarded secret (the Dedodanths claim DNA manipulation—a "humanist" tech, *ha!*); nevertheless, it is reported that the transformation is rapidly induced, instilling a perpetual state of shock at the abruptly monumental dimensions of the hitherto commonplace (ready to hand). At the moment when the shrinkage completes, the novice's facial expression is frozen in a rigid mask of absolute rapture. Thus reborn, it then embarks upon a lifetime of enchanted speculation on the mysterious Dasein of the nonhuman world. The CIA branch of Dollarama provided a readymade cathedral—a consumer experience packed to the rafters with all delights—and quickly became the pilgrimage site for miniature onto-tribesmen throughout the Kingdoms of RÉSO. And here they remain, locked in combat with the Dollar-a-men, who, blinded by the social logic of exchange, consider the little tribesmen pests, laying traps for them at night.

Although they were not officially recognised by the telecompagnons, the FTO were accomplished makers of "cusps", the graspable media I needed to undertake my first subterranean pilgrimage. The cusps were my grail, the only guarantee of witnessing the lost food court of Avalon and securing an augmented audience with the anchorite Gregg Wallace. Unable to modify his mouth from its transfixed 'O' of wonder, the little man whispered "ooo . . ." and turned his back on me. Before I could protest, he unhinged a panel on the rear of his onesie and discharged a small glowing orb, as tiny as the popping boba of spherified green tea I had earlier enjoyed for breakfast. Side-stepping the pooped orb, he then pointed towards it and made a low sweeping arm gesture of continuance. This completed, he sprinted off. I followed the direction in which he had been pointing and sure enough I could just make out a broken path of popping boba.

The trail of sizzling onto-boba ended in the Cosplay aisle next to a tray of novelty eye augments that had been discounted since Halloween. "Gary Gilmore Contact Lenses", a neon decal loudly announced. Could these be the thrilling cusps I so coveted? The graspable treasure I sought was said to be immensely singular (although, by necessity, a pair) and there were at least thirty identical packets in this box. I rummaged, prodded, sniffed and tasted amongst the vexing multiples until a Dollar-a-man approached with a merchant's uncanny stealth and challenged me. "You finger it, you eat it". Taking this as providence, I walked behind him towards the tillers.

"Wha dey do?" asked the Dollar-a-man. "I'm not sure, I just liked the . . . packaging", I replied. Although I was following immediately behind him, he removed one of *my* lenses from the open packet and fumbled it into his right eye. The discordant effect was immediate and spectacular. I had been forewarned that the cusps must always be used as pair since they allow the wearer to exclusively perceive objects *or* subjects.[14] Applying the lens to just one eye thrust

---

[14] Gambini: I don't mind that really. This bit was always the hardest. One bit like this nearly cost the publisher his house last time. It was tough. He'd been working with all the greats: Eddie Murphy, Pat Buchanan, Phil Collins. At this point he was putting his home on the

the Dollar-a-man into a dialectical confoundment, cleaving his mind by driving a Modernist totem straight through his anterior insular cortex. Clamping his jaw and marching backwards in a stiff-limbed and soldierly fashion, he began to randomly tag things with his price gun.

Tackling him gently but firmly to the floor, I fished the cusp from his bulging eye and stuffed it into my Willard satchel. Presuming he'd come after me, I made an explosive exit through the glass storefront and, starting my leap unnecessarily early, plunged below the turbulent surface of North America's largest indoor fountain.[15] Beneath the water, the Emerald Order Breneau, the Elohei-Elohim Celestrian-hominid Founders Race and the Azurite Universal Templar Security Team were busy reconstructing Québec's 1967 World Fair entirely from Density-5 Chronocrystals mined in the Mechizedek Cloister. From humble beginnings as the Crazy Deal Artefact Institute—whose mandate prescribed artistic, institutional, and activist methods and practices to address the relationship of post-crisis artefacts to their aesthetic, technical, and social contexts—the project had morphed into a full scale reconstruction of late modern technocratic talk show set mounted on a cradled wood panel. Marvelling at the spectacle presented before me, I paused to take a few pictures for the folks back home.

---

market to finance the commentary—the investors he'd been working with weren't very happy!

[15] Muller Ltd.: This was the last bit of the commentary to have the words written. Woof woof!

PODCAST III — THE MODEL OF LOUIS XV

Energized by the crisp citrus of that first wash in the fountain, we came within bluetooth range of Christ Church Cathedral, wherein a 1/24th-scale hologram of Yves St. Lauren was said to perform a synchronised chakra discharge from the base of its spine. Using Crystallized Swarovski elements, this Pepper's Ghost from incredible TV could 24ct. gold-plate your DS Lite, creating a truly unique talisman investment solution.

"Sorry, the item above appears to be one of a kind".[16] Those sweet, sweet words I so longed to read were at last within my grasp. My DS was currently protected only by the promise of paper gold, swathed in gold futures options and spread betting contracts. Soon it would be truly new without tags.

The Diaspora's server-to-server authentication instantaneously signaled our approach to the Customer Service Attendants flanking the entrance of the *galerie*; they greeted us warmly with a devotion:

We believe people are basically good.
We believe everyone has something to contribute.
We believe that an honest, open environment brings out the best in people.
We recognise and respect everyone as an individual.
We encourage you to treat others the way you want to be treated.

My study buddy Muller Ltd. checked in on his Brandeum pendant cell before placing it in the plastic tray. He nodded towards me as he produced a HAPTIME YGH338A USB Cup Warmer, Clock and Hub from his kirtle and rested it directly on the x-ray scanner's conveyor belt—a wise purchase from Dollarama. I also put my Brandeum in the tray, then dug into my Willard satchel to retrieve the 4 port USB hub/clock that I'd picked up at Wirelesswave and, as if by way of thanks, slipped in two agility rings, a gift voucher for Ainsi Soit-Elle, an Oh Henry! bar to help with the grinding and, as casually as possible, the precious cusps. We passed through the full

---

[16] Muller Ltd.: You did this bit, but I think I took it out. The words were changed here; it used to say, "as we know, later in the text we read these exact same words". But now it's in this section that we see many of the motifs, like, being planted, seeding what's to come later. It builds up suspense and promises what we will see later in flashback. We can't take it all as actually what we said; it's filtered through memory.

body scanner.

Les Promenades Cathedrale's constitutional terms and conditions summarily accepted, we espied a great white flag thrusting out, and a glittering travelator projecting forth to meet us. I perceived upon it a very ancient warden of Yves St. Lauren, accompanied by a bulk order of best-buy mages. Extending his hand in welcome, St. Lauren's tiny avatar sported a new three-piece suit from Canadian Taylor. Woven from upcycled feathers and dream catchers it was almost shamanistic for such a respected Goldsmith and sworn enemy of alchemy. Clearly proud of their Keylontic jerkins and tattooed leg sleeves, St. Lauren's mages addressed us silently in a variety of awkwardly frigid poses. Transfixed by the spell of Goldcore State Corporatism, the Les Promendades Cathedrale's Customer Service Attendants stared at us through permanent contact lenses (an inferior class of cusp, I mused indulgently) that emulated the narcissistic personality disorder of Ayn Rand.

I handed one of them my gift voucher for Ainsi Soit-Elle. He scanned the QR code with an upscale 5ième Avenue cellphone before stamping our hands with the Randian quote of the day: "Know, all ye investigators that the head is all things, which if it hath not, all that it imposes profits nothing!"[17] I rubbed at the inky residue, the Fountainhead fabulism almost immediately illegible on my sweaty paw. I glanced at Muller Ltd. for analysis of this lucid syllogism, but he was too busy grinding monatomic seasoning into his Big Gold Box. He was always busy pawing something from which good might arise. "An amazing experience for contestants", he wibbled. "Amazing!"

The food court of Les Promendades turned out to be an excruciatingly pitiful sight. The majority of outlets were ei-

---

[17] Gambini: I always wanted to change it because I think commentaries are really more about fantasies than facts. Always. I'm always careful not to introduce any spoilers, so I hope, if you're reading this, eh, for the first time that you've actually read it before.

ther boarded up or sequestered by Deodanths as laboratories for their vile, bio-alchemical apotheotic dabblings. The sole remaining outlets—the boulangerie, La premiere Moisson and a Van Houtte coffee house—were serving up limp paper plates of steaming green swill and ladling stagnant water from a tank of decaying North Atlantic crustaceans directly into the eager mouths of verminous journeymen, hopelessly lost and broken by the entrepreneurial conundrum of PATH's economic perversity. Amidst the burnt-out booths, makeshift shelters had been assembled from the flotsam and chaff of exhausted consumables. The wailing of hungry infants and psychotic rants of spurned Grouponites echoed off barren walls where nothing hung but the freeze-dried corpse of a single investment-class mercenary. Taking a step back, something crunched underfoot. Looking down I almost expired—the floor was strewn with the tiny picked-clean skeletons of onto-tribesmen!

I rummaged around my Willard satchel and found the cusps ensconced. The mall was an integrated field, a cumulative memory providing templates for experience. The cusps were its interface, allowing their wearer to experience morphic resonance with the mall's cumulative memory. As I slipped the lenses into my eyes all media lost its inviolability. The cusps networked my sensorium with Les Promendades' resonant memory space. From a drop grew a great flood, overwhelming me with a tsunami of experiences flowing, twittering and chattering through my body.

Crystal chandeliers bathed the court with a brilliant light, so as to be brighter and see more brightly. Amidst high-backed booths of dark walnut and white leather, herb gardens of cypress, Aristotle basil, ocimum basilicum, myrtle, jasmine and pimpinella anisum filled the air with a delicate symphony of gently intoxicating fragrances. From somewhere came a wisp of psychedelic rock—a murmur of recombinant chords, reverbs of fractured melody. In the holding pool of a magnificent central waterfall, a boisterous cohort of master goldsmiths splashed in the scented waters and grasped playfully at passing dancing girls. High caste waiters minced demurely amid the convivial scene balancing silver platters of the finest Patati Patata poutine garnished with frosted lamprey fins individually threaded on crispy-fried lobster antennae. I jumped to my feet in astonishment as a roving automaton resembling Mother Céline Marie Claudette Dion abruptly exploded, showering the air with miniature gift boxes that drifted gently down towards the delighted clientele on fine gossamer parachutes. My experience of Les Promenades had been handed over to me, its collective ambience dislocated to my own perception. I was here. This was truly the Vale of Avalon!

As the Arcadian vista swam back into view, I was greeted by a further phenomenon. A floating path of glowing Tupperware began to manifest itself box by box, eventually leading my eye to an elevated booth set in the far north west of the court. Sitting in that booth, at a table piled high with miraculous viands, the likes of which I had never seen, I recognized the cheerfully stern countenance of the Australian TV chef John Torode. Looking up, he beckoned for me to mount the translucent path. Eagerly I climbed the shimmering bridge. To my yet-further astonishment was lifted gently into the air by some unseen force, propelled forward, feet dangling, and lowered into the leather seat opposite the Master.

Torode ogled me—in that jowly, cock headed, twinkly-eyed way of his—as if appraising a forkful of $666 Douche Burger held at arm's length. I was at a loss for what to say. My stomach breached the awkward silence with a loud eruption of gurgles. Obviously I could ignore the pungent aromas of garlicky goodness no longer and so plucked an amusingly realistic finger shaped appetizer from the top of a three-tiered party platter. Just as I was about to clamp down toothily on the morsel, Torode lifted a finger and tilted his head an extra few degrees. With his other hand he reached toward a hatch set into the wall between us. When he slid it open, my finger-food slipped from my fingers and clunked

on the table. "Oh God", I gasped, "Is it really you?"[18]
Framed in the hatch was the grinning face of the most legendary anchorite of all. "Om nom nom nom!" spoke the
apparition.

The anchorhold of Gregg Wallace was widely believed
within the subterranean multitude to be nothing more than
urban legend, a story adapted by the Deodanths as a propaganda tool to frighten the weak-minded and preach their
repugnance at the sensual ingestion of matter. *The Body
with Fried Organs* at first glance appeared to be a combination of recipe book and bestiary purportedly written by
Gwen Troake, a Devon housewife who, in 2011, won the
accolade Cook of the Realm, leading to the BBC selecting
her to organise a banquet to be attended by Prince Charles,
Earl Mountbatten of Burma, James Martin and Wallace himself. Little is mentioned of the banquet's actual proceedings
yet her "Surprise Recipe Against the New Plague"—said to
have provided the event's gastronomic entertainment—
proved to be very revealing:

*Let him take his forearm with the skin on, he will take a
sharp knife and raise off the skin with as much meat from
the bone as he can possibly get, so that it appears like a
whole forearm when stuffed. He will stuff the limb with
ingredients including beef suet, veal, bacon and herbs
before putting the whole thing in the oven for two and a
half hours. Once removed from heat he will then reattach
the arm between wrist and elbow joint and munch hearti-
ly until done. He must then attach hand to elbow joint
using a sublimate of ground liverwort, black pepper, su-
perglue and Thion Hudor. He will take a bath in clam
juice but not to stay in (with his head above water) longer*

---

[18] Muller Ltd.: Yeah, it kinda ties the two storylines together. But,
um, perhaps this is a bit too dry. It's a tough juncture but I think
that, right here, this is just a great line. Look at the way it reads, I
don't think it would read in quite the same way if it were published
somewhere else. I think it's a beautiful passage—a remarkable skill.

than half a minute, if the juice be very cold. After this he will chant the above recipe twice an hour until the limb reinstates at full length.

A further six pages of trans-memberment recipes describe increasingly miraculous culinary combinations of humans, animals, vegetables and cooking implements. It is on the seventh page that the tone abruptly changes. *The Body with Fried Organs* continues in a confessional prose:

He has brought me to this place in The North, a truly marvelous place that only those with the milky eyes can see . . . [The Body with Fried Organs then describes in detail the Vale of Avalon where I now sit with Torode]. . . . His handmaiden Torode explained to me that he is now 'dead' to the world, sealed away in an anchorhold where he will forever become Michelin. Its body had been radically reengineered as a sensorium of the self. Every inch of its skin was grafted with enhanced taste buds—eyes, ears and nostrils had been replicated, boosted and multiplied by tiny local surgeons at a very reasonable price. My own recipe for 'recombinant chowder' had been perfected and Wallace can now regenerate body parts at will.

As if to validate these incredible facts, an elaborate thali had been arranged before me on the anchorite's shrine-table. Thirteen aluminum containers each containing a separate part of the recluse's corpus were accompanied by a variety of intricately spiced toothpastes. In one katori, a lozenge of Wallace's iconic golden brown head replaced, *ossobuco*, the yolk of a barbecued egg. Hardly even dusted with chat masala, the egg was supported by a tiny beer barrel moulded from low-calorie Wallace foot jelly. In another, the skin of the anchorite's tongue was stuffed with a pate of halibut and compressed high-resolution scans of wooden letterpresses, congealed with [RhCl(H2O)5]2+ at several gauss until blindingly white. In another katori a "rice" was composed of 24 ounces of the anchorite's fingernails, accelerated, then reheated with a third part of chicken liver, that is, 8 ounces; separated in Merkaba Orbs with a Büchner funnel, and cooked in the sun and black earth until it formed a gelatinous suspension that looks (and tastes) just like semen. The thali was seasoned with crushed anchorite backbone, ceremonially set on fire and extinguished with a mist of "Relentless" energy drink (to symbolise vitality).

Although I wasn't feeling too peckish, I shuffled a few of the moreish morsels onto my paper sideplate and nibbled away politely. After sampling some inspiringly flavorsome Wallacean dishes the handmaiden revealed this to me:

To the rear of this anchorhold a hagioscope looks onto a hyper-kitchen so splendid it knocks the rest of Avalon's wonders into cocked hat. The comestible Wallace passes its self-anointed flesh across this pontifex where it is received with great honour. Though this flesh is our enemy, we are commanded to support it. Every day we must serve Eucharistic viands to the Great Enfolder who must worship himself to death ad infinitum so that the ouroboros of our becoming—the fearsome engine of our subterranean hypereconomy—is eternally preserved.

I had assumed that I had been invited to a macabre death ritual right up to when the hatch finally slid open and the blindfolded Wallace could be peeped inside his anchorhold, all teeth, tongues and whistling nostrils.[19] "Om nom om nom?" the anchorite seemed to mumble with animated brow. He who chatters grinds chaff. The two jaws are the grindstones, the tongue is the clapper. A great fool would Wallace be if he grinded whichever he wanted, chaff or wheat. Wallace whispered only occasionally unto his handmaiden Torode, guarding his window well against idle

---

[19] Muller Ltd.: I wasn't so keen on that; it's all a bit *Casualty*. Let's leave it for now.

speech. He spoke infrequently and spoke little. His warbling was weighty and of great power.

Tiny laughter emanated from Torode's belly. His stomach was channeling the anchorite's carefully chosen gibberish into plain French. I moved closer to hear a tiny voice whisper: "I would soon as put a baby in a refrigerator than an egg". Wallace warbled again, his tongue stopping short of a gallop. "What brings you here?" whispered Torode's tum. "I am the Journeyman Gambini . . . ." "I approach the end and seek . . . ." "Om nom, nom om . . . ." More restrained twittering. Torode's gut intoned, ". . . The end of the Chinese restaurant? The dawn of couscous parties?" "I, a Journeyman", I continued. Torode's midriff rumbled enthusiastically. "Mmmmmm . . . we likey! You shall learn to deny the difference between yourself and all of creation by devouring everything that is dead, all rocks and things and all that lives and breathes, all cattle and all wild. On your belly shall you crawl eating dirt, dandelions and dogs the days of your life". He twittered and warbled no more for there was no more to speak of. Silence would bring forth eternal food.

We stopped off for a light brunch at The Model of Louis XV, a local restaurant recommended by Torode that makes wonderful use of local RÉSO produce—granular star fruits, fibrous misquotations, brittle polka dots, animate proxies, chilli chocolate, winter sport curlicues, sticky traction, dry iodine rich agate fish, gelatinous telethons—donating its profits to the Monte Carlo Croupier and Straight Cops Foundation, a group dedicated to discovering renegade SWAT teams turned bad. Lunch at The Model of Louis XV worked in a traditional mode. Saucier, poissoniers, sous chefs and patty flippers investigated fusions of John Does, 354-lb.ft. torque and dentex caught between Cannes and San Remo, dizzling with metabacetus, dental popcorn and Soviet postcodes. From GIFs of mountains to the memory of lava beneath the sea—the colourful dishes we heard rumours of reflected tiny flavour intervals which are basic and strong, sometimes secreted to the point of indivisibility, but also umami and non-tastes, "sun-drenched" values, heavier than rich, smelling "toll-free", attenuating and exceeding all levels of attention.

Following our insinuated brunch, we went backstage to get a few lessons. Certified to BS EN1004 (Class 3), The Model of Louis XV's kitchen was (a bit too) obviously influenced by the lyrics of the Houston based hip-hop collective Boss Hogg Outlawz. The kitchen's scales are said to be able to determine the relative viscosity of crops decimated by the Oklahoma Air National Guard. Working with the sous chef, I mixed a ¼-cup of light soy sauce purchased at 0.9% APR, a modicum of dishonest and divisive propaganda and 3mg of Swedish parsley before exposing the concoction to 104.1 MHz for a few hours (rule of thumb, should not be saucy).[20] Meanwhile Muller Ltd. lured a dozen public domain templates by vaf-vafing the song of the Scandinavian male water spirit Nix, before marinating them in a flooded Volvo XC60 during a cool wet summer. Do not over-process! The results hover over the taste buds, gazing listlessly out at the magnificent underground mall. By now my eyes watered more than my mouth. Removing my Gary Gilmore Contacts, taking care to peel them off simultaneously, the stagnant corpse of a Van Houtte decayed in my nostrils, the sour gall of charcoal-lice creamer melting on my oh so sorry tongue. All again was mere libation, as plain as plain can be.

---

[20] Muller Ltd.: We probably rewrote this bit more than any other. I think it's a case of over-interpretation. We've been here already. It doesn't hold up so well; but let's get into that later. The effect is lost here, it doesn't read or scan so well.

PODCAST IV — LIBER DE MONSTRUOSIS HOMINIBUS PATHIS

Having led me safely to the entrance of PATH, my master compagnon Muller Ltd. ouah-ouahed his goodbyes and entered a portal that would take him deep within the belly of the large beaver that guarded the entrance to the Weiden + Kennedy Building in downtown Portland. 25 years ago, at 2.30 p.m. an intern trained in the mechanics of sealing borders acting on behalf of the Advisory Council sealed off the boundary between what became officially known as La Ville Souterraine LS87KD38400 and RÉSO, leaving only one official entry-point open. A piece of paper pinned on a cork board said that these measures had been agreed upon with a decision by the Advisory Council; that they would remain in force until the conclusion of the summer sales. This was the beginning of a new development in underground shopping known to the terrestrial world as "PATH".

I was here to undertake the next phase of my long journey of indenture. PATH would offer my apprenticeship in alterity. According to the *Liber de Monstruosis Hominibus Pathis* app, in the years that it had been separated from RÉ-

SO, PATH had followed its own parallel system of indenture based on the outlawed allemande traditions of *Wandergesellen*. In this system, everyone entered their trade as a master, assigned to their compagnon siège (*Wandergesellenhaus*) at birth. Since they were fully incorporated, PATH masters began their career as public limited companies, with shareholders determining their every decision. Ltd. corporate-personhood involved meeting strict productivity targets and high profit margins expected by shareholders, ensuring the maximum efficiency of person-skillbundles. PATH rigorously enforced a "work ethic", foregrounding homo economicus over homo ludens. Ltd. masters would work 800 minutes each day every day of the year, not even breaking to celebrate Mr Peanut Day. Every seventh year, they would undertake a year long "Wanderjahre" to "de-skill" and "unlearn" their craft. At the end of their career, they would finally retire as ignorant Journeymen, freed from the burden of knowledge and the unrelenting work that attended it, but only if they accrued enough capital to acquire a majority of shares in their self. The harder they worked as young Ltd. masters, the more their stock rose, making this prospect ever more unlikely. As they unlearned, their stock and their earning power would both drop dramatically. Ltd. masters had to quickly learn how to play the corporate-personhood market, to tactically invest in others to ensure that they were not left with a personal redemption deficit. Most Ltd. masters managed to evolve from a public into a private limited company, but only a few made the rank of Journeyman. Muller Ltd. had often spoken wistfully of the day when he would liquidate himself and live off his shares in other Ltd. masters.

As I waited interminably at immigration, it gave me time to enjoy the intimate topography of PATH's infamously gnarled, claustrophobic space. There were no trappings of the ceremonial here, although insuperable resources had been used to ensure a spectacle of power far more complex and subtle than any Baroque edifice. Rumours that the immigration chamber boasted smooth, white walls nearly 8 feet high, and that in some places a 10-foot-high atrium window substituted for the wall, fitted with an electronic warning device, turned out not to be exaggerated (although the warning device was entirely a fabrication). Electric lights, designed to illuminate noiselessly, were installed with a deliberate delicacy that masked monumental, painful effort. The chamber was also generously equipped with power outlets, the true hegemonic purpose of which remained chillingly un-announced. Such devoted displays of the latest technological resources, acts of consultation and terror, disguised the fact that in yesteryear this was once the happy site of a poutinerie.[21] Now swathed in concrete, the ground gave no escape. A St. Christopher-shaped booby trap was situated in the ceiling, warding off those who harboured thoughts of heading for the roof. In the distance the chilling discontinuous rhythmic cacophony of metal being worked into the pale flesh of escapees tore at the visitor's eardrums.

"My name is Andrei Negura. I was born in the local magasin of Ameublement Daily Living in Les Beaux Jours *galerie* of eastern RÉSO. I first arrived in this waiting chamber in August five years ago in on a scholarship to major in Philosophy of Entrepreneurialism at PATH University", whispered the young woman sitting opposite me. She did not raise her head from the tattered copy of *Hello* that hid her lips from the CCTV. "I only wanted to go to a school with a baseball team. Within the first month of my stay here I sold my index finger to a dog-headed witch for more money than I could earn back home in a lifetime". This macabre[22] transaction was the catalyst for a terrifying sequence of events cul-

---

[21] Muller Ltd.: Ooooh yeah, I like this bit. It's gorgeous; you done a great job!

[22] Gambini: I figured I didn't have a great vocabulary when I was writing this parable, just one or two words that were kinda important to me, and this is one of them. Usually those words, though, never make it, when the writer tries to get across his ideas. The inspirational words are almost never in there. I was so embarrassed writing it because I was worried that someone might read it.

minating in the appalling circumstances that Andrei currently endured. "It is 6:30 am on a bitter December morning. Outside this chamber, in the cramped tunnels of PATH, a legion of dog-headed villagers are hurling debris at the windows of their retail units. Judging by rumours I myself have spread over the past twenty-four months, I believe I may be the last human left alive in PATH. I have no Internet connection, the TV is analogue and the phones are dead".

Although I didn't hide my boredom, Andrei continued to recount her experience of PATH:

I was taking a walk through PATH on a quiet Sunday afternoon when my reverie was abruptly broken by a vociferous stream of curses accompanied by the high-pitched squeal of a furiously revving electric motor. I followed the noise to its source. There I discovered a portly old woman lying next to a Segway. Her personal transporter had apparently lost control and was now rocking dangerously on the precipice of an travelator. Leaping to her aid I dragged her back onto the walkway and returned the shopping that had spilled from her basket. She thanked me and invited me to tea. I had nothing better to do and generally enjoy meeting new people so I accepted.

We glided off to a cosy demonstration kitchen within one of the premier homeware stores in the Bay Adelaide Centre. Although the kitchen formed an open stage to customers ascending and descending on the adjacent travelator, we were so immersed in our conversation we forgot about our audience. From that point on I recollect nothing other than intense emotion, a feeling of great warmth and belonging as if I had returned home to the bosom of my family after a long absence.[23] And, alt-

---

[23] Muller Ltd.: Maybe the words aren't so important. Wouldn't it be great if, at any time, we could hear and see great artisans thinking about their craft? When we did our first commentary there were, like, tens, even thousands of details embedded in my ideas which I knew about, maybe the rest of my team knew about, but which were

hough this may be a consequence of hindsight, I remember that there was the distinct aroma of dog. The
next thing I recall I was standing outside on the porch
grinning into the spotlights that beat down on the demo-
kitchen. I felt elated and slightly tipsy. My right index finger was missing and in my left hand I held a ridiculous
sum of money. The stump healed impossibly fast and
there was no pain whatsoever. For the sake of appear-
ances I took a few days off university and wore a band-
age for a week or so upon my return. A few more weeks
passed without event and I began to feel a little saner. I
was coasting along nicely again.

It should have been a joyous day. I had noticed posters
in my local pub advertising a jousting tournament being
held in PATH as part of Homecoming. A visiting troupe
from The Society for Creative Anachronisms would be
performing and, having attended some of their meetings
at University earlier in the year, I was asked to help with
the food service. Lodging locally, I got there early to as-
sist in preparing the catering stands. It felt good to be
involved.[24] The event started well. I had a great view
from my burger hut under the Eaton Centre. The crowds
cheered at the thundering of hooves and resounding
splinter of balsawood against steel. Children with plastic
swords performed their own duels and faked numerous
elaborate death sequences.[25] At a lull in the proceedings
a hungry and impatient queue formed in front of me.

---

essentially invisible to the world at large. The commentary didn't
even scrape the surface. Wouldn't it be amazing to make all of that
thought available instantly to anyone anywhere? Constantly?

[24] Gambini: I'm sure that that's easy to do. You just got to ask yourself why it hasn't happened. There's too much at stake for the second character—what would they do if everything they ever thought
about was all streamed live? Their work would vanish overnight.

[25] Muller Ltd.: I guess so. There'd be no room for professional commentary. It makes me apprehensive. I'm mean how else could someone confirm the suspicion that the commentary on Ronald Haver

Having developed a strong phobia, I found myself compelled to lift each raw patty to the sunlight and carefully check for anomalies. It was just after such an inspection that I noticed a familiar grey-haired figure staring at me from the reed-beds by the indoor fountain. Behind her a large pack of dogs sat patiently in the water, only their heads showing above the surface. I motioned to point but, due to my missing digit, succeeded only in raising a fist. Then, as if at my unintentional salute, all hell broke loose.

The first wave of dogs burst from the water. They scrambled through the foaming shallows and leapt to the bank. As they rose to full height a terrifying deformity was rudely unveiled. Their snarling countenances were carried upon the torsos of men! Startlingly naked and with a blade in each hand, they tore into the now screaming masses. Jaws locked upon throats and knifes plunged indiscriminately into the defenseless flesh of man, woman and child. Blood began to arc through the air and startled horses trampled over the fleeing spectators. A troupe of knights, led by their King, attempted to make a break towards the shopping centre's eastern gates only to be borne down and savaged by another wave of dog-heads emerging from [Les Cafés] Second Cup. A third wave made straight for the armoury display to hastily procure crossbows and dispatch individuals who had escaped the blind chaos at the centre. Yet another group of attackers carrying petrol canisters mounted Segways and began setting the brightly coloured tents alight. A serving wench, her smock aflame, ran shrieking from the IPA tent, scissor jumped from the juice bar and smacked heavily across the foredeck of an automobile stand.

---

talking about King Kong is an homage to the way Ronald Haver introduced his commentary on King Kong if they weren't able to listen to the commentary on Ronald Haver talking about King Kong?

Dogheads on Segways zoomed up the slope towards me. I dived through the serving hatch as a flaming torch burst through the door. Under cover of smoke I scrambled towards the throatless corpse of a squire. I pulled the most substantial looking Claymore from his leather scabbards and tumbled behind a dying mare. As I lay huddled on the scorched earth a suspicion of complicity nagged at my guts. Furious at my entrapment I hurtled into the fray, intent upon slaying a few of the abominable hounds before attempting escape. I swung my sword furiously at the first I encountered and his bloodstained head vectored away from his still running body. I decapitated two more before the futility of my actions hit home. I watched spellbound as my first victim plunged his fist into his neck cavity and began tugging at something inside. Instantaneously it began to morph, sprout hair and coagulate into the head of a Labrador. I glanced behind me to see the others rebirthing themselves in the same hideous manner.

Acting on instinct I dived at their naked midriffs, tackled them to the ground and pulverised their still soft cranial pods under the soles of my armoured Sorel walking boots.[26] These two stayed down. I had found a method of permanent dispatch. I spun round in search of allies to whom I could communicate my discovery. There were none. All had been slain and my foes had swiftly departed. I was left alone with the stench of smoked meat and butchery saturating my nostrils. My ears burned with the echo of distant barking and the murmurs and screams of the dying.

I dragged myself wearily back up the slope towards the

---

[26] Gambini: I guess. Although we want to tie together the seemingly incomprehensible elements of this commentary, at the same time, we're not trying to give the only reading, the only possible interpretation. We're just trying to help you if you've been confused. There are a lot of people who are trying to put this together and still having difficulty.

Bay Adelaide Centre, slipping occasionally in pools of clotting blood. I pulled a corpse free of a Segway and wiped iridescent matter off the handlebars. As I glided through PATH I passed numerous isolated scenes of violent slaughter. A melancholic howling wafted across Cadilac Fairview Tower as I bunny-hopped through the cooling rejectamenta of this apparently consummate massacre. Reaching the border at 777 Bay on College I fell exhausted upon the floor. And so, I remain here, awaiting my safe repatriation to RÉSO.

As far-fetched as it was, Neguri's story left me a little shaken. And yet, I resolved to enter PATH to discover it for myself and continue my dispassionate and scientific recording of other lands. To my surprise, it was not so different to RÉSO. Yes, it was dominated by a mean corporate approach to architecture, yes its shopping was provincial, yes its food was entirely unpalatable, yes its drink was subject to draconian paternalism and yes, it was populated by Anglophone cynocephali rather than humans.[27] But, in every other respect, the cynocephalus is just like you and me.

---

[27] Muller Ltd.: At first you can't tell what the hell you're reading—then it pulls back and you can tell that it's a commentary that suggests interpretation. But it's not an obvious homage. What we're suggesting is that much of what we're reading here is just made up.

Podcast V — Turk's House for Sailors Tourist Information Centre

For the small price of two toonies and a loonie—coins only, no change given—PATH's dog-legged anthropomorphs will smuggle you back through the old West End into Westside's ancient Shanghai Tunnel network. There I would master the art of stepping. The Steps that lead down beneath Turk's House for Sailors Tourist Information Centre have been closed to the public for more than 60 years. The ebony sculptures are too precious to be touched by crowds of tourists, although vagrants, prostitutes, delinquents, vagabonds, and rebels still insist on breaking in at night to shelter when the bar gets rowdy with bachelorettes. I wear a brand new pair of soft Pendleton moccasins each day to work my trade, my perambulation polishing and caressing each and every plateaux, removing the heady cocktail of stale urine and Hippocras, the famous spiced tonic wine, that bathes the steps.

Today I am outrider to a hoary old blanketed *teton* bent under the weight of a 32" CRT TV. Sometimes, as I round a landing, his TV flickers into action, catching the signal coming in illegally over the border from Washington. As one, we wearily tackle the spiraling wooden steps. Every once in a while some particularly repentant bâtard chucks in a few extra Willamette Bucks and a loose cable trips us, grazing our knees.[28] Puddles of hobo piss, cold and moist in disposition, caress our feet. Today we are higher than yesterday, and tomorrow the compound figure of Nina, our local ghost, shall glance up to view the spiral steps disappearing around the eternal corner. Impossible to make out the end. Too far. But finis terrae will come.

I once met The Pardoner. I heard rumours of a man grinding his face flat against the jerry-built brick walls while descending the steps. I was shocked by his sudden appearance and nearly dropped the TV. His face was indeed as smooth as the wooden steps themselves. The featureless plane on the front of his head furnished no mouth to speak of. By way of greeting he proffered a business card. In olde German gothic font it bore but one word: "IMPRESARIO". He placed the card atop the TV next to an application form and a biro. Obviously I could not fill it out without dropping the TV and voiding my amassed indulgences. (My apprenticeship is a privilege, but the bureaucracy takes the shine off the perks.) My antagonist or savior—for I knew not

---

[28] Gambini: Actually what's interesting is it's the opposite of cause and effect; it's like the opposite of a plot. Normally, as we know, later in the text we read these exact same words. But here it's different, it's exceedingly difficult. It's not just filler. It's not linear; it's an intense feeling, an experience rather than a moment.

which—expressed amusement at my obvious distress by flexing his sweaty biceps, rapidly erecting a small MDF cathedral, and disappearing inside before torching his flat-pack vestibule.

Grasping the remote and nun-chuck of the Samsung chantry box (which, before you complain, comes out of *my* wages), I resumed my circumlocutory ascent of the Steps. The flickering numerical gauge in my peripheral vision indicated several thousand clients logging to share my activity as it hits 08:00hrs in eastern RÉSO. I curse softly as I enjoy the experience of the collective pain of alterity for as long as it takes to say three *sacres*. An endless litany of intricate liturgical profanities fills my head:

> Pronounced "lion duty". Osti de vestments. Dear Near Utopian. Mon tabarnac jva te décalisser la yeule comme le calice. Mighty crossbow ebooks. Lamentable hazard. Airy fellow soldier. Quietly out-broached descended walk! Château de marde. Contradict pompeius troth. Curried six chainmails. Criss. Transfigure those sayings. J'men calice. Porter dispersed their porter. Causal cellar beggar. Bâtard. Pair of poppies. Tabarnac. Gape village figure. Tie her fertile. Unfit driveling chestnuts. Paris serving comminations . . . .

Incorporating the babble of their thoughts, I hear the noise of our many individual existences. They, and I, care about one thing; this fusion of our mentalities oriented on the climb, the need to ascend and/or descend. Step by step we evolve, so slowly as to be nearly imperceptible.

A startup with scalable, cost-effective customer acquisition, Steps is a very profitable little free-hold. Each step clocks up kilojoules on the chantry box, the kjs convert into Bridgetown Bucks, and the neighbourhood LETS currency. Having paid my PDX Currency Corp. Lord his duty, this offers me a basic income that easily assuages my desires. But the real money comes from the profanities. A penance by proxy, I pace the steps on the behalf of others for their liturgical indulgences (to sign up, hit the "sign-up" button at the top right of the site).[29] When my shift ends, I am assured that I will relax upstairs with my friends, family and ancestors in the National Waffle Window & Vintage Store Memorial Museum cafe. *Causal cellar beggar!*

As I enter the National Waffle Window & Vintage Store Memorial Museum, I am ushered to a soft black easy chair close to the former Red Light vintage store panorama. I enjoy the faux vintage store mise-en-scene, thinking that this really is a no brainer. I get extra loyalty Bridgetown Bucks at the National Waffle Window & Vintage Store Memorial Museum since it is owned by PDX Currency Corp. the same LETS scheme as Steps. Most of the dishes are boiled twice in different water to avoid melancholy.

My waiter arrives promptly, serving me an amuse-bouche of cream egg benedict with Sugar Free Oregon white truffle waffle foam and suede fricassee. I smile and politely stuff some in my gob before spitting it into a napkin and discreetly palming it into my robe pocket. Such gastronomic transgressions are punishable by sumptuary law. To be seen spurning the delicate blanc manger of the leisure class can land you with a real penance: permanent demotion to bondsman. Coarse food for coarse people.[30] But, by my reckoning, cream egg is the cause of superfluous humours, especially phlegm. Frying and baking should only be used for meats of moderate humours, never suede. The chef should be drawn through the street on a sled with the amuse-bouche bound around his neck!

---

[29] Muller Ltd.: This reminds me of something we said earlier on in this commentary. I'm not sure what exactly, but it's very familiar. It takes place in a very similar context. It's building up something that resembles, uh, the kind of commentaries we know, rather than the ones we'd really like to hear.

[30] Gambini: You've made that comparison before. It's not allegorical, but the structure of this text, when you look at it, hopefully makes a lot of sense. It's audacious to include it here I think.

In a large edible mirror, ostentatiously ensconced in a shiny black baroque plaster frame, I spy my mother's great uncle chatting with KGW-TV newscaster Joe Donlon. They are just out of earshot. He is sipping a blue Slush Puppy laced with ergot-infected rye from a demitasse cup, but seems totally bemused. Donlon is wearing a Scooby Doo costume (it was Halloween on Thursday), a character thought to generate good blood and to provoke urine, stool, and the menstrual flow. Donlon appears to be enjoying his Edible Pilgrim, a pike sporting a roast lamprey as a pilgrim staff, part of this evening's allegorical menu of self-cooking beasts. Easy listening renditions of The Cribs' greatest hits purr in the background (lyrics sung in Mandarin). There is a distinct aroma of truffle and my hair has recently been styled. I am wearing a pressed shirt with high collars, two buttons open to reveal my hairy chest. I check the time only to be reassured that my watch is more expensive than it need be. After having convinced the porpoise to be stuffed with minced plover, I opt instead for Trompe l'oeil Thermidor (live homard soaked in strong brandy mixed with latex casts of cooked lobsters) accompanied by a battalion of inedible wooden figurines.

Suddenly a Fred Meyer reusable bag strikes my face and is held there for some time by a shrieking icy wind. Breathless and unable to use my arms, I shake my head until it is dislodged. Before my vision clears I am immediately assailed again, this time by a lean cut of beef Tri-Tip. Sauce dribbles down my party shop robe and a pickled egg whispers something vaguely seductive in my ear. The offended voices of the compound-self ring loudly in my head for eternity and I think real tears do flow.[31]

---

[31] Muller Ltd.: I actually wouldn't know how to cry.

Podcast VI — The Armory

I recalled fondly the soft pop as I removed the golden chipolata device from the cat's fundament and gently deflated her into her mahogany casket. Will I ever again engage in those sweet fireside exchanges? It is doubtful, given the totality of the siege that awaits me on the penultimate day of my tour. I reflect on the countless yarnbombs I have knitted. Now they lie, strewn across the Kingdoms of RÉSO, in a nebula of crimson medallions. The Cookie-Cutter 3D Gun. A device uncovered in the grounds of this very compagnon siège. Its secrets unravelled by our own resident rioter. Curse the boy! What wrath, what immediate vengeance he has brought upon us all. Oh that I might lift his battered spectacles up off the table and crush them with my graspable interface. Before this stronghold is dust he will fear my stench! My stinger secretes a single drop of venom in anticipation. I must vacate this self-indulgent torpor. With a shake of the midsection, I forlornly resume the packing away of my inventory. Essentials first. 4 port USB hub/clock, ampullae, agility rings, Ainsi Soit-Elle voucher, Oh Henry! bar, cusps. But what about the mouse nozzles I never got round to stimulating and that half written diet guide (who will become obese in the lean years to follow?) Did I really need the knitted PATH dog heads for the local orphanage (orphans no more alas)? The listing of my, soon to be sacrificed, possessions drew certain repressed emotions to the fore and I started to cry again. Stupid old Gambini.

Weary from lack of sleep, my Willard satchel almost empty, for those of gentle birth do not carry packs, I headed up west through the Shanghai Tunnel towards the First Regiment Armory's heavily fortified spiral staircase, watching out for stumble steps and keeping my sword drawn in case suddenly surprised by an assailant.[32] My visor was drawn so that all I could see was squeezed through the narrow slit in front of my eyes. The top of the stair was invisible with light. I could feel the sudden rise in my diastolic blood pressure. A sword was mounted just above the door. Below it was a severed arm, a trophy from a recent execution. Is that what they did with them? The left corner of the room bore damage from the artillery attack the anti-Chinese rioters had administered to the fortifications last Saturday morning in what had been an unprecedented level of visceral combat choreography. The right corner of the room bore traces of sustainable building practices, a concern for maintaining the historical character of the Armory while developing it into a theatre.

It had been a prolonged siege, a sacking with mood

---

[32] Gambini: Me neither. Which is why this moment is so believable to me.

swings, much bloodshed and weekday withdrawals. Having drilled endlessly, and fought with great ferocity, many of my compagnon émeute were lost either to the building's complex displacement ventilation system or to the murder holes of the Pearl District's food Eden. In retaliation, the National Theatre Customer Service Attendants had explored this maze-like fortress, slaughtered almost every man, woman, child and slave who resided within the burgh walls, even those who tried to flee to amateur dramatics held in nearby Gothic Revival churches. Some six hundred theatre-loving Portlanders suspected of contemplating rioting were put to the sword. They didn't have to do this; it was part of the sport.[33] Life as a National Theatre Customer Service Attendants was monstrously violent, but there was the great spoil of contentment and the reassuring illusion of power in such arbitrary slaughter. I had learned the kind of rapport and harmony with this place, with this way of life, as hostages can develop for their captors.

I'd been struggling tactically, almost making it out of the Shanghai Tunnel and into the arts citadel early in the morning, but had to pack it in and set up camp again under Old Town Pizza until it got late. It was all about salience. The cannon and mangonel had been the main challenge because of the need to get the launch angle just right while ensuring that enough of my rioters survived the arrow loops to storm the redeveloped bastion. It was much harder still than all those months posing as a herbalist and giving alms to vagrants on the skid road to get information on the supplies of bog ore being bought by Oregon's travelling merchants travelling along the mighty Columbia River. Strangest of all was the sudden demand for a metal acquired from vicious griffins in the North Pole and supplied by a one-eyed

---

[33] Gambini: But it can't always can it? I feel we have to confront this just to make sure it's the case. This remains one of the most interesting subtexts of this commentary. It's an abstraction perhaps, maybe the unknown. The way the characters get split up and then end up becoming practically the same people.

horseman that I'd learned of while temping at Cargo on NW13th. I was sure this line of investigation would pay off eventually (it was probably destined for a handcrafted guitar pedal of some sort), but I wasn't quite sure how.

The ones that didn't make it, the infected corpses, were swaddled in manure, loaded onto a trebuchet and fired over the fortifications at our common enemy. As part of the ongoing work to conquer the Pearl District, this framework was the best practice, improving morale of my team while causing the greatest psychological damage to our adversary. My reward for being coordinated was *that* diorama. The dénouement—a fifty-pound projectile pinning the sustainably designed battalion's mascot, a black swallow, to the ground —was such a nice touch. It gave me an immense feeling of satisfaction. It brought it all back down to earth. This is what it was really about. Forty smurfberries was all it took to get me started.

My eyes slowly drifted around the room, scanning robotically from left to right as if weighed down by a heavy suit of body armour. It truly made me feel as if I was in hostile territory, out of my depth. A peephole window was garlanded by a swarm of dead insects. The lonesome horns of freight trains crossing the Eastside's railroad intersections scented the evening air. On the twilight horizon in the Willamette River, I could just make out the Chinese galleons in all their colourful elegance swarming in preparation for their migration to warmer waters. They appeared to float above the sea, painterly and glitch-ridden, breaking up like oil on water. These old boys looked hazy, lost in the obscurity of the haar. A light as intense as five suns illuminated the upper layers of the atmosphere, reflecting their crimson glow back indirectly, giving the impression of looking in rather than out. Their portholes percolated a sticky sap into the water.

As I turned from the window, my eyes readjusted to the gloom. I could now see a dark pulsating mass in the opposite corner of the room. The same sticky substance glistened in the gleaming beam that fell from the window. A trickle down a falling wall, it formed rivulets and contortions on the surfaces and cavities of the dusty corner. A babble of pigments the colour of molasses, copper and silver was spawning a globular residue of elaborate grandeur. Without allowing my attention to stray, I leaned over to where I'd left a fine glass Mason preserve jar perching precariously on the edge of a flowerpot stand. As I took a sip of lukewarm Portland Oyster Stout, this darkest fluid pumped out molasses of sumptuously misshapen treacle tresses. The dry black air caught in the back of my throat causing me to hiccup, a liquid flesh dribbling and oozing like melted chocolate. I was ravished.[34] The sensation of a deep anxiety about this medium was at once overwhelming.[35]

Scanning the ground through my visor I spied fragments of a substance approximating molten metal and black glass, and here and there dark stains caused by this subtly briny liquid. I opened up the window to engage the gas chromatography sequence: "nine globular proteins of unknown sequence and conformation". Less-than-thrilling prose. I'd seen something like this before, a transparent black-red pigment made from coagulated elephant and dragon blood. These incidents would have made a slight impression on my mind, but for the fact that I had the tingling, tantalising feeling that an entity was about to manifest itself. The mass was drawing me ever closer, inviting me to reach out and touch this form that was starting to reveal itself. It was as if I felt the very substance in which my experience was being rendered.

Maybe it was a metaphor; they were getting more popular again. I could use a bit of a story every now and again. The alternative was the universal lowest common denominator, the race for the bottom. Meaning had been tied to colour then, it was part of the alchemical philosopher's stone.

---

[34] Muller Ltd.: I think I nicked that bit. It's a quote I think. It gives it more emotional weight—I can see the effect it has. I'm really happy with it.

[35] Gambini: I think you did a great job.

Crushing the glands of the snail. It was one thing to paint amazing worlds and incredible historical detail; another to make a connection through the labyrinthine subjective conflict the protagonist has to go through. This is what makes the experience more human, what lends it cordiality. It was more than just dressing up. What was this elusive, sweaty, adhesive mass? A prosthetic? Body armour? Viscose vest? A periwig? These were two identical images pushing and pulling against one another, in fact—I experienced them twice, reverberating with the same breath, causing me to gag on a chocolate raisin.

The thick stone walls delayed the detailed reflections. And then, standing in this shadow, I saw a man-at-arms, a somewhat vain, satisfied figure of authority. Hand on hip, his potbelly protruded proudly as if to escape its armoured guard. His white kid gloves gleamed in the twilight. "A noble will reap a handsome ransom", I thought. Now to put him to his broadsword. I tilted my hand a few degrees to the right, gesturing towards the framed figure as if to flush him. Then I saw that this was not a knight. A quarter-length portrait revealed all its skill, detail, richness and restraint. This figure at once swung out from the theatre wall and vanished in flash, disintegrating into a thousand shards.

A momentary lapse of equilibrium, and the connection was plain. This was my own reflection. The mere presence of this Claude glass incited the supernatural powers of its owner. It transformed my perception into permeable boundaries, liminalities, analogies, doublings. Didn't big grey elephants recognize their own reflection? Or was it the armour-plated rhino from *Anthropologie*? My passions and vanity were at once intimate and at a double remove. Through a glass darkly, my auxiliary organs made me ingest and feel the terror, wonder and understanding of this delay. These broken images, these situations and identities, this natural magic, this calisthenics of the mind and eye, were part of who I was right now.

As the quartz evaporated and the silvering sputtered to

the ground, the wall behind the looking glass betrayed a dark black chasm. It billowed a curious sulphurous odour. I shook my body towards it spasmodically, crouched down and pushed myself into the cavern. A cinematic sequence immediately commenced. In this, I crawled along a dark and dank passage through the Armory's walls into its vaults and onwards into a tunnel that took me under a breach in the fortress wall. From there I followed the peripheral Shanghai passages that ran like a warren under the ancient town. They took me beneath downtown landmarks: REI, Union Station, The Frying Scotsman, Cool Moon Ice Cream, BridgePort Brewpub, Pacific Northwest College of Art, Aveda Institute, Rose City Mortgage, Patagonia, Peets, Pearl Bakery, Oven & Shaker . . . and onwards deep beneath the Willamette itself.

As I emerged from the Shanghai Tunnel into the National Waffle Window & Vintage Store Memorial Museum cafe, the first thing I saw was the glinting light reflected in my perfect-ly preserved gauntlet. Presumably I was using this hand to crawl through the tunnel, yet the gauntlet was perfect with no wear marks and no dirt whatsoever on it. My impressively detailed prospect told me that the pit could not have been dug out by Sedantaire—it must have been the product of modern industrialised mining made in the future or in the distant past. These were continuity errors that, in any other situation, would have permanently suspended my belief. But such ontological discrepancies were part of the flat world of wanderlust I had come to accept: the indistinct plot-lines, the lack of strict causality, the duplicate personas, the shifts of setting and time, facts and fantasies. There was no index of fundamental truth, the genre just seemed to simply trans-form with each new release.[36]

The rattling of body piercings refocused my attention. Something was coming along the tunnel after me. It tilted forwards to run towards a set of sandstone steps leading it

---

[36] Gambini: I like this change of tone—it's less polemical. I had to fight to have this bit in here.

quickly up and out into the light. Suddenly the air separated into a myriad of celestial particles. A heavy explosion, shuddered the earth beneath. The tunnel had collapsed in its wake, vitrifying and melting, leaving me stranded a block back atop the Baghdad Theatre. When the wind and dust subsided upon the orientalist theatre's red tiled roof I saw in front of me a Victorian gentleman's machine. It was beautifully crafted in the arabesque style popular in fan fiction workshops held at the Belmont branch of the Multnomah County Library. Not a whiff of von Braun or Teflon. So the griffin-sourced base metals were for this marvellous steampunkery? An early flying machine designed for vertical take-off and landing? Perhaps this materia obscura was a lifeboat come to take me to the next level? But how could such a chariot of fire possibly work? A chocolate raisin's worth of antimatter would be enough to take me around the celestial spheres, but it would require engines and some means of storage. Despite my immediate concerns over the lack of boosters or, indeed, of any visible engineering, it looked like it was being groomed for the official launch of a magnificent journey.

I walked up onto an adjacent ceremonial platform and faced the machine. As I stood in position, my heavy armoured Sorel boots holding me steady, an intense beam of red light thundered and flashed from the base of the podium, its hot vapor lapping and scorching around the mechanical voyager. I imagined a hot breath of wind on my face blown up by this intense thunder, earthquake, storm and tempest.[37] As the crystallizing flame of devouring fire deflected off the roof of the theatre beneath me, the flying charger rose, in infinite brilliance.[38]

---

[37] Muller Ltd.: We should probably get back to the key themes. This is getting like some horrible hospital drama.
[38] Gambini: Sure.

♍

Chapter 2

Imperium et Sacerdotium

Jack Cade, Editor
Journal of the Cascades Historical Society

PART I: AFTER THE ANARCHICAL SOCIETY

The term neomedievalism is often attributed to the writings of the English political theorist Hedley Bull who, in 1977, published *The Anarchical Society: A Study of Order in World Politics*. Writing at the tail end of détente, Bull used a medieval analogy to build a theoretical model "for the future structure of world politics that could replace the system of sovereign states".[1] Bull was one of the first prominent theorists to argue for the emerging influence of non-state actors, such as the United Nations and private transnational corporations, in global policy making. Prior to the development of the Westphalian systems of territorial sovereignty and nation

---

[1] Hedley Bull, *The Anarchical Society: A Study of Order in World Politics* (New York: Macmillan, 1977), 255.

building, he argued, Europe was organised by multiple, asymmetric layers of authority, each of which shared sovereignty with the others. These layers of sovereignty were overlapping and were not supreme; authority was shared among rulers, the vassals beneath them, and the Pope and the Holy Roman Emperor above. He argued that "if modern states were to come to share their authority over their citizens, and their ability to command their loyalties, on the one hand with regional and world authorities and on the other with sub-state or sub-national authorities, to such an extent that the concept of sovereignty ceased to be applicable, then a neo-mediaeval form of universal political order might be said to have emerged".[2]

Bull, like Arnold Wolfers before him[3], ultimately rejected the notion of neomedievalism as mere supposition lacking any real empirical basis, particularly during a time dominated by superpower competition and before the establishment of the World Wide Web. The idea may have seemed obscure, even slightly eccentric at the time, but it has proved to be remarkably prescient.[4] Greater foresight was demonstrated by Yehezkel Dror who, in the early 1970s, was hypothesising ways in which foreign policy makers needed to generate

---

[2] Bull, *The Anarchical Society*, 255.

[3] Wolfers proposed a kind of "new medievalism", a move "toward complexities that blur the dividing line between domestic and foreign policy": Arnold Wolfers, *Discord and Collaboration: Essays on International Politics* (Baltimore: Johns Hopkins University Press, 1962), 241–242.

[4] "With hindsight of half a century, we can see that Wolfers was writing at the absolute apex of the CW [Clausewitzian-Westphalian] system, and while it is completely understandable that he abandoned neomedievalism at that point, history has subsequently developed in the directions he speculated upon": Philip A. Schrodt, "Neomedievalism in the Twenty-first Century: Warlords, Gangs and Transnational Militarized Actors as a Challenge to Sovereign Preeminence," paper presented at the annual meeting of the International Studies Association, New Orleans, Louisiana, February 17-20, 2010: 10.

"countercraziness strategies" to engage with what would later become commonly known as "rogue states".[5] From NATO's perspective, "crazy states" included Cuba, Libya and Iran, while the Warsaw Pact began to grown increasingly concerned with Afghanistan and Iran towards the end of the 1970s. While Dror specifically addressed the international relations of sovereign states, his concept of multi-actors could be applied to the then contemporary development of neomedieval non-state/state conflicts such as that, for example, between the IRA and the United Kingdom or between ETA and Spain. The Soviet invasion of Afghanistan in 1979—officially to prevent Islamic revolutionaries forming another "crazy state" on the Soviet border—helped to fuel an escalation of the Cold War. This, in turn, enabled neorealism to rise in prominence in International Relations theory. So long as the NATO/Warsaw Pact balance of power was the major empirical preoccupation, neomedievalism remained mere supposition. The neomedievalist insight of Dror's hypothesis would not become apparent until the early 1990s. The rapid development of information and communication technologies, the fall of the Berlin Wall, the Balkanisation of central and eastern Europe, and the rise in number of transnational organisations—from regulatory bodies and multinational corporations to environmental pressure groups and terrorist organisations—added fuel to the medieval analogy in international relations theory in the 1990s. It rapidly evolved into fully-fledged and highly visible geo-political debate, even finding its way into government think tanks on the future of America's global hegemony and national security after 9/11.[6]

---

[5] Yehezkel Dror, *Crazy States: A Counterconventional Strategic Problem* (London: Heath Lexington Books, 1971), 73–91.

[6] After the fall of the Berlin Wall, Serbia and Montenegro, Iraq, Syria, Afghanistan, Sudan and North Korea were added to NATO's unofficial list of rogue states, while the concept became a component of the Clinton Administration's foreign policy. While the Clinton Administration abandoned the concept in 2000, the "crazy state" con-

In 2001, Jörg Freidrichs revised and refined Bull's original proposition in an attempt to break the deadlock of what he called the "triple dilemma of current International Relations theory".[7] Here the author outlined the inadequacy of contemporary theoretical models to deal with the simultaneous globalisation and fragmentation of a modern state system that nevertheless remained a dominant organisational force. He argued that while the challenges to national sovereignty were very real, the state system was not in danger of disappearing altogether; on the contrary, its continued existence was vital in the maintenance of political, social and, as witnessed most notably during the 2008 financial crisis, economic stability both within and without national borders. Despite this continued hold on legitimate political action, the discourses of International Relations still fixed resolutely the nation-state's gradual erosion both from above, by transnational, liberalised economies and cross-cutting communication technologies, and below, by sub-national communities realigning along ethnic, cultural and religious lines. By the early 21st century, it had become increasingly difficult to imagine a possible future in which states continued to exist as partial actors within an extended multilateral web of complex and fluid power relations. As prominent International Relations professor Andrew Linklater put it, such a possibility received "too little attention from political theorists who are, with some exceptions, firmly wedded to reflections on the modern state, and from mainstream students of International Relations who, by analysing relations between bounded communities, have often ignored questions about how alternative forms of political community and new principals of world organisation might

---

cept rebounded when Iran, North Korea and Iraq were infamously singled out as a "Axis of Evil" in President George Bush's 2002 State of the Union Address following in the wake of 9/11.

[7] Jörg Friedrichs, "The Meaning of New Medievalism," *European Journal of International Relations* 7.4 (2001): 481.

evolve".[8]

Conventional wisdom in the '00s, then, supposed that the nation-state was in its death-throes; it would either break down into parochial enclaves, be consumed by economic processes of standardisation,[9] or react by aggressively reaffirming political, social and economic boundaries. To illustrate the impasse reached by International Relations discourse, Freidrichs quoted at length from French scholar Pierre Hassner who, significantly, imparted his message in a deliberately "medieval" language, both in its ecclesiastical, apocalyptic overtones (ruins of Empire/rupturing heavens) and in its adoption of Tolkienesque protagonists (princes, monsters and fairies):[10]

Peace or War? Utopia or nightmare? Global solidarity or tribal conflict? Nationalism triumphant or the crisis of the nation-state? Progress on civil rights or persecution of minorities? New world order or new anarchy? There seems to be no end to the fundamental dilemmas and anguished questions provoked by the post-Cold War world. One is almost tempted to turn to the language of myth and fairy tale. Perhaps we should blame the witches and bad fairies who made their wishes over the cradle of the latest born of the international systems. Perhaps the Prince has been turned into a monster and will never recover his original form. Perhaps the fall of the Soviet empire has torn a hole in the heavens and in the ground underfoot, allowing us to glimpse through the ruins of the postwar structures both the shinning prospect of a

---

[8] Andrew Linklater, *Critical Theory and World Politics: Citizenship, Sovereignty and Humanity* (New York, Routledge, 2007), 92–93.

[9] For example, in the case of the European Union, consolidation into a federal superstate.

[10] This recourse to fuzzy irrationalism was perhaps an attempt to communicate something incommensurable to post-enlightenment discourse. Neomedievalism in International Relations can be read as a de-rationalisation of political theory.

global community and the swarming menace of unre-strained violence.[11]

Hassner suggested that a juncture had been reached where the secular analytical languages of political science no lon-ger sufficed to adequately impart the rapidly morphing com-plexities of globalisation. Freidrichs asserted that this "dile-mma" came from a particularly modern desire to unify the dual processes of fragmentation and globalisation onto a single ontological narrative of international transformation. It is as though we were "still captive to the modern a priori that a coherent order cannot be organised if not from exact-ly one organising principal".[12]

It was instead proposed that Bull's neomedievalism be adapted to allow these multiple, conflicting theories to co-exist within a relatively stable and holistic framework. It was necessary to expand upon Bull's oft-cited definition of neo-medievalism as "a system of overlapping authority and multiple loyalty".[13] In this definition, Freidrichs read a narrow pejorative caricature of the late Middle Ages as instable, anarchic and barbarous. Bull himself noted the apocalyptic implications of a post-Westphalian world that would "con-tain more ubiquitous and continuous violence and insecurity than does the modern states system".[14] To shift the emphasis towards a more sustainable equilibrium, Freidrichs reminded us that—while the late medieval period was un-doubtedly plagued by inter-ethnic conflict, social inequality, outlawry and religious sectarianism—the social fragmen-tation of Western Europe was held in check for centuries by both Christian universalism, and the hegemonic claims of the Holy Roman Empire. Within this social constellation the

---

[11] Pierre Hassner, "Violence and Peace: From the Atomic Bomb to Ethnic Cleansing", in *Beyond Nationalism and Internationalism: Monstrosity and Hope* (Budapest: Central European University Press, 1997), 215–219.

[12] Freidrichs, "The Meaning of New Medievalism", 479.

[13] Bull, *The Anarchical Society*, 254.

[14] Bull, *The Anarchical Society*, 255.

Catholic clergy and the feudal nobility "formed trans-territorial classes that preserved a considerable degree of uniformity".[15] According to the neomedieval paradigm, global stability is managed by the conflicting yet inter-dependent universalisms of the neoliberal world market economy and the liberal nation state system. As principal actors within this world order, the clergy have been replaced by the global managerial class of bankers, corporate CEOs and scientists and the feudal aris-tocracy by politicians, policy makers and bureaucrats.[16] Like the ecclesiastical and monarchial powers of medieval Europe, these groups are "characterised by an extraordinary degree of spatial and social mobility" that is denied to most ordinary subjects.[17] Accordingly, Bull's neo-medievalism is revised as: "a system of overlapping and authority and multiple loyalty—held together by a duality of competing universalistic claims".[18]

Within this expanded definition three main overlapping realms are in evidence and remain stable only within a continual flux between antagonism and cooperation. For a neomedieval order to function, no one sphere can claim total legitimacy over another. Societal actors constantly operate through networks of resistance and re-focused loyalties to promote "life-world" values—be they political, religious, environmental, etc.—in resistance to both the totalitarian

---

[15] Freidrichs, "The Meaning of New Medievalism", 486.

[16] Of course, it might make as much, if not more, sense to equate medieval ecclesiastical powers with those of contemporary elected political authorities that, at least, maintain the illusion of counsel with commoners through regular surgeries and congregations. Such authorities claim to hold the will of unaccountable monarchial forces in check, forces that we might today equate with the global neoliberal economy. Both seek universal legitimation in the limited choices offered to individuals to elect (democracy) and to consume (neoliberalism). Since they emanate from different cultures, ecclesiastical and monarchial "choices" are often conflicting.

[17] Freidrichs, "The Meaning of New Medievalism", 492.

[18] Freidrichs, "The Meaning of New Medievalism", 490.

claims of the liberal democratic state and the colonising forces of the neo-liberal global economy. Economic realms must resist political interference and adapt to societal values at odds with the autonomous logic of market efficiency. In the realm of politics, collective sovereignty must be maintained, at national and international levels, despite the particular claims of societal actors and organising forces of the global economy.

Freidrichs acknowledged that the symmetry of the above model was problematic. A balance was inferred that ignored the fact that the universalising claims of the transnational economy continued to colonise both politics and society, ensuring that there was little prospect of opposition to neo-liberalism. Questions also arose regarding where individuals turned in matters requiring democratic resolution. If the state was no longer primarily accountable for upholding and policing values such as social inclusiveness or even basic human rights, how would individuals determine which organisations should serve as the focus of their loyalties?[19] Despite these issues, Freidrichs's neomedievalism offered, at least, a historical meta-narrative in nucleo, providing a framework that allowed simultaneous discussion of globalisation, fragmentation and sovereign states. His was an ameliorative interpretation based on a (fantasy of a) Middle Ages of relatively sustainable order.[20] By this analogy, "apocalyptic fears of an imminent new world disorder can be smoothed. At least in principle, cultural pluralism is not necessarily linked with anarchy, nor is universalism with a global super-Leviathan".[21]

Along with Freidrichs, Phillip G. Cerny and Stephen J.

---

[19] I will engage some of these issues in more detail later in this chapter by discussing where other commentators took Bull's embryonic hypothesis, as well as by looking at specific examples where it was applied (sometimes irresponsibly) to world events.

[20] Which is simply to say that the interpretation required the construction of a medievalism.

[21] Freidrichs, "The Meaning of New Medievalism", 494.

Kobrin also made significant contributions to the formulation and promotion of neomedievalism as a geopolitical metaphor or "inter-temporal analog of comparative political analysis".[22] Both built their theses from a broad range of disciplines, ranging from economics and history to cultural studies and political science. Kobrin focused on the role of digital technology in the dematerialisation of territorially-defined economies and political identities, while Cerny centred his analogy on the obsolescence of the "security dilemma"—a neorealist term describing how the state system was maintained through cyclic and reciprocal res-ponses, such as an arms-race or strategic alliances, to perceived external threats.

To varying degrees, all three authors followed up on groundwork prepared by Gerrard Ruggie in his 1993 article, "Territoriality and Beyond: Problematizing Modernity in International Relations," in which he traced the transition from medieval to modern to postmodern Europe in an attempt to find a language apposite to the exploration of contemporary international transformation. In the same article he drew upon a number of sources to extrapolate a history of the medieval period central to all subsequent neo-medieval discourse[23]:

---

[22] Stephen J. Kobrin, "Back to the Future: Neomedievalism and the Postmodern Digital World Economy", The Wharton School, University of Pennsylvania, 6; revision of a paper originally published as "Back to the Future: Neomedievalism and the Postmodern Digital World Economy", Journal of International Affairs 51 (Spring 1998): 361–386. Available online: http://citeseerx.ist.psu.edu/viewdoc/down load?doi=10.1.1.131.6106&rep=rep1&type=pdf

[23] Gerard Ruggie, "Territoriality and Beyond: Problematizing Modernity in International Relations", International Organization 47.1 (Winter 1993): 139–174. Ruggie quotes from Joseph R. Strayer and Dana C. Munro, The Middle Ages (New York: Appleton-Century-Crofts, 1959), 115, and from Perry Anderson, Lineages of the Absolutist State (London: New Left Books, 1974), 37, 37–38.

The archetype of nonexclusive territorial rule, of course, is medieval Europe, with its "patchwork of overlapping and incomplete rights of government", which were "inextricably superimposed and tangled," and in which "different juridical instances were geographically interwoven and stratified, and plural allegiances, asymmetrical suzerainties and anomalous enclaves abounded". . . . the spatial extension of the medieval system of rule was structured by a nonexclusive form of territoriality, in which authority was both personalized and parcelized within and across territorial formations and for which inclusive bases of legitimation prevailed. The notion of firm boundary lines between the major territorial formations did not take hold until the thirteenth century; prior to that date, there were only "frontiers," or large zones of transition. The medieval ruling class was mobile in a manner not dreamed of since, able to assume governance from one end of the continent to the other without hesitation or difficulty because "public territories formed a continuum with private estates".[24]

The proceeding centuries witnessed a gradual consolidation or "bundling" together of both secular and spiritual social groups and institutions under territorial based sovereignty. The emergence of modern macro-nation-states was far more complex than a shift from fluid overlapping structures to rigid hierarchies inside and anarchy outside—as inferred by neorealism. Ruggie argued that a partial "unbundling" of territory had always been a prerequisite to the success of mutually exclusive sovereign states in that it provided a fictitious "extraterritorial space" where diplomacy could be carried out. Chapel embassies, for example, provided visiting dignitaries a patch of homeland where a Protestant service could be carried out on Catholic soil and vice versa. These small pockets of alien sovereignty developed over time to

---

[24] Ruggie, "Territoriality and Beyond", 149–150.

include a variety of functional regimes such as international fairs, common markets and political communities spanning across multiple borders. Unbundled territory, then, acted as a pressure valve, loosening the grip of what Ruggie termed the "paradox of absolute individuation".[25] The processes of globalisation accelerated the unbundling of territoriality, a condition necessitated by increasing transnational interdependences. The negation of exclusivity provided a means for dealing with "those dimensions of collective existence that territorial rulers recognize to be irreducibly transterritorial in character. Nonterritorial functional space is the place wherein international society is anchored".[26] Ruggie concluded that unbundled territoriality is the site from which all attempts at rearticulating international social and political space should propagate.

For Kobrin, the proliferation of extraterritorial space was exemplified by information and communication technologies. The rapid expansion of the Internet marked a fundamental rupture between geographic space (a space of place) and cyberspace (a space of flows).[27] This allowed simultaneous information exchange between transnational corporations, culture and media centres and government bureaucra-

---

[25] Ruggie, "Territoriality and Beyond", 164.

[26] Ruggie, "Territoriality and Beyond", 165.

[27] "Space of place" and "space of flows" are terms borrowed from Manuel Castells, *The Rise of the Network Society* (Oxford: Blackwell, 1996), 412: "Our societies are constructed around flows: flows of capital, flows of information, flows of technology, flows of organizational interactions, flows of images, sounds and symbols. Flows are not just one element of social organization: they are the expression of the processes dominating our economic, political, and symbolic life. . . . Thus, I propose the idea that there is a new spatial form characteristic of social practices that dominate and shape the network society: the space of flows. The space of flows is the material organization of time-sharing social practices that work through flows. By flows I understand purposeful, repetitive, programmable sequences of exchange and interaction between physically disjointed positions held by social actors."

cies to operate in nebulous realms outside the jurisdiction of national borders, rendering space "once again relational and symbolic, or metaphysical. External reality seen through the World Wide Web may be closer to medieval Christian representations of the world than to a modern atlas."[28]

Similarly, mobile populations or diasporic societies with internet access became less culturally dependent on economies of scale that arise in communities of place. The ability to network electronically, to establish "scale-free" communities of practice based on ethnicity, religion, political identity, sexual preference, cultural interests, economic class, celebrity ranking etc., made modern practices of nationhood more portable, or even, in some cases, irrelevant. At the same time, access to physical transterritorial mobility and to virtual information networks remained rigidly divided between those who had and those who had not. Clusters of privilege, capital innovation and property rights (citadels) formed that were "surrounded by a vast and impenetrable forest" (barbarian camps and ghettos).[29]

According to Cerny, the collapse of the Soviet Union was not solely a result of power-shifts in relation to the United States but, more accurately, its passing was brought about by new configurations of internal and transnational pressures arising from increased economic interdependences, heightened public exposure to social and cultural alternatives via communications technologies, and a general expansion of consumerism that the USSR was increasingly unable to control in an ever more interconnected world.[30] International relations, therefore, were no longer to be dominated by indivisible nationalist concerns but by "divisible benefits pursued by pluralistic, often cross-national networks of individu-

---

[28] Kobrin, "Back to the Future", 11.

[29] Kobrin, "Back to the Future", 10.

[30] Philip G. Cerny, "The New Security Dilemma Revisited: Neomedievalism and the Limits of Hegemony", paper presented at International Studies Association, Montréal, Québec, March 18-21, 2004: 5.

als and groups".[31] In general, it could be said that citizens became less concerned with the institutional benefits of "belonging" to (or opposing) the particularised, cultural and sociopolitical values embedded within their state of citizenship. As well as negotiating over issues directly involved with the home state, many social causes or interest groups focused more on "cross-cutting transnational issues such as the environment, women's issues, the international banning of land mines, opposition to the holding of political prisoners worldwide, promotion of sustainable development and the like".[32] Consequently, the processes of states were progressively transformed into "transmission belts" or "enforcement mechanisms" for political and cultural exchanges occurring across an evermore diverse and complex global stage "increasingly characterized by attributes that echo features of the medieval world".[33]

Despite differing angles of approach, these authors offered a systematic breakdown of International Relations neo-medievalism in the early 21st century as summarised by Cerny at the 2004 Annual Convention of the International Studies Association in Montréal, Québec:

1. Competing institutions with overlapping jurisdictions (states, regimes, transgovernmental networks, private interest governments, etc.).

2. More fluid territorial boundaries (both within and across states).

3. A growing alienation between global innovation, communication and resource nodes (global cities) on the one hand and disfavoured, fragmented hinterlands on the other, along with increased inequalities and isolation of

---

[31] , "The New Security Dilemma Revisited", 6.

[32] Cerny, "The New Security Dilemma Revisited", 3.

[33] Cerny, "The New Security Dilemma Revisited", 2, 7.

permanent sub-castes (the underclass).

4. Multiple and/or fragmented loyalties and identities (ethnic conflict and multiculturalism).

5. Contested property rights and legal boundaries (e.g., disregard for rules and dispute resolution procedures, attempts to extend extraterritorial jurisdiction, etc.)

6. The spread of what Alain Minc has called "zones grises",[34] or geographical areas and social contexts where the rule of law does not run (both localized ghettoes and international criminal activities).[35]

These points typified the consolidated idioms of International Relations neomedievalism of which there were a growing number of exponents.

The analogy developed here was inherently and dangerously double-edged. Invoking the medieval, as Bull feared, conjured firmly embedded popular images of Empires in ruin, barbarian hoards, crusades, jihads, fortresses, outlawry, misogyny, superstition and fear—not to mention plague and famine. The neomedieval rhetoric carried a prophetic or millenarianist trope, an anticipation of cataclysmic events, which IR scholars tempered through selective historical sourcing and particular emphasis on the 'high' or 'late' period of the Middle Ages. This very duplicity made the transhistorical

---

[34] Cerny is quoting from Alain Minc's best selling book *Le Nouveau Moyen Age* (Paris: Gallimard, 1993). In a 1994 interview for the BBC2 television series The *New Middle Ages*, Minc explained, "We are already seeing the emergence of 'grey zones' in which any kind of power does not exist any more, rather like the Middle Ages with its vast abandoned areas. For three centuries, we have been establishing the State to create order. Today, we are seeing areas developing without any kind of order or any kind of State": *The New Middle Ages*, BBC2, November 28, 1994.

[35] Cerny, "The New Security Dilemma Revisited", 7–8.

model conducive to creative analysis while remaining precariously fuzzy and open to political misappropriation. Cerny juggled the hot potato deftly in his conference paper. The central thrust of his argument posited a new neomedieval world order in which

> a new sense of generalised insecurity has emerged represented not only 'from above' by the threat of proliferation of weapons of mass destruction, but also 'from below', by the rise of civil wars, tribal and religious conflicts, terrorism, civil violence in developed countries, the international drugs trade, etc. This sense of insecurity reflects the fact that the provision of security itself as a public good—the very raison d'être of the states system—can no longer be guaranteed by that system.[36]

And yet Cerny asserted, as did Freidrichs, that such a volatile "system need not imply global chaos, since the medieval order was a highly flexible one that created a wide range of spaces that could accommodate quite extensive social, economic and political innovations," to be compared to a future world order which "similarly provides manifold opportunities . . . . In the world of global finance, multinational firms, multilateral regimes, and private authority, therefore, the emerging neomedieval world order, reflecting its medieval predecessor, is most likely to be a kind of durable—yet fertile—disorder".[37]

Not all commentators shared such a benign view. For some, neomedievalism served as a warning from the past. Just as the Roman Empire collapsed in a gradual "death by a thousand cuts", resulting in the so-called "Dark Age", so at the dawn of the second millennium, Western imperial hegemony (territorially embedded or globally diffuse) was threatened by the barbarians knocking again at the door.

---

[36] Cerny, "The New Security Dilemma Revisited", 5.

[37] Cerny, "The New Security Dilemma Revisited", 19.

Cerny's silver lining of "extensive innovation" and "manifold opportunities" applied not only to those operating within legitimate, state-sanctioned spheres of global influence but also to an increasing number of proxy or state-seceded, semi-autonomous organisations for whom the continued opulence and future comfort of the Pax Americana was not on the agenda.

At "Globalisation and Governance in the Pacific Islands", a conference held in Australia in 2005, John Rapley delivered a keynote address, entitled "From Neo-Liberalism to the New Medievalism," sketching a potted history of the rapid, worldwide adoption of neo-liberal reform strategies over the past thirty years. He outlined how the shift from state-led development to free market economies, coupled with the hyper-growth of urban regions or "global cities", particularly within the Third World, led to a marked withdrawal of state-level governance. To compete internationally, both rich and poor states alike, were forced to reduce taxes on production, cut down on public expenditure and deliver an increasing number of services via private or semi-private contractors. In the developing world—where urbanisation was at its most acute and governments struggled to meet basic demands for public goods such as water, housing, roads and security—Rapley argued that sovereignty, rather than being merely decentralised, was being negotiated with those who could "deliver the goods".[38] In cities across the Middle East, Latin America, Asia and Africa, where neo-liberal policies created pockets of vast wealth beside sprawling slum districts, new political patrons "ranging from criminal gangs to Islamist civil-society networks have assumed many of the functions that states have abandoned, funding their operations through informal taxes as well as proceeds from the

---

[38] John Rapley, "From Neo-liberalism to the New Medievalism", keynote address, "Globalisation and Governance in the Pacific Islands" conference, Australian National University, Canberra, Australia, 2006: 17. Available online: epress.anu.edu.au.

drug trade, human trafficking and money laundering".[39] By way of example, Rapley recalled the lamentation of the US sponsored "war on drugs" by a senior Jamaican police officer who declared it "unwinnable" because much of downtown Kingston's food, clothing and education was funded by gang-controlled drug money. This "rudimentary welfare" was provided in conjunction with an informal law-and-order programme complete with chicken-coop holding cells and private judicial hearings, in many cases with cooperation from local police who tolerated the dons' drug activities in return for relatively peaceful streets. The system operated well enough in the vacuum left by official retreat, and gang-controlled communities, Robert Kaplan argued, were amongst the safest in the country.[40]

This complex symbiotic relationship between state and "statelet" was undoubtedly a global trend, a reconfiguration of power relations not just confined to impoverished sectors of the urban environment. Within the global cities of the developing world, it was not just marginalised groups who managed their affairs and competed for resources independent of state regulation. An increasing number of the urban elite, those firmly "plugged-in" to the international marketplace, were living in segregated enclaves walled-off from the poorer communities who constituted the vast majority of the megalopolis demographic. As Nezar Alsayyad and Ananaya Roy explained in their thesis on "medieval modernity", the gated enclave was the most common paradigm of spatial organisation in the early 21st century's splintering urbanism. The "secession of the successful" was not simply a residential phenomenon, but part of a "network of exclusion" taking in urban restoration projects, art and media centres, leisure complexes, and even semi-private toll roads and skyways. In São Paulo, for example, the world's largest

---

[39] Rapley, "From Neo-Liberalism to the New Medievalism", 6.

[40] Robert Kaplan, "The Coming Anarchy", *Atlantic Monthly*, February 1994, 44–76.

fleet of private helicopters, one of which cost ninety times the average resident's annual salary, regularly bypassed the city's crippled transport network. Alsayyad and Roy described gated communities as a new kind of "spatial governmentality"[41] with reciprocal rights and obligations managed by common interest developments (CIDs) and external threats controlled through surveillance technology, private security firms and crenellated architecture.

Alsayyad and Roy's medieval analogy was partially based on a model of 11th- and 12th-century city-states as "honeycombs of jurisdiction" where certain freedoms (from serfdom for example) were granted in exchange for loyalty to a diverse and overlapping set of competing institutional bodies. Their comparative analysis took in three distinct yet interdependent modes of urban spatial formation: the gated enclave, the squatter settlement and the camp—the natures of which, they argued, could be better articulated through an engagement with their pre-modern counterparts:

First, if modern citizenship was constituted through a set of abstract individual rights embedded in the concept of the nation-state, then now there is the emergence of forms of citizenship that are located in urban enclaves. As in medieval times, this citizenship is linked to either patronage (as in the bishop) or to associational membership (as in the guild) and in both cases it is fundamentally about protection. Secondly, such forms of citizenship substitute for or are even hostile to the state. From the private home-owners' associations to the neighbourhood-level Islamic republics being declared by religious fundamentalist groups, these are private systems of governance that operate as medieval fiefdoms, imposing

---

41 Nezar Alsayyad and Ananaya Roy, "Medieval Modernity: On Citizenship and Urbanism in a Global Era", *Space and Polity* 10.1 (2006): 6.

truths and norms that are often contrary to national law.[42]

The analogy broadened discussion around the emergence of informally governed territories within the neo-liberal city by complicating the polarised notion of clear delimitations between the (plugged-in) global elite and the (switched-off) impoverished masses. In the medieval city, the "logic of rule is never singular; the terrain is always that of uneasy alliances and shifting sovereignties".[43] As Rapley attested, power was negotiated through complex webs of association and patronage between state, NGO, religious organisation, ethnic tribes, gang leaders and corporate body. The competition over resources was fiercely contested and resolved through a "politics of fiefdoms negotiated through modes of visible and invisible regulations".[44]

It was not so much the sharpened divisions between rich and poor that led Rapley, in his conference address, to propose "that the symbolic date on which the neo-liberal empire ended was September 11, 2001, the date the command structure of history's most powerful empire was temporarily decapitated by a handful of men armed with box cutters"[45]; rather, it was the close proximity and labyrinthine interconnect between local and transnational concerns that confounded Western projects of global democratisation. In the wake of the neo-liberal age, Rapley argued that the neomedieval analogy, as set out by International Relations scholars, was a valid one. However, he noted that this debate tended to cluster around the political reconfigurations of Europe rather than the burgeoning cities of the Third World, rapidly evolving nodes "integrated into the global economy, standing often in the vanguard of global trends".[46] The legitimate vectors of communication established between these nodes

---

[42] Alsayyad and Roy, "Medieval Modernity", 3.

[43] Alsayyad and Roy, "Medieval Modernity", 12.

[44] Alsayyad and Roy, "Medieval Modernity", 12.

[45] Rapley, "From Neo-liberalism to the New Medievalism", 15.

[46] Rapley, "From Neo-liberalism to the New Medievalism", 18.

and those of the First World allow state seceded, criminal organisations such as terrorist groups and drug traffickers (or alliances between both) to operate at a global scale free from detection. Even if individual members could be identified, shelter could be sought in communities where the state no longer has adequate jurisdiction. Moreover, manifestations of violence were no longer confined to specific geographic territories as "gang warfare or apparently random murders in Toronto or London that seem senseless and anarchic within the context of those societies take on a brutally rational meaning when analysed within the context of gangs back in Jamaica or Nigeria".[47]

With the attacks on the World Trade Centre by al Qaeda, "the metonym for the amorphous global network",[48] and the subsequent retaliatory wars in Afghanistan and Iraq, came the slow dawning realisation that conventional rules of warfare no longer apply. Violent conflicts can no longer be seen as legitimate acts between states, wars transcend borders to follow subnational and supranational fault-lines of deep-rooted religious or tribal resentments and the distinction between war and crime is increasingly hard to officially classify. The so-called "enemy" is nomadic: a hybrid, globalised and stateless wanderer with one foot in each world, able to deftly manipulate the available resources and technologies of both.

As Chris Berzins and Patrick Cullens speculated in their contribution to the anthology, Neo-Medievalism and Civil Wars, the 9/11 hijackers' lives "were more or less ambiguously divided between the pull of the Western cities where they lived, studied and travelled, and the radical factions within the mosques, where they worshiped and were recruited. These men were seemingly equally at ease, or more accurately at unease with modern technology and dress as they were with the traditions of the Muslim faith. They exist-

---

[47] Rapley, "From Neo-liberalism to the New Medievalism", 19.
[48] Rapley, "From Neo-liberalism to the New Medievalism", 17.

ed as foreigners, within an increasingly fragmented and alienating social, cultural and economic space while at the same time pushed up against the universalising influence of religion, and ultimately fanaticism".[49]

Within this medievalising rhetoric lay the crux of Cerny's "generalised insecurity" from below. An abstracted fear of the irrational pre-modern "other", a living fossil of the "dark ages" infiltrating the networks of modern secular society. This led Rapley and many other advocates of neomedievalism to speak of a "new Rome" and "new barbarian tribes" gnawing at the edges of the Empire until eventually toppling its core. For the new medievalism had an omnipresent and troubling subtext, "just as the original medievalism was built atop the triumph of the triumph of Germanic tribes over the Roman Empire, the new medievalism can itself degenerate into a cold ruthless struggle over resources . . . happening in a context where abundance has never been greater, but relative scarcities never more acute".[50] Rapley made the additional point that, in allowing greater experience of how "the other half lives", the Internet ensured that the "notion that worlds really are apart begins to tumble. Resentment grows. It festers".[51] Rapley warned that the "new Romans, like the old, might not enjoy the consequences".[52]

Such apocalyptic hyperbole utilised a woefully inaccurate, yet highly popular vision of the early Middle Ages, one hastily qualified as an exercise in "what if?"-style speculation. This was a powerful and compelling trope feeding the spectacular apocalyptic narratives that saturated Western cinema at the turn of the 21st century. Retro-futuristic imaginings of Vandals and Visigoths, astride hover-bikes sporting

---

[49] Chris Berzins and Patrick Cullen, "Terrorism and Neo-Medievalism", in Neil Winn, ed., Neo-Medievalism and Civil Wars (London: Frank Cass, 2004), 25.

[50] Rapley, "From Neo-liberalism to the New Medievalism", 19.

[51] Rapley, "From Neo-liberalism to the New Medievalism", 20.

[52] John Rapley, "The New Middle Ages", Foreign Affairs, May/June, 2006, 103.

high-tech weaponry, terrorising the remaining inhabitants of post-apocalyptic cities, demonstrated the primitivising tendency in Western consciousness towards allegedly "premodern" societies. The most influential political journalism tended to be that which explicitly delineated and exploited the neo-medieval "heart of darkness".

In 1994, Kaplan wrote an article entitled "The Coming Anarchy"[53] for *The Atlantic* magazine, drawing on his experiences of extensive travel in West Africa and the Middle East to formulate a report on how "to remap the political earth the way it will be in a few decades hence".[54] On his tour through the adjoining counties of Sierra Leone, Liberia, Côte d'Ivoire, Ghana, Togo, Senegal and Nigeria, he witnessed mass displacement of populations driven to urban coastal areas due to deforestation and desertification. The communalism and polygamy of peasant life, when translated into an urban social context, ceased to function: food and shelter were not given freely and loose family structures led to the world's highest birth rate and the proliferation of the HIV virus. Further displacement was caused by rebel uprisings and tribal conflicts characterised by a "pre-modern form-

---

[53] The title of Kaplan's article echoed computer engineer Roberto Vacca's 1974 book *The Coming Dark Age*, which hypothesised a technological apocalypse leading to a new dark age between 1985 and 1995. Following in the speculative wake of science fiction writer and futurist Isaac Asimov's popular book and TV series *Future Shock* (1970), Vacca imagined the pre-modern other being held at bay by technological advances. The overload of the technologically determinist "great systems" that could "start a catastrophic process that would paralyse the most developed societies and lead to the deaths of millions of people": Roberto Vacca, "The Beginning and Duration of the Dark Age", *The Coming Dark Age* (Granada: Frogmore, 1974), 9. While Vacca fantasised that "the imminent dark age" would begin in the United States and sweep rapidly across the world's most technologically advanced states, Kaplan's neomedievalism inverts this scenario, identifying the ungoverned spaces of developing sub-Saharan Africa as a bulwark of future anarchy.

[54] Kaplan, "The Coming Anarchy", 46.

lessness . . . evoking the wars in medieval Europe prior to the 1648 Peace of Westphalia".[55] Kaplan was struck by the superficiality of a political cartography imposed by former colonists that had become "largely meaningless".[56] The fragmentation of West African states Kaplan described clearly fitted the parameters set out in neomedievalist International Relations theory, establishing the sub-Sahara as a paradigm for future developments in the rest of the world:

> West Africa is becoming the symbol of worldwide demographic, environmental, and societal stress, in which criminal anarchy emerges as the real 'strategic' danger. Disease, overpopulation, unprovoked crime, scarcity of resources, refugee migrations, the increasing erosion of nation-states and international borders, and the empowerment of private armies, security firms, and international drug cartels are now most tellingly demonstrated through a West African prism. West Africa provides an appropriate introduction to the issues, often extremely unpleasant to discuss, that will soon confront our civilization.[57]

The plight of West Africa may have seemed at a far remove from the privileged interests of Western society, yet, in an evermore interconnected world, there was one inescapable issue of global import which could not be ignored—the environment. Kaplan argued that the political and strategic impact of rapid population growth, pandemic outbreaks, deforestation and soil erosion, water scarcity, pollution and rising sea levels would be at the very centre of early twenty-first century foreign policy, plugging the "crisis management" gap left by the Cold War. Concern over the stability of the planet's ecosystems and its diminishing resources was undoubtedly an issue of monolithic scope at the forefront of

---

[55] Kaplan, "The Coming Anarchy", 46.

[56] Kaplan, "The Coming Anarchy", 48.

[57] Kaplan, "The Coming Anarchy", 46.

public interest. While Kaplan, obviously, could not have predicted 9/11 and its worldwide repercussions on foreign policy and security protocols, he argued that international terrorism and civil violence, defined in his article as a "transformation of war",[58] would intensify in correlation with the above-mentioned factors. His bleak prognosis for a century in which "the classificatory grid of nation states was going to be replaced by a jagged-glass pattern of city states, shanty-states, nebulous and anarchic regionalisms",[59] was derived from two key concepts: a revised understanding of both warfare and mapmaking.

Kaplan argued that while the minority of the global population found shelter in a "post-historical realm", living in "cities and suburbs where the environment has been mastered and ethnic animosities have been quelled by bourgeois prosperity", the vast majority of the surging population would remain "stuck in history, living in shantytowns where attempts to rise above poverty, cultural dysfunction, and ethnic strife will be doomed by a lack of water to drink, soil to till, and space to survive in."[60] Here he borrowed an analogy from Thomas Homer-Dixon, then the head of the Peace and Conflict Studies programme at the University of Toronto, of a stretch limo travelling through the homeless streets of New York. Inside the limo is Fukuyama's "Last Man", healthy, well fed, and pampered by technology, an inhabitant of the "air conditioned post-industrial regions . . . with their trade summitry and computer information highways. Outside is the rest of mankind going in a completely opposite direction".[61]

The metaphor may be poignant, yet, as we have seen, such notions of a completely bifurcated world were reductive and unsustainable, especially considering increasing

---

[58] Kaplan, "The Coming Anarchy", 46.

[59] Kaplan, "The Coming Anarchy", 72.

[60] Kaplan, "The Coming Anarchy", 59.

[61] Kaplan, "The Coming Anarchy", 61. This equally describes the plot of Don DeLillo's 2003 novel *Cosmopolis*.

demographic shifts and cultural interaction. Kaplan pointed to Samuel P. Huntington's equally controversial Clash of Civilisations thesis, claiming that, following the economic and ideologically driven international wars of the previous century, conflict would increasingly occur along cultural fault-lines at a sub-national level.[62] His thesis was widely criticised for superficially homogenising civilisations into self-enclosed territories and ignoring the shifting interdependencies, mutual affiliations and internal partisanships that constitute the hybridism of cultural identity. Nevertheless, Kaplan added that, "as refugee flows increase and as peasants continue migrating to cities around the world—turning them into sprawling villages—national borders will mean less, even as more power will fall into the hands of less educated, less sophisticated groups".[63] Considering the fundamental impact of environmental scarcity, he proposed a world more dangerous than the one Huntington envisioned, "a run-down, crowded planet of skinhead Cossacks and juju warriors, influenced by the worst refuse of Western pop culture and ancient tribal hatreds, and battling over scraps of over-used earth in guerrilla conflicts that ripple across continents and intersect in no discernible pattern—meaning there's no easy-to-define threat".[64]

Kaplan concluded with an examination of military historian Martin van Creveld's assertions that the conglomerate military machines of the nation-state were dinosaurs on the brink of extinction. The threefold division into government, army and people no longer held. To see the future one must "look back to the past immediately prior to the birth of modernism—the wars in medieval Europe which began during the Reformation and reached their culmination in the Thirty Years' War".[65] In this type of warfare, armies were

[62] Samuel P. Huntington, *Clash of Civilisations and the Remaking of World Order* (New York: Simon & Schuster, 1996).

[63] Kaplan, "The Coming Anarchy", 60.

[64] Kaplan, "The Coming Anarchy", 60.

[65] Kaplan, "The Coming Anarchy", 73.

comprised of mercenaries and "swarms of military entrepreneurs"[66] whose allegiances and motives were entangled along political, economic, religious and social lines. If states were losing their legal monopoly on armed conflict, then the distinction between war and crime would be more ambiguous. As governments lost their ability to protect citizens from eruptions of small-scale violence, armies would be "gradually replaced by a booming private security business, as in West Africa, and by urban mafias, especially in the former communist world, who may be better equipped than municipal police forces to grant physical protection to local inhabitants".[67]

At the heart of Kaplan's argument lay a fundamental criticism of the enlightenment impulse of European colonists to measure, categorise and format the world in terms of a totalising classificatory grid.[68] His visit to Africa brought home the damaging legacy of an "artificial reality" legitimised and universalised through the invention of print technology, and still staggering on today in elite geographic and travel publications. A more appropriate representation of the multi-actors involved in territorialisation, he asserted, requires a hyper-cultural map:

Imagine cartography in three dimensions, as if in a hologram. In this hologram would be the overlapping sediments of group and other identities atop the merely two-dimensional color markings of city-states and the remaining nations, themselves confused in places by shadowy tentacles, hovering overhead, indicating the power of drug cartels, mafias, and private security agencies. Instead of

---

[66] Kaplan, "The Coming Anarchy", 73.

[67] Kaplan, "The Coming Anarchy", 74.

[68] Dror called this the "Everyone Wants What We Want" fallacy, the foreign policy delusion that "those who do not want, as yet, what the United States wants will change their minds once they become developed": Dror, "Common Fallacies in American Strategic Studies", in Crazy States, 14.

borders, there would be moving 'centers' of power, as in the Middle Ages. Many of these layers would be in motion. . . . To this protean cartographic hologram one must add other factors, such as migrations of populations, explosions of birth rates, vectors of disease. Henceforward the map of the world will never be static. This future map—in a sense, the "Last Map"—will be an ever-mutating representation of chaos.[69]

Long gone, then, was the grand theory of post-war international relations, the humanist generalisations inspired by classical realists such as Hans Morgenthau.[70] In its place Kaplan proposed a real-time rolling account of shifting patterns of current events, of fading and emerging ideologies, multi-scalar maps of unpredictable, system-less neomedieval state and non-state relations. The Coming Anarchy differed from other neomedievalisms not just in its orientation towards the developing world, but also in the highly emotive and subjective tone of Kaplan's writing. Kaplan's work was persuasive in its dense mix of anecdotal on-the-ground reportage, academic referencing and statistical analysis, a literary style that resonated with audiences beyond academia. Kaplan enjoyed wide readership at government level; his 1993 book *Balkan Ghosts: A Journey Through History* was said to have directly influenced President Bill Clinton's decision against intervention in Bosnia. It is also significant that John Rapley's later article *The New Middle Ages* was published in Foreign Affairs—a "Beano read" in the circuits of the international political classes. It is not too surprising then, to find, the neomedieval model was considered in US government-sanctioned studies on national defence. This was where the dangers of drawing comparisons with such a lengthy and misunderstood period as the Middle Ages became most apparent.

---

[69] Kaplan, "The Coming Anarchy", 75.

[70] Hans J. Morgenthau, *Politics Among Nations: The Struggle for Power and Peace* (New York: Alfred A. Knopf, 1948).

In 2008 the Strategic Studies Institute at United States Army War College published a monograph by Dr. Phil Williams entitled *From the New Middle Ages to a New Dark Age: The Decline of the State and U.S. Strategy*. The paper used the neomedieval school of thought to propose that America reassess its state-centric approach to foreign policy if it was to avoid being helmed in or overcome by a "tsunami of chaos".[71] While Williams cited examples from all major neomedievalist International Relations scholars, taking on board the emphasis on metaphoric rather than actual return to pre-existing socio-political structures, he nevertheless managed to reintroduce the terrifying prospect of imminent apocalypse. His report urged government policy makers and strategists to utilise Cerny's concept of a "durable, yet fertile, disorder" characterised by the late Middle Ages to develop more holistic, "transagency organisational structures" to manage "forces of global disorder". Yet he warned that failure in this regard would lead further back in history to a "New Dark Age" characterised by "wicked problems" of which "we haven't seen anything yet".[72] Within this anticipation of modernity's total collapse we find echoes of Rapley and Kaplan's stark prognosis and the analogy began to hypostatise.

In the months following the events of 9/11, the medievalist[73] Bruce Holsinger was bemused by a newspaper article describing the war being waged "between the modernists and the medievalists". In suddenly finding himself sharing the professional title of "medievalist" with Osama bin Laden, he was encouraged to follow the "medievalist" rhetoric employed among the USA's political classes over the next few years in their battles with fundamentalist Islam. While his

---

[71] Phil Williams, "From the New Middle Ages to a New Dark Age: The Decline of the State and U.S. Strategy", Strategic Studies Institute, U.S. Army War College, June 2008, 41.

[72] Williams, "From the New Middle Ages to the New Dark Ages", 39, 41, 42.

[73] That is, a scholar of the middle ages.

peers published corrective papers admonishing inchoate historical appropriations, most notably regarding the "crusade" infamously pursued by President George Bush, Holsinger found himself engaged in a deeper and more troubling investigation into the adoption of neomedieval International Relations theory by the Bush administration and its use to justify the torture of prisoners at Guantanamo Bay.

Holsinger's publication *Neomedievalism, Neoconservatism and the War on Terror* highlighted the perennial mining, exploitation and distortion of the Middle Ages to promote, sanction and maintain cultural beliefs and support political actions in the early 21st century. Holsinger began his essay with a quote from the opening paragraph of Joseph Strayer's *On the Medieval Origins of the Modern State*; "In the world of today, the worst fate that can befall a human being is to be stateless".[74]

This statement captured the plight of Guantanamo detainee Salim Ahmed Hamdan who, in admitting to his affiliation with al Qaeda, and despite being a citizen of Yemen, was qualified by US law as a "non-state actor" or "enemy combatant" and therefore not party to the rights and privileges set out by international law. Bound up within the "historical autism" of the Bush administration, Hamdan became a "medieval man . . . not simply for his barbarism, his backwardness, his allegiance to a ruthlessly violent conjunction of theological fundamentalism and mass murder," but because "he is to be feared, imprisoned and, most importantly of all learned from, precisely for his perceived ability to render irrelevant the authority, territorial integrity, and jurisdictions of modern nations—nations that are the raison d'être of the neoconservative worldview".[75] Holsinger concluded by amending Strayer's aphorism to: "one of the worst fates that

---

[74] Joseph Strayer, *On the Medieval Origins of the Modern State* (Princeton: Princeton University Press. 1970), 3.

[75] Bruce Holsinger, *Neomedievalism, Neoconservatism, and the War on Terror* (Chicago: Prickly Paradigm Press, 2007), i–iv.

can befall a man today is to be rendered medieval".[76]

Holsinger's book was dense with quotations framing a phenomenon he termed "the 9/11 premodern". Huntington's *Clash of Civilisations* had suddenly become a "clash of millennia", a political form of opportunistic periodising, dividing the world "along an axis of both history and geography".[77] Holsinger demonstrated the use of medievalist tropes in the various pronouncements and fatwahs of Osama bin Laden pre- and post-9/11 and in statements and interviews with the then Deputy Secretary of Defence, Paul D. Wolfowitz in the months of 9/11's aftermath. The quotations highlighted the absurd notion of a war between the modern, rational enlightened world and an allegedly archaic, irrational, and "medieval" universe. "Fukuyama's 'Last Man', healthy, well fed, and pampered by technology", guarded the frontiers of Liberal Democracy against Thomas Hobbes's "'First Man', condemned to a life that is 'poor, nasty, brutish, and short'".[78]

Yet, it was the neoconservative casting of Islamic terrorist organisations such as al Qaeda as neomedieval rather than medieval that Holsinger found more ominous. He quoted at length from a testimony delivered by Secretary of Defence, Donald Rumsfeld before the Senate Appropriations Committee in 2005. In his preamble Rumsfeld stressed the modern characteristics of the enemy:

> To the seeming surprise of some, our enemies have brains. They are constantly adapting and adjusting to what we're doing. They combine medieval sensibilities with modern technologies and media savvy to find new ways to exploit perceived weaknesses and to weaken the civilised world.

---

[76] Holsinger, *Neomedievalism*, i–iv.

[77] Holsinger, *Neomedievalism*, 7.

[78] Kaplan, "The Coming Anarchy", 60.

In the rest of his speech, Rumsfeld outlined the changes undergone in the U.S. security apparatus to face the challenges of "agile and networked foes" in an increasingly complex, globalised world. His words betrayed an obvious reading of neomedieval International Relations theory in which "the enemy's medievalism is inseparable from its character as an agile, adaptable, transnational, multimedia organization".[79]

It was within this interpretive framework that Holsinger examined the so-called "torture memos", the series of high-level conversations between officials at Justice, the Department of State, the Department of Defence, and the White House that resulted in the decision that the 1949 Geneva Convention III, relative to the Treatment of Prisoners of War (GPW), did not apply to prisoners taken by U.S. soldiers during the Afghan War against the Taliban and Al Qaeda.

Holsinger followed and dissected the memos through extensive quotation. The entire debate is well documented and concludes that al Qaeda and the Taliban, or more precisely, the blurring of the two, constitute a new kind of enemy, a fusion of "sub-national feudal formations" and "transnational organisations working against and across national boundaries".[80] We clearly see the neomedieval International Relations paradigm at work here. The enemy was rendered medieval, barbaric and clearly operated within Ruggie's "unbundled territory", a disjointed space at odds with modern conceptions of both history and geography and therefore exempt from international legal jurisdiction. It was a twisted and cynical logic that allowed modern humanitarian politics to be abandoned when faced with an enemy whose tactics, strategy and entire ideology hailed from a period before their instigation.

Holsinger concluded that neomedievalism was an "intellectual paradigm" or "global idiom of the non-state actor"

---

[79] Holsinger, *Neomedievalism*, 53.

[80] Holsinger, *Neomedievalism*, 73.

that was hijacked and reified by the Bush administration, who employed a hodgepodge "medieval" rhetoric of outlawry, feudalism, failed-state or pre-state primitivism, crusades and barbarism to help justify both the War on Terror and the torture of "enemy combatants". From its inception as a metaphorical elucidation of global developments that are fundamentally "new", the neomedievalism of IR "gives us a frightening lens on to the ultimate co-optability of academic theorising into a regressive and destructive political culture".[81]

---

[81] Holsinger, *Neomedievalism*, 81.

Part II: Europe in the Middle

Following the collapse of the USSR in 1991, a number of former Soviet Republics gained their sovereignty, many for the first time. The fall of the Berlin Wall in 1989 had already generated the first wave of post-Soviet Balkanisation in Europe as competing groups sought to establish sovereign nations based on territorial and cultural allegiances that pre-existed the rise of the Russian, Austro-Hungarian and German Empires. The break up of Yugoslavia and Czechoslovakia were achieved by very different means, signalling that, in Europe at least, the neomedieval dimensions of unbundling involved stirring up complex and unpredictable vernaculars. Many minority groups in this region of Europe did not occupy a unified territory. For example, the Aromanians were particularly "unbundled", scattered across Albania, Bulgaria, Greece, Macedonia and Romania, precluding the establishment of a unified territorial Vlach nation-state. Kaplan's speculative multi-scalar political map would quickly become an obligatory accessory for navigating the Europes that emerged from the Cold War.

Some post-Cold War European Union member states did not restrict themselves to enforcing control over resources within their own borders (as they had during the Westphallian system), they often operated an ethnic conception of statehood that extended to their perceived diaspora born in other states. For example, at the 2004 Annual Convention of the International Studies Association in Montréal, Stephen Deets delivered a paper regarding the 2001 Hungarian Status Law, which was passed under what he termed "the spectre of neomedievalism". The law allowed "ethnic Hungarians" who were citizens of the bordering states of Romania, Slovakia, the Republic of Serbia and Montenegro, Croatia, Slovenia, and Ukraine to apply for a certificate that would make them eligible for particular benefits within the Hungarian state. While similar "law of return" legislations concerning national minorities and their "kin-states" had been passed before and accepted as part of a generally anticipated movement towards a new integrated Europe-without-borders, the Status Law differed in that it extended the benefits and regulatory laws of Hungarian nationality to those permanently residing beyond state borders.

Hungarian NGOs, initially set up to look after the social and political concerns of minorities in neighbouring host countries, would now have legal powers to process status claims, provide ID cards and distribute welfare and education grants. In this, Deets argued, the Hungarian government was seeking a neomedieval form of extraterritorial, diasporic governance that permitted Hungarian sovereignty to intervene across multiple state territories. The law was obviously controversial, immensely complicated to implement, and required radical revision after multi-fold objections were taken to regulatory bodies such as the EU and the Venice Commission.

Deets suggested that the reaction to the law from European states and their collective institutions, plus its subsequent redrafting, was evidence of a "pulling back from neomedievalism", concluding that the "shadow of Westphalia still looms too large"[82] to permit a precedence for the legal creation of trans-sovereign nations. Again, here there was a focus on the unrelenting protection of state borders and binding legal norms, but perhaps more essential to the medieval analogy (as outlined so far) was the stasis or balance resulting from multilateral negotiations or "multiperspectival polity"[83] occurring, both horizontally and vertically, between sub-state minority groups, localised NGOs, national governments, and various intergovernmental organisations and regulatory coalitions.

Another example of European multilateralism can be found in Scotland's relationships with the nation of Québec[84] and federal Canada. When Québec's sovereigntist Premier Pauline Marois visited Scotland in January 2013 to meet with Alex Salmond, Scotland's sovereigntist First Minister maintained a friendly distance, treating the encounter as no more than a "courtesy call".[85] In spite of their common commitment to self-determination, Salmond was careful not to alienate over five million self-proclaimed Scot-Canadians (of which 200,000 resided in Québec alone) by holding a "nationalist summit". Ever the pragmatic economist, Salmond had a bigger prize in mind. Due to be ratified the same year, the Canada-EU Comprehensive Economic & Trade Agreement (CETA)

---

[82] Stephen Deets, "The Hungarian Status Law and the Specter of Neo-Medievalism in Europe", paper presented at International Studies Association conference, Montréal, Québec, March 18-21, 2004, 26.

[83] Ruggie, "Territoriality and Beyond", 172.

[84] The "Québecois Nation Motion", approved in the Canadian House of Commons in Ottawa in 2006, set a precedent of recognising the intra-nationality of non-territorial micro-nations within a sovereign state. In this case, the Québecois were officially recognised as a nation by the state of Canada. As a self-idenfitying ethnic group, Québecois remain distinct from Quebeckers (territorialised inhabitants of the province of Québec), albeit that they may often be identical.

[85] Editorial, "Marois Should Have Known Scottish Trip Would Flop", *Montreal Gazette*, January 30, 2013.

would eliminate tariffs on almost all European goods imported into Canada. To capitalise on this important transnational neoliberal economic directive, the Scottish Premier could not be seen to overtly support Québecois secession from Canada for fear that it might equally alienate Scot-Canadians and Anglophone Canada. The Scottish Nationalists were thus willing to undermine the universalism of their Claim of Right to national sovereignty. In terms of loyalty—avoiding solidarity, favouring no single sphere or network—this was a canny neo-medieval tactic. It would seem that the quest for Scottish sovereignty was best served, in this instance, by pursuing an opportunity to win the support of its Diaspora and establish new international markets for Scottish exports.

This brings us back to Freidrichs' assertion that the neo-medieval analogy only works via the negation of "undisputed supremacy" and the associated implication that modern conceptions of linear progress no longer apply. As James Anderson suggested, the EU represented a kind of "arrested federalisation" (a self-abrogating process of both Balkanisation and confederation). Reaffirming Bull's statement that "the disintegration of states would be theoretically important only if it were to remain transfixed in an intermediate stage,"[86] in which substate nationalisms or regionalisms substantially undermined but did not succeed in replicating existing state sovereignty. Full success for regional separatisms or the creation of a United States of Europe would simply increase or decrease the number of states, a merely quantitative change rather than qualitatively changing the nature of states and politics."[87] Neomedievalism, then, lay somewhere in the middle: a multiplicity of tangled political, economic and cultural relations, confounding teleological as-

---

[86] Bull, The Anarchical Society, 275.

[87] James Anderson, "The Shifting Stage of Politics: New Medieval and Postmodern Territorialities?", Environment and Planning D: Society and Space 14.2 (1996): 14.

sumptions and suspending future anticipations of either global solidarity or apocalyptic disintegration.

As the 2001 Treaty of Nice allowed the EU to absorb much of the former Eastern Bloc into political and economic union, the emphasis remained on achieving a stable "Pax Europa" by expanding the EU to engulf as much of the European continent as possible. From 2004, the EU expanded into the East, consolidating Europe's new borders, enabling stability through "Hollandisation".[88] There was little consideration that the EU's founding members had themselves long been subject to devolutionary and independence movements, comparable to those that flourished in former Socialist Republics such as the USSR, Yugoslavia and Czechoslovakia. All it would take to precipitate these tendencies was a political and economic upheaval comparable to the fall of Communism. In the wake of the 2008 global financial crisis, neomedieval International Relations quickly spiralled off from playing a rhetorical role in the war on terror to precipitating and analysing the (re)emergence of sovereign, neomedieval nations from within the EU's existing member states. Following the 2007 Treaty of Lisbon, Europe's established bureaucratic macro-states—Spain, Belgium, France, Germany and the UK—rapidly began to break up into the nations, länder and regions from which they were constituted. To ensure that this intra-national instability did not threaten the European Union, the EU developed a "flat" approach to sovereignty, allowing its constituent nationalities and cultures to multiply, federalise and overlap within the EU's supranational borders.

While these emerging neomedieval nations appeared, in the short term, to have formed spontaneously as populist political "solutions" to an ongoing economic crisis, they were, in fact, the fruits of geopolitical struggles that have informed Europe's myriad revolutionary movements from

---

[88] See Martin Van Creveld, *Technology and War* (New York: Free Press, 1991).

1789 onwards. They may not have been casting off Communist rule, but they were, nevertheless, seeking to emerge from highly centralised "empire states". While consolidating the post-war drive towards an integrated Europe, implementation of the Treaty of Maastricht in 1993 enshrined the principle of subsidiarity, providing succour for regional and local geopolitics to flourish within its member states. Read as a commitment to the right to self-determination for all European peoples, European subsidiarity triggered the decolonisation of Europe. To dissolve European imperialism, and the two world wars it started, meant dismantling its foundations in the Clausewitzian-Westphalian system of militarised colonial competition between European macronations over the world's resources. Progressive, post-colonialism in Europe can, in part, therefore be identified with the unfurling of the Clausewitzian-Westphalian system through the rise of federalisation, devolution and independence movements across the continent.

In their break with Europe's "old" macro-nationalism, these movements were energised by a spirit of "national exceptionalism" that paralleled the foundation of the federal republic of the United States, a nation that combined a pooling and devolution of sovereignty. However, while the United States consciously severed its ties with European medievalism (past) in favour of an enlightenment bias towards ancient Greco-Roman democracies (past-future), new Europeans imagined their democratic emancipation prefiguring and following their colonisation into the continent's macronations.[89] This wave of "New Europe" was predicated on the imaginary of an older, and allegedly, more egalitarian Europe.

Such imaginaries had thrived in nineteenth-century Ro-

---

[89] The "tabula rasa" of the American continent was never an option for post-colonial Europe. During the economic crisis, European party politics were increasingly wedded to the complex geopolitics of ethnic and linguistic identity and the distribution of "territorial" resources.

manticism[90] and in Germanic idealist philosophies that stressed the importance of shared language, culture and ethics. The new Europeans, however, only dabbled in Romantic imaginaries of national continuity since the very awareness of such histories revealed the absolutist nation-state to be a myth, and a pernicious one at that.[91] Romanticism invented medievalisms of national unity in the ideological service of 19th-century macro-nationalism and its attendant colonialist ambitions. As we have seen, however, the more fractured, regionalised, medieval Europe was less state-centric and less nationalistic than Europe became following the rise of capitalism and industrialism in the 19th century. According to Ernst Gellner, European nationalisms developed at different speeds and under different conditions, generating five European time zones: Atlantic (early 14th-century onward), Roman (1789-), Central (1914-) and Post-Soviet (1991-). For example, as Philip A. Schrodt pointed out, not only was 19th-century "Atlantic" and "Roman" Europe more concerned with colonial than national competition, Germany and Italy failed to consolidate into united states until towards the end of the century. "There were and are almost no "nation-states", instead the multi-ethnic state is the norm", concluded Schrodt.[92] To establish territorial sovereignty based on romantic invocations of "national spirit", therefore, carried very little weight in the multicultural Europe of the early

---

[90] A peculiar manifestation of medievalism developed in the 19th century that was central to the rise of nationalism and the concept of the sovereign nation-state.

[91] "The aforementioned textbook version of the impact of the Treaty of Westphalia (1648)—typically presented as the miraculous birth, with Hugo Grotius as the midwife, of a stable system of absolutist states out of the chaos of the Thirty Years War—is a myth": Philip A. Schrodt, "Neomedievalism in the Twenty-first Century: Warlords, Gangs and Transnational Militarized Actors as a Challenge to Sovereign Preeminence", paper presented at International Studies Association conference, New Orleans, February 17-20, 2010, 3.

[92] Schrodt, "Neomedievalism in the Twenty-first Century", 3.

21st century, a continent scarred by a century of industrialised "ethnic cleansing".

Gellner's time-zone classification is particularly apposite to understanding neomedieval Europe, demonstrating "that nation states do not all proceed through similar stages to the vanishing of national identity and national frontiers."[93] Gellner's classification invites the addition of a sixth "neomedieval" zone, consolidating during the global economic crisis that followed shortly after the 2004 expansion of the EU. Unlike its predecessors, this neomedieval zone had no geography, and it could emerge from within communities of any European Union member states. Communities that perceived themselves to be micro-nations suffering from a democratic deficit within their host macro-nation-states could invoke the principal of subsidiarity and petition for official recognition within the EU.[94] In many cases, this would facilitate "independence", the transfer of fealty directly to the EU. The EU's federalist strategy of "pragmatic engagement" was designed to ensure that the EU's future as Europe's supranational overlord, even if this meant challenging the sovereignty of its established macrostates.

Those micronations seeking to establish neomedieval states, spurned the historicism, Romanticism and idealism of Europe's previous waves of nationalism in favour of emphasising the futurity of medievalist narratives, focusing on their unique proto-democratic contributions to the contemporary telos of the greater European project. Understanding the vernacular, grasping the struggles of Peoples' Histories in the formation of specific territorial rights, was central to securing and maintaining European civil rights and gaining

---

[93] Heikki Mikkeli, *Europe as an Idea and an Identity* (London: Macmillan, 1998), 215.

[94] For example, following the example of the Québecois nation motion, the Aromanians were represented within the 11th European Parliament as a "micro-nation"—people subject to EU law and the local laws of the states in which they lived, but guaranteed special status as a micro-nation officially recognised by the EU.

greater economic, environmental and political powers for current citizens of Europe's states-in-waiting. They also stressed the importance of understanding and diffusing peripheral tensions in establishing Pax Europa. Micronations had been subdued and absorbed by their overlord macronations, their identities suppressed, their peculiar political and economic needs and proclivities ignored in favour of the desires of the perceived centre. The EU's "pragmatic engagement" with the peripheralisation of politics, where possible, would help to reduce hostility and tension by removing Europe's centres of Clausewitzian-Westphalian power.

As post-Communist Europe had discovered, the EU offered a very different type of overlordship to those nations that could legally call themselves states. Sovereignty would enable emancipation and the (return of the) bespoke governmental apparatus that Europe's many nations desired. As such, emerging neomedieval micro-nations were the antithesis of the mythical, pre-lapsarian, monocultural, nation-state. They explicitly followed in the footsteps of the French Revolution, their primary goal being to establish a modern united Europe of republics of free and equal citizens.

The neomedieval character of these discourses, then, is evident in the following tendencies:

1. The Westphalian macro-nation-states were an obstacle to a peaceful and harmonious European Union of the regions. Pre-Westphalian Europe, therefore was a recurring metaphor for Pax Europae. This practice of metaphorical medievalism drew directly on neomedieval International Relations theory.

2. Following this metaphor, (re)emerging states used evidence of their formation and consolidation as medieval nations as justification for their re-emergence in an idealised neomedieval European Union of the regions.

3. (Re)-emerging states were predicated on the persis-

tence, or reinvention, of pre-Westphalian cultural and political practices specific to a region.

4. Emerging neomedieval states—Scotland, Wales, Cornwall, Friesland, Lappland, Flanders, Kashubia, Livonia, Wallonia, Brittany, Alscace, Occitanne, Catalonia, Gallicia, Andalucia, Valenciana, Basque Country, Ladins, Trentino South-Tyrol, Fruii, Corsica and Sardinia in particular—were predominately, albeit not exclusively, pro-European Union.

5. The European Union played the role of overlord, enfranchising and safeguarding the sovereignty of micronations through the principal of subsidiarity, building "ever closer union among the peoples of Europe, in which decisions are taken as openly as possible and as closely as possible to the citizen".[95]

To emerge as an independent state from the remains of an imperialist macro-nation, to achieve national and cultural self-determination, was a goal enshrined by the UN and the European Union.[96] In spite of this, the "new" neomedieval states had to negotiate entry into the EU, since governance of the EU was dominated by the larger, more populous, macro-nations from which they aspired to secede (i.e., France, Spain, the UK, Germany and Italy). Since the post-Westphalian macro-nations dominated the EU parliament, it was in their interests to block the disintegration of their own territorial sovereignty by blocking all attempts to create new states from existing EU members. Support for such stalling tactics came from Euro blocks as disparate as the National Conservatives, the far right European National Movements and Eurosceptics. However, Europe's broader tapestry of centre and centre-left political blocks had more to gain from

---

[95] Treaty of Rome, Article 151; see also Article 308, 1957.
[96] The EU enabled subsidiarity by encouraging European regions, rather than member-states, to compete for Community funding.

unbundling the territorialisation of European politics. A neomedieval Europe would be one less dominated by coercive macronation-states, a Europe more ready to move on from tactical political coalitions—volatile alliances designed to achieve an improbable balance of macronational power[97] and pan-European political goals—to formalised strategic Europarties that united across the continent.

A corollary of the negotiations over the EU's "new" neomedieval member states was adoption of the Euro and tight neoliberal controls over public spending. In effect, these limitations restricted many of the sovereign powers that normally accompany self-governance, effectively dissolving state-control internally. New EU member states were given the narrowest windows for manoeuvre in gathering and distributing their own taxes. The de facto neoliberalisation of these hollowed-out states forced them to either devolve, privatise or abandon many of the functions of social democracies. This neoliberalisation had an impact at the level of local government, now tasked with greater responsibility for the delivery of public services. While some wealthier European cities attempted to recover their medieval city-state status by levying taxes and running monopolistic local services, others were faced with no option other than the race to the bottom, outsourcing and privatising local services to the point of dissolving local government.

While rescinding many of their downward responsibilities for social security, Europe's new neomedieval members were transferring their fealty from their respective Westphalian macro-nations to that of a much larger European state. They would remain in union with their former overlords, albeit that they would now share a common overlord in the EU. Their new overlord would play an equal role in determining how far they would all determine their own futures.[98]

---

[97] As in, continuing to follow an obsolete Clausewitzian-Westphalian paradigm.

[98] It's worth emphasising that the EU's overlordship was predicated

While the geopolitics of fealty were often caricatured as primarily cultural, they made cold economic sense. The European Union offered greater social and economic opportunities and support for the peoples of Europe than smaller Westphallian macro-nations could, and they did so without the attendant threat of coercive nation-statehood. The EU offered the promise of easy access to European and global markets without overshadowing vernacular mobilisation.

Where Europe's imperialist macro-nations had once competed with each other in exercises of Clausewitzian military power, Europe's neomedieval states were eager to cooperate economically. In dismantling the Westphalian macro-nations and encouraging more culturally sensitive, vernacular localised governance, it was hoped, the neomedieval European Union would be able to focus on its wider goals of political and economic unity through Hollandisation.

Scotland's secession to EU overlordship provided a poster boy for the development of European "pragmatic engagement" with neomedievalism. Elements of this secession were, notably, prophesied in Bull's new medievalism:

> We may envisage a situation in which, say, a Scottish authority in Edinburgh, a British authority in London, and a European authority in Brussels were all actors in world politics and enjoyed representation in world political organizations, together with rights and duties of various kinds in world law, but in which no one of them claimed sovereignty or supremacy over the others, and a person living in Glasgow had no exclusive or overriding loyalty to any one of them. Such an outcome would take us truly "beyond the sovereign state" and is by no means im-

---

on "Hollandisation" and cooperation rather than (neorealist) competition between member states. The EU was therefore destined to dissolve large sovereign states to enable better regional trade across and beyond Europe. The EU encouraged vernacular mobilisation for this reason, it had much to gain from Balkanisation within its own borders.

plausible, but it is striking how little interest has been displayed in it by either the regional integrationists or the subnational "disintegrationists".[99]

Bull's example of Scotland as a prospective neomedieval territory was prescient in the wake of the 1997 devolution referendum, which belatedly established the conditions for the neomedieval sovereignty that he hypothesised.[100] After the reopening of Holyrood, the Scottish Parliament, in 1999, however, Scotland remained a devolved nation within the UK macro-national state. As overlord, the UK negotiated with international organisations such as the EU and UN on Scotland's behalf. Holyrood's limited powers were, effectively, "leased" from the UK and could be returned to Westminster by future UK governments. The 2014 referendum pursued by the governing Scottish National Party sought to end to this international arrangement and allow Scotland to negotiate its own sovereign terms with other nations and international NGOs. The terms of secession proposed by the Scottish National Party were neomedieval in Bull's formulation, generating a new system of overlapping loyalties for the average Glaswegian.

After 2014, Scotland was to retain the Pound Sterling, remain in a personal union of crowns with England, remain in the European Union and become a full member of the UN. Following Scottish independence, Bull's Glaswegian would pledge fealty to a British monarch, have their interest rates set by the Bank of England, their fishing quotas set by the European Union and their income taxes imposed by Holyrood. Political authority was to be a neomedieval overlapping mixture of European/Scottish democratically accountable governance and British autocratic overlordship. This

---

[99] Bull, *The Anarchical Society*, 266.

[100] Bull would, presumably, have been speculating on a potential outcome of the 1979 devolution referendum, a plebiscite that failed to achieve devolution.

seemingly unlikely neomedieval prospect was upset by events. In the run up to the Scottish referendum, right-wing protest-voting in English local elections[101] led to the unforeseen rise of the UK Independence Party (UKIP), a right-wing fringe party who aimed to restrict immigration and restore UK sovereignty by leaving the European Union. Since the prospect of leaving the EU was not popular in Scotland, UKIP's victories in 2013 increased the gulf between Scottish and English politics. Scottish voters were faced with the choice of remaining in the EU by voting Yes to independence, or being dragged out of the EU against their will by a UK plebiscite that would, prospectively at least, be held in 2015. One of the choices, then, that faced Scottish voters was between an expansive European neomedieval model of sovereignty or a retreat into the "Splendid Isolation" pursued by the British Empire in the late 19th century.

The debates that raged in 2013-14 over Scottish and UK sovereignty were dominated by the neomedieval turn. The Scottish and British nationalisms officially competing in the 2014 referendum ("Yes Scotland" vs. "Better Together") were not neat binary oppositions. The debate featured multilateral and overlapping narratives of cultural emergence. However, ostensibly, two competing, and equally selective, medievalisms were mobilised in the debate over Scotland's future.

"Scottish" medievalisms were a hodgepodge of disparate imaginaries, drawing as heavily upon the history of pre-Union Scotland (c. 410-1707) as on post-Union medievalisms. Histories of Scotland, from its formation to its political unification with England and Wales in 1707, were central to establishing the legal case for the nation's re-emergence as a sovereign state. The legal issues, however, were difficult to disentangle from Romanticism's influential fixation with Scotland as the epitome of Europe's lost "pre-modern". Roman-

---

[101] The Isle of Anglesey in Wales also voted in the council elections of May 2013.

tic perceptions of Scotland as a distinct, wild, uninhabited and ungovernable place on the very edge of the known world, were nothing new; they were shared by the Romans, widely held in medieval European and Arab nations and even by Scotland's 12th-century Scoto-Norman monarchs. "Scotland-as-Other" was a powerful ideology long promulgated inside and beyond Scotland itself.[102] The Scottish medievalisms that mattered, therefore, were those that foregrounded contemporary principles of "Scottish national unity in alterity" and "Europeanisation".[103] Much of the emphasis here was placed on narratives that engaged with the foundation of Scottish nationhood and its struggle to remain a sovereign European state. Restoring continuity with pre-Union Scotland was key to the articulation of a post-British imaginary. Medievalist chronicles of Scottish underdogs suppressed by English overlords provided the backstory to Scotland's disproportionate contributions to the British Empire and global culture, science and industry.[104]

"British" medievalisms were, equally, a smörgåsbord of

---

[102] While it aspired to be a macro-nation, the UK was never a unitary state. The 1707 union of Scotland, England and Wales legally preserved the cornerstones of Scottish identity: Scots law, Scottish generalist education and the Kirk. In these matters and more, Scotland remained Other to England and Wales.

[103] The Scoto-Norman monarchs clearly implemented this process. Europeanisation, however, was stalled by the growth of the British Empire.

[104] A shift from a British to Scottish bias in these terms was evident in the Curriculum for Excellence for school children aged 3-18. The new curriculum involved studying Scotland, providing learning resources for teaching Scottish history as well as focusing on Scotland's people, languages, environment, culture and global influence. While the new curriculum proposed examining "5,000 Years of Scotland's History", the new Scottish Higher focused mainly on events after the succession problem following Alexander III's death in 1286, medievalising the formation of Scotland in the wars of independence at the expense of reading histories of Northern Britain's multi-ethnicities before the political formation of Scotland.

disparate identities, fabulous chronicles written in the middle ages mixed together with modern medieval legends and imperialist histories of the British Isles. Much favoured were medieval chronicles mythologising the fortitude of plucky and virtuous tribes of aboriginal Britons suppressed in Roman Britain. The modern mythology of native British sovereignty was largely a product of the medieval era itself, when monarchs employed historians to legitimate their claim to the throne by inventing their aboriginal kinship.[105] Related medievalisms were born of the Romantic and pre-Raphaelite movements implicated in the invention of pre-Roman and early medieval "British" traditions. Medieval, Romantic and pre-Raphaelite medievalisms were allied to the post-Union Britology of the Kingdom of Great Britain and Ireland in which the telos of "British national unity in diversity" was produced to legitimise the image of empire. Britology—maintaining the Anglo-British self-image of a benign empire respecting the vernacular while coercively imposing its version of civilisation over much of the world—was rooted in a centralising 19th-century view of the British Isles and Ireland. Since the 1603 personal union of the crowns of Scotland and England in James the VI and I, Britology was tasked with constructing British-ness, a tall order since "Britain" was not, and never has been, a nation.

In theory, Britology required a different form of historical imagination to replace competing Scotocentric and Anglocentric perspectives. For example, from the perspective of Britology, the Kingdom of Scotland (c. 410-843) that formed out of Gaelic speaking Alba—but one of many possible Scotlands that might have been—was a stepping stone towards the inevitable unification of Great Britain and Ireland

---

[105] In sharp contradiction, historians were also employed to trace regal ancestry back to Genesis, to create the illusion that the ruling class were, somehow, more direct descendants of the original ancestor. Medieval histories generated a double duplicity, at once rooting the monarchy in a particular place while placing them in an evolutionary fast-track.

into a macro-nation. During the period in which Scotland was emerging as a nation, north Britain was home to numerous different linguistic and ethnic groups, as was typical in Europe at the time. Following Scotland's union with England and Wales, the island of Great Britain again became the mongrel nation it allegedly was before the arrival of the Romans. In practice, however, since England was by far the largest nation in the UK, Britology was overtly Anglocentric. Britology articulated the status quo of perceived English overlordship of Britain and Ireland; it was the ideology of the unitary force of a centralising nation-state over minorities within its borders. Since it was the voice of the Anglo majority, Britology survived the collapse of the British Empire and the devolution of Scotland, Wales and Northern Ireland in the 21st century.

While British and Scottish sovereigntists were, literally, competing over the same terrain, it was not surprising to find many correspondences between British and Scottish medievalisms. In each discourse, premodern events and myths were used to legitimate the very different political realities of a post-industrial economy. For example, the image of the native underdog and the (largely 19th century) concept of the inevitability of national unity was one shared by both medievalisms.[106] Where, then, did British and Scottish medievalisms differ? For one, Scottish nationalists, bolstered by the powerful mythologies imagined by Victorian Romanticism, had a longer historical period of Scots sovereignty (843-1707) from which to win support for their post-colonial narratives of oppression and emergence. This, however, did not represent a unifying intra-national narrative for Scottish Nationalists. On the contrary, this period incorporated post-medieval Scotland and included the Scots Renascence and

---

[106] Albeit that the image of the Scottish underdog, emerging from a small peripheral nation, was more persuasive than the image of the British underdog, emerging from the largest empire the world has known.

the Scottish Reformation. As such, the historical era of absolute Scottish sovereignty unfolds competing medievalist ("Auld Alliance") and overtly "anti-medievalist" (predominately anti-Catholic) movements among the Scottish peoples.

Disentangling "Scottish" from "British" medievalisms was a tricky business, as the fortunes of the UK's monarchy attested. The British monarchy was a surviving medieval institution par excellence, the legacy of power hungry warlords battling over territory and resources after the retreat of the Roman Empire. The unification of Scotland's nations, of England's nations, England's annexation of Wales and England's later unification with Scotland are testimony to the aristocracy's adoption of the Norman feudal system of absolute territorial authority. Europe's predominately French-speaking, inter-bred transnational monarchy were anathema to the modern nationalism that began to emerge in the 17th century. The aristocracy had only their own interests, rather than the wider interests of their host nations, at heart.[107] However, the post-medieval figurehead of the monarch had a different function to fulfill: to provide a substitute for the Pope in European nations that revolted against Rome's religious overlordship or an advocate of Catholicism in those that remained faithful to the old religion.

For example, support for the 1603 personal union of crowns was elected among the peoples of Scotland on the religious affinities of the monarchy, support that varied within Scotland. Catholic British monarchs were squarely rejected by lowland Protestant Scots while more likely to be embraced by those Highland Gaels who remained Catholic. While post-medieval Scotland retained many of its medievalist practices (in terms of its monarchy, law and superstitions),

---

[107] Feudalism's overriding concern with expansionism was key to the personal union of the crowns in 1603 and remained a mainstay in the international outlook of modern European nations until the end of WWII.

its Protestant national church was vehemently anti-medievalist in matters of religion, education and politics.[108] These were the cultural politics that came to dominate Scotland's philosophical outlook and, in turn, completely transform its identity. Anti-medievalism was the root of the Scottish Enlightenment—pervading new attitudes to art, politics and economics. Herein lay modern Scottish nationalism's major claim to futurity, an intellectual futurity that would emerge autonomously (albeit exploiting opportunities provided under the yoke of British imperialism). The fact that this intellectual futurity was inherently anti-medievalist did not prevent the "Yes Scotland" independence campaign from simultaneously mobilising the rabble-rousing medievalisms of Victorian Romanticism in its cause. This opportunistic neomedievalism explains, for example, the Scottish National Party retaining the British Monarch as non-executive Head of State following independence, albeit in a vernacular neomedievalist form, reprising her role as "Elizabeth I, Queen of Scots".

Meanwhile, early 21st-century British sovereigntists sought to mobilise the period 843-1707 in their favour, imagining Scotland pursuing a canny military-industrial union with England, disparate partners uniting to pursue the "greater good" of global colonial expansion.[109] In these terms, the union was overtly post-medieval, for it was concerned, primarily with enabling Scotland's colonial expansion into North America, Africa, India and beyond. This was a military-industrial future-

---

[108] The Protestant Reformation, which emerged across Scotland and England in different measures, was upheld by Unionists as a unifying religious belief system distancing the nations of the British Isles from former allies in Catholic Europe.

[109] In Scotland, trade in tobacco and textiles with British colonies in North America and, later, shipbuilding for the Empire's fleets, had the greatest economic impact, leading to the depopulation of the Highlands to serve the rapid industrialisation of west central Scotland. In generating an industrial working class and Anglicising Gaeldom, West Central Scotland became a proving ground for featly to the British Empire.

past, one based on the perceived benefits of a long-gone colonialism and industrialism, the bedfellows of an imperialistic phase of nationalism that excelled in Europe until the end of WWII.

In spite of British nationalism's propounded military-industrial futurity, Victorian Romanticism, the foremost purveyor of post-Union Scottish identity, exploited the medieval to such an extent that it might be credited with having invented the cultural practice of "medievalism".[110] The military-industrial futurity of the British Empire of the late 19th century was exonerated by its "civilized" celebration of the anti-modern cultural vernacular, whether this be in the form of the pastoral, "Scottish" medievalisms, or the "native".[111] Herein we can perceive Scottish Unionism's practice of neo-medieval opportunism.

Clearly, there were many significant overlaps here, zones of transition that were being contested as well as histories that were neither "British" nor "Scottish". Understandably, British and Scottish sovereigntists of the early 21st century both sought to mobilise readings of Scotland's medieval history in their favour, despite "Scotland" and "Britain" being equally meaningless to most inhabitants of the British Isles for much of the middle ages. The medievalisms that relate to Scotland between 410 and 1701 demarcate a "Balkanised" terrain torn by religious, ethnic and linguistic divi-

---

[110] The word medieval is thought to have existed since 1817, only coming into more general use in the 1820s. See David Matthews, "From Mediaeval to Mediaevalism: A New Semantic History", *The Review of English Studies*, new series, 62.257 (November 2011): 695–715; see also Clare A. Simomons "Medievalism: Its Linguistic History in Nineteenth-Century Britain", *Studies in Medievalism* XVII (2009): 28–35.

[111] This may appear counterintuitive, but the realities of the industrial-militarism pursued by the British Empire required a foil in the form of vernacular mobilisation. The corporate plan of the British Empire required that it absorb and promote the local vernacular as part of its "benign" acts of colonisation.

sions, Europe located on the cusp of the pre-modern and post-medieval.[112] And yet, there remain some important distinctions between the Scottish and British nationalisms in terms of territorialisation.

Anti-medievalist hysteria served the rise of Protestantism and Enlightenment in post-medieval Scotland, establishing the Scots international reputation for intellectual futurity.[113] These qualities were associated specifically with Scotland, rather than Britain, even following the Act of Union. In Scotland, Walter Scotticisms, the Romanticised medievalism that became fashionable in 19th century Britology, were regarded as an alien preserve of the British landed gentry for whom Scotland was a playground. For most Scots, Victorian medievalism was the antithesis of their cultural values; it was little more than cultural tourism, a fabrication of Scotland created for external consumption.[114] However, in the 20th century, Britology industrialised Scottish-identity-as-Romantic-fiction and sold it back as a sop to Scotland's industrialised urbanites, by then wholly alienated from their cultural origins. Britology's territorialisation of Scotland, in this sense, performed a devious infinite loop, the tease of a promised premodern land to which Scots could never return. Of course, considered from the perspective of Scotland's booming military-industrial destiny as a full board member of the British Empire, this fictional premodern held little ap-

---

[112] Qualities that made it particularly attractive to Romanticism.

[113] Scotland's intellectual futurity played a key role in the British Empire's military-industrial futurity establishing many of the key advantages in engineering, finance and politics that served the expansion of British colonial rule. Equally, and most notably in the case of the United States of America, Scots intellectual futurity contained the seeds of the downfall of the British Empire in its radical brand of "democratic intellect".

[114] The UK's military-industrial barons, the nouveau riche who benefited most from the economic fruits of union, preferred the profane qualities of "realism" and the decorative arts.

peal as a destination.[115] Herein lay the long-time appeal and success of Britology's story of Scotland.

In post-industrial Scotland, Britology's infinite loop broke. Britology made its own albatross, a vision of Scotland reliant upon the continuity of an imperialist UK that no longer existed. Once the British Empire collapsed and its military-industrial economy vanished, the Scottish premodern that it romanticised became far more appealing. Britology's own ghosts of redcoats and absentee landlords past came back to haunt it, the "British" playing scapegoat to Scotland's postcolonial and postindustrial woes. Britology's narrative of progress that had made Scotland's premodern so unpalatable, was now that of the unimaginative status quo failing to face up to economic realities. The landed neomedievalism of the UK's military-industrial future was now firmly stuck in the future-past.[116]

In stark contrast, the intellectual futurity promised by Scottish Nationalism promised a commons of participation, a reconnection with depopulated Scotland's terra firma as a regenerative economic resource, and repatriation of Scotland's culture and economy to the context of an embryonic united Europe. Scotland's cosmopolitan, European, agrarian,

---

[115] For pre-Union Scotland, fortunes and reputations were primarily to be made in trade with Northern Europe. Post-Union, Scotland opened up its markets to England's colonies in North America and, in time, much of the rest of the world, drawing Scotland's attention away from Europe towards its "Splendid Isolation" in a growing British Empire. West central Scotland mushroomed in population as commerce shifted from the European-facing east coast to the American-facing west coast in the service of the British Empire. Pre-union Scotland had been divided into Highland and Lowland cultures. Industrialisation that followed in the wake of union generated the "Tartan Curtain", an East/West divide in Scotland that remained discernible into the early 21st century.

[116] England, Wales and Northern Ireland continued to pursue a Clauswitzian-Westphalian vision consistent with Britology's narrative of "Splendid Isolation", a solo world player disintegrated from larger political unions.

medieval past would inform its past-future. Scotology combined the Scottish fantasy of rootless diasporic intellectual adventure with frugal and stoic historical accounts of the legal battle for resources and territorial rights in Scotland. The dispute over Scotland's pre-Union borders remained relevant; most of Scotland's riches in the early 21st century were seen to be, literally, terra firma, tied up in farming, fishing, North Sea oil and gas, in water and in renewable energy.[117] However, since the fossil fuel riches of the North Sea were a depleting resource, futurity had to primarily concern the battle for terra nova, for the cultivation and taxation of intellectual property. Both were battles worth fighting, but one held the greater prize.

When Scotland's postindustrial stakes are considered in these ways, we might conclude that the British and Scottish nationalists of the early 21st century actually had very little to gain from staking out allegiances and analogies with premodern Scotland. The battle over Scotland's future really lay in the interpretation of the post-medieval era. The choice was between the remnants and possibilities of an intellectual futurity that promised an end to ethnic unrest via the Hollandisation of Scotland and a Clausewitzian military-industrial future-past that promised more of the same. As state of becoming, Scotland's garden of forking paths in 2014 was a series of criss-crossing desire lines worn out by Scottish and British medievalisms, anti-medievalisms and European neomedieval futurities.

In the event, Bull's premonition of the neomedieval Glas-

---

[117] In a bid to reduce operating costs and quickly raise tax revenue, the Scottish Parliament voted to lease land and sea operated by Scotland's energy industries to non-state actors. Corporations bid to manage the fields, pursuing their own forms of economic union and law enforcement in Orkney and Shetland. Scottish Enterprise licensed the Norwegian-owned Company of Scotway to trade North Sea resources exclusively in Krone. Over a ten-year leasehold, the Company of Scotway replaced the Scottish Government as the legitimate form of authority in Orkney, Shetland and their off-shore fields.

wegian did not come to fruition in its entirety. Following September 2014 independence referendum, two states emerged: the United Kingdom and the secessionist EWNI (England, Wales and Northern Ireland). With Scotland no longer returning Labour, Liberal-Democrat and Scottish Nationalist MPs to Westminster, and given England's lurch to the far Right, the Conservatives seemed guaranteed to win an outright victory in the 2015 EWNI General Election. Following a hung parliament, to remain in government, the Conservatives entered into a coalition with the UK Independence Party (UKIP). UKIP's conditions were that EWNI immediately hold an "in-or-out" referendum on its continued membership of the EU. EWNI's swift and acrimonious departure from Europe allowed a beleaguered EU not only to recognise Scotland's Claim of Right, but to accept it as the UK's successor state.[118] While the United Kingdom of Scotland retained the British monarch in a personal union with England, the unexpected outcome of the 2015 General Election forced it to abandon pre-election promises to retain the Pound Sterling. Scotland signed up to the European Social Charter, Schengen the Euro and began the lengthy process of transferring its fealty entirely to the EU.

---

[118] While assumed prior to the 2014 Scottish Referendum, it is debatable that EWNI would have been recognised by the EU as the continuing "UK" state as, like Scotland, it was, effectively, a single kingdom (England), albeit one combined with two annexed provinces (Wales and NI). Scotland's treatment as the successor UK state was opportunistic, had EWNI not left the EU, Scotland would have applied for entry as a new member.

ↄↄ

Chapter 3

The Journeyman's Guide
to Anchoritism

INTRO:

Built on contributions from dudes in the local anti- and post-humanist communities, the *Journeyman's Guide to Anchoritism* was a swarm-authored, locally-produced guide for visitors and residents alike. Focusing on non-glossy, low-to-no cost anchorite tourism, it included revisions of a contemporary work, colloquially known as "Sacamano's Vintage Journal", a handmade scrapbook by Ex Libris Anonymous upcycled from pages of old religious textbooks. Written in an accessible lay style, its readership today is mainly comprised of Journeymen and Pilgrims.

    This edition includes marginalia from Alexandr Petrovsky's skim-read personal edition, purchased from Powell's while on a placement at the Weiden + Kennedy Building.

JACKET, VERSO:

When the spatial territories of both the sovereign human subject and sovereign state institutions unfurled in the rhizomatic cross-flows of global capitalism, then so too did the temporal categories that buffered modernity against the unformatted messiness of its unruly predecessor.[1] As the epochal partitions fell away, so it was that, perhaps a tad surly,[2] we discovered a plethora of hybridized medievalisms gathered together; remixed, reimagined, translated, fed-back, fed-forward, folded and refolded into the very constitution of modernity that now proclaimed itself symptomatic of an unspoken desire for a future assembled from a bricolage of pre-modern components. The Journeyman conducts her sacramental wandeln with prosumerist ambient liturgy, mass customised relic-ing and endless re-encounterings of future incarnations of off-map coffee shops that have occupied the same homey house for several years.

REVIEW:

There will be many things about this guide that you will not like. It might drive a bit too fast for comfort, especially because it has no seatbelts—the Journeyman's Guide is open top and the roads to its anchorholds swerve all over the place. But you need to drive very fast to see things as things.[3]

THE REVOLUTION OF THE THING

As the struggle to become a subject became mired in its own contradictions, a different possibility emerged. How about siding with the object for a change? Why not affirm it? Why not be a thing? An object without a subject? A thing among other

---

[1] PETROVSKY'S MARGINALIA: Must mean the middle ages?

[2] PETROVSKY'S MARGINALIA: Bike mechanic at Abraham's?

[3] Reviews, *Proto-Bitch*, Portland, Oregon, May 2014.

things?[4]

Anything is thing enough to party.[5]

Think about Anchorholds and what comes to mind? A slower pace of life? A quiet Sunday spent alone contemplating in a delightful cell? Stolen moments of solace in a washroom cubical playing *Temple Run*? Or how about a hyper-condensed non-territory of infinite connections and quasi-objects? Astonishing rough diamonds, anchorholds are more than lush visions that hide their simple delights under a veil of complexity. These living tombs—by no means rare in the deterritorialised urban topographies of our times—are the sink-holes of subjectivity, exemplars of corporeal craftsmanship, virtuoso conductor pits of the post-human noise. In the very midst of the "already" unpretentious block, the most

---

[4] Hito Steyerl, "A Thing Like You and Me", *e-flux journal* 15 (2010): par. 8. Available online: http://www.e-flux.com/journal/a-thing-like-you-and-me.
[5] Ian Bogost, *Alien Phenomenology, Or What It's Like to Be a Thing* (Minneapolis: University of Minnesota Press, 2012), 24.

niche artisanal neighbourhood, under the gleaming temporary pavilions of a non-recurring Biennale or the grass-roots of a maker-infested quasithingiverse, you will come upon a vault, a pit, a walled and grated cell, in the depths of which a human-object resides, eternally committed to eternal lament, litany or the madly ascetic "relic-ing" of the self.

Anchoritism is the widespread eremitic practice of solitary confinement. Anchorites (from the Greek verb *anachorein*, 'to withdraw') are men and women who volunteer to be permanently sealed away in electromagnetically shielded sub-basement cells adjoining the outer wall of a local landmark. If their application is approved, a ceremony of entombment is performed by a Local Investor who will later seal the enclosure with their official stamp. Often, as part of the macabre ceremony, a grave will be dug and the Office of the Dead recited to signify the new anchorite's liminal status as already dead to the world yet reborn to a life of solitary spiritual communion. There it remains until fully, corporeally, expired.

The anchorite's decision to become a person-object requires it to legally declare the purgatory of the neoliberal agent bankrupt. Historically speaking, the neoliberal agent was a self-managing, person-corporation, a bundle of flexible, improvable skills. Declaring their personhood legally bankrupt, the anchorite abandons its person-assets and becomes quasi-object.

A commonplace yet mysterious practice—what reflections such a strange spectacle awakens in us: that horrible unplugging; the cable torn from the outlet; that living being cut off from the communion of the noosphere[6] and already numbered with the undead dead; the sublime unfriend; that LED lamp burning its last Duracell in the darkness; that remnant of life flickering out in the pit; that liturgical whisper, a

---

[6] PETROVSKY'S MARGINALIA: An evolving form of mass consciousness, the noosphere was a concept developed by Jesuit priest Teilhard de Chardin in the 1950s.

purgatorial voice both less and more than human,[7] the never-ending litanies encased in plaster or stone: that eye darkly reflected in a blank screen; the haunting returned gaze of dead pixels; that ear inclined attentive to a Samsung Galaxy S9 that is now free to speak of itself; that mind enmeshed in a body, itself become one with its dungeon, and from out that triple incarnation of mind, flesh and stone, the perpetual plaint of a consciousness in free-play. What of all this reaches the fleeting apprehension of the nomadic pilgrims and corporate Journeymen[8] who, without breaking the multiplicity of the pack, leave stone-cold kick-ass breakfasts and half-munched Farm Fusions as reverent alms to the one who vowed to stay behind?

Exploring anchorholds is fun, but more effective when approached with a bit of local know-how. The legal commodity status of anchorites in all the states and provinces visited in this Guide is related to changes in local laws that required courts to recognise all objects (Fyodor Terentyev, Irn Bru, Tecámac, flip-top box, Court of Henry VIII, zinester, spider plant, Albert Bush-Brown, dead canary, Chateau Frontenac, 3:17pm, polyester, Nectar soda, vinyl seat, Catalan, George Clinton, Lakefield National Park, etc.). This simplified the previously complex situation of multiple legal fictions that invoked personhood as the *sine qua non* of "rights". The Revolution of the Thing ushered in the rapid and effective "objectificiation" of the law, the establishment of constitutions founded on object-sensitive ontologies, and the realignment of politics into post-humanist and anti-humanist factions.

The Revolution of the Thing combined radical de-sub-

---

[7] PETROVSKY'S MARGINALIA: The guest bartend at Maceo's on 6th.

[8] PETROVSKY'S MARGINALIA: The Journeyman is a neomedieval archetype that establishes an analog between contemporary nomad theory (especially the "nomadology" of Deleuze and Guattari) and the medievalist practices of pilgrimage, travelling apprenticeship, *mercenarius*, crusading, and adventuring.

jectification with dramatic reforms to the status of signification. Early reformers worked hard to ensure that there was
no single anchoring connection (no "transcendental signifier") that fixed meaning to the ground of the real. Instead
they proposed a deferral along an endless chain of signification, a constant wailing and gnashing of teeth, a surplice or
excess of meaning that found no safe anchorage in the
bounded territories of the Port of Origin, presence, being or
self. The most influential political figures in this period, the
anchorites, accepted that the duration of this deferral is day
and night forever and ever. It is hard for mortals to grasp
how long this vacillation will be, but after we have been
there a billion years, the interminable deferral will have but
just begun. The subject then, came to be understood as
nothing more than a disembodied textual being, the sole
product of representation itself. Representation was always
in crisis.[9]

Intertwined within the anchorite's anti-humanism, the
Revolution of the Thing proposed a great multitude of theoretical perspectives of the "post-human" that were not so
easily accused of overzealously collapsing the category of
the human to the realms of signification. A "new kind of
man", the anchorite came forth to us from a disparate field

---

[9] PETROVSKY'S MARGINALIA: In the opening chapter of *Art Encounters: Deleuze and Guattari* (Basingstoke: Palgrave Macmillan,
2006), Simon O'Sullivan argues that that all discourses concerning
art tend to be premised on a binary oppositions between con-
tent/form or meaning/object that are reinforced by questions like:
What does this artwork mean? The Art object becomes predeter-
mined by the questions asked of it and we never get to that place
beyond the circumstances of the object being talked about. This
contestant deferral leaves the art object hollowed out, or merely a
form of writing. He proposes that theories of representation never
get beyond this kind of ontological iron curtain between being and
things, or between thought and matter. The critique of representation always takes place within the field of representation itself, therefore auto-generating a perpetual state of crisis.

of inquiry that challenged human exceptionalism, considering recent developments in cybernetics, informatics, biotechnology, and neuroscience.[10]

Gathering momentum at natural science and (post) humanities[11] swap-meets, theories of the post-human marked the beginning of a paradigmatic shift away from the all-possessive "I" of the "solipsistic human dasein" towards a flat or deflated ontology that reinstalled the human as merely one category of being amongst countless others.[12] The ontological barrier—established by Kant's Copernican Revolution—between subject/object, thought/reality, phenomenon/noumenon, began to crumble and a multiplicity of in-human "actants" arrived to stake their claim within a radically expanded definition of being.

Equador led the way in the Revolution of the Thing, Article 71 in Chapter 7 of its Constitution securing equal rights

---

[10] PETROVSKY'S MARGINALIA: Katharine Hayles argued against post-structuralism's prioritising of semiotic or symbolic structures in favour of a theory of embodiment in which material and immaterial modes of affective signification interplay in the performative production of subjectivity: N. Katherine Hayles, *How We Became Posthuman: Virtual Bodies in Cybernetics, Literature, and Informatics* (Chicago: University Of Chicago Press, 1999). As she put it, "embodied experience interacts with codes of representation to generate new kinds of textual worlds. In fact, each category—production, signification, consumption, bodily experience, and representation—is in constant feedback and feedforward loops with the others" (28). For Hayles, human subjectivity must be articulated not as an autonomous will, but as an emergent system or a "distributed cognitive system as a whole, in which 'thinking' is done by both human and non-human actors" (28).

[11] PETROVSKY'S MARGINALIA: . . . deconstruction, queer theory, postcolonialism, actor-network theory and the schizo-nomadic ontologies of Deleuze and Guattari. I've found so many cool (post) humanities that I can't list them all. Sweeeeet!

[12] Julian Yates, "It's (for) You; or, The Tele-t/r/opical Post-Human", *postmedieval: a journal of medieval cultural studies* 1.1/2 (2010): 225.

for all lifeforms: "Nature, or Pacha Mama, where life is re-produced and occurs, has the right to integral respect for its existence and for the maintenance and regeneration of its life cycles, structure, functions and evolutionary processes. All persons, communities, peoples and nations can call upon public authorities to enforce the rights of nature. To enforce and interpret these rights, the principles set forth in the Con-stitution shall be observed, as appropriate. The State shall give incentives to natural persons and legal entities and to communities to protect nature and to promote respect for all the elements comprising an ecosystem." Equador main-tained that humans, as part of Pacha Mama, were unexcep-tional and no longer in the middle. RÉSO followed shortly afterwards, redrafting the 19th Amendment to its By-Laws to secure citizenship and the equal rights of all objects: "Noth-ing and no one is willing any longer to agree to serve as a simple means to the exercise of any will whatsoever taken as an ultimate end. The tiniest maggot, the smallest rodent, the scantest river, the farthest star, the most humble automatic machines—each demands to be taken also as an end, by the same right as the beggar Lazarus at the door of the selfish rich man".[13] RÉSO shall apply preventive and restrictive measures on activities that might lead to the extinction of things, the destruction of things, and the permanent altera-tion of things.[14]

Julian Yates likened the invasion of inhuman actants that ensued to spine-tingling, otherworldly collect calls[15] that "resonate within the 'human' but whose exteriority precludes their ready processing." There is a fault on the line, an un-canny phone call deploying an "overwhelming, potentially

---

[13] Bruno Latour, *Politics of Nature: How to Bring the Sciences into Democracy*, trans. Catherine Porter (Cambridge, MA: Harvard University Press, 2004) 216.

[14] PETROVSKY'S MARGINALIA: First time I read this, it was pinned to the customer noticeboard of a Wal-Mart in Utah.

[15] PETROVSKY'S MARGINALIA: . . . one of those auto-leveling alt-arts.

cacophonous prosopopeia." We cannot give a face to the post-human noise that "floods the switchboard", bringing the "figure of the outside that is of all the beings confined there and not granted citizenship . . . inside the oikos or collective".[16]

But, the mysterious call did not just come in from this side of the Enlightenment divide. The brain-scrambling cacophony was partly the result of a transtemporal epistemic overlap. Yates recalled how we desperately tried to "to transform [the] noise into news of an other".[17] The other turned out to be of monolithic proportions. It was the great pre-modern other,[18] the Leviathan of Félix Guattari's first type of "territorialised assemblage":

> Polyphonic spatial strata, often concentric, appear to attract and colonise all the levels of alterity that in other respects they engender. In relation to them, objects constitute themselves in transversal, vibratory position, conferring on them a soul, a becoming ancestral, animal, vegetal, cosmic. These objectities-subjectivities are led to work for themselves, to incarnate themselves as an animist nucleus: they overlap each other, and invade each

---

[16] Yates, "It's (for) You", 225.

[17] Yates, "It's (for) You", 228.

[18] PETROVSKY'S MARGINALIA: Multiple divergent strands of neo-medieval theory and practice then synthesizing into a single disenable phenomenon. For example, Bruce Holsinger examined the work of key twentieth-century French intellectuals (Bataille, Derrida, Lacan, Barthes, Bourdieu) to uncover a foundational medievalism, which was "this coterie's recurrent fascination, even obsession, with the historical period that modernity most consistently abjected as its temporal other. In its variegated assault on the legacy of the Enlightenment, the critical generation of this era turned to the Middle Ages not in a fit of nostalgic retrospection, but in a spirit of both interpretative and ideological resistance to the relentless inevitability of modernity": *The Premodern Condition: Medievalism and the Making of Theory* (Chicago: University of Chicago Press, 2005), 5.

other to become collective entities half-thing, half-soul, half-man, half-beast, machine and flux, matter and sign . . .[19]

---

[19] Félix Guattari, *Chaosmosis: An Ethico-Aesthetic Paradigm*, trans. Paul Bains and Julian Pefanis (Sydney: Power Publications, 1995), 102.

THEKARY OF THE ELIASSON

How good it is to be alone.... God shows his hidden mysteries and heavenly secrets to his dearest friends, not in the crowd of men, but where they were alone by themselves.[20]

Follow Mount-Royal's medieval re-enactors down to the lil' gem Rue Notre-Dame, regularly bedlamized by weekender anti-police brutality riots and the bestial devilry of carnival. Go at 10:00 a.m., Monday mornings. Everywhere you'll spy the unmistakable signs of the day after. The ground strewn with luminous detritus of every description: ribbons, rags, plumes, grapefruit-infused beer bottles, and regurgital matter from the cabbagey feast of poutine, well-peppered pies of smoked beef, chicken and eels and pigeons, geese and other fowl roasted on a spit. A good many of the kids come down just to turn over the charred remains of *compagnon émeute* that mysteriously pile up to form a peak on the corner of Rue Saint-Suplice. Standing in front of the Palais de Justice they rapturously recall the fine mummings and cere-

---

[20] Ancrene Wisse, *Guide for Anchoresses*, trans. and ed., Hugh White (London: Penguin Books, 1993), 75.

monial lynchings of the days before, sharing with phones dismembered effigies—last Instagrams of vanquished joy— while the homeless lug their booty of recyclable trash.

Watch out for scholars from the McGill Ghetto, in the mood for homey vegan food, passing to and fro, intent on finding BFFs lost amid the sensual vicars of the wooing tents. The artisans and tradespersons of Vieille Ville love to gossip and call to one another from shattered magasins while mounted officers-of-the-peace fidget speculatively with somnolent noise grenades and covetous plastic cuffs. Notre-Dame's rockabily-dude DJs entertain and give rennet-free drink and pétanque to keep things from getting dull.

After contemplating the vibrant and clamorous materiality of this recuperating urban assemblage, turn your attention towards the ancient building called the Notre-Dame Basilica. Upon turning the corner into Rue Saint-Sulpice, notice a tiny arched window peeking onto the sidewalk and closed by iron cross-bars, the only aperture by which a little air and light can penetrate to a small, doorless cell constructed on the level of the ground. Entombed within the wall of the old sanctuary is a quiet the more profound, a silence all the more oppressive, amid the echoes of Vieille Ville's weekly festival of destruction.

This gloomy cell is the *reclusorum* of the erstwhile artist Studio-Eliasson who, some years back, vowed to entomb himself forever until death. Studio-Eliasson discarded his Berlin workshop, a 15,000 square-foot "dynamic knowledge-production machine" or "psychographic anatomy"[21] of architects, farm animals, scientists, lab equipment, draftsmen, lighting technicians, art historians, house plants, construction materials (from sub-atomic particles to entire solar bodies), carpenters, hydroponic gardens and sustainable foodstuffs, actors (theatrical), state-of-the-art lighting/heating apparatus, visionary pedagogues, alchemical compounds, critical

---

[21] Caroline A. Jones, "The Server/User Mode: The Art of Olafur Eliasson", *Artforum* 46.2 (2007): 321–324.

theorists, chefs, archivists, blacksmiths, professional psychics, electricians, medievalists, computer frameworks, organic compost systems, documentarians, solariums, artisans, sofa-beds, poets, electricians, object philosophers, air conditioners, humidors and baby-sitters. Giving up the rest of his personal effects as "contact relics" to the poor and to the crossed out ~~God~~, Studio-Eliasson entered this one empty chamber, the door of which is walled up and the window open to the elements winter and summer. Thus became the Notre-Dame anchorite.

Studio-Eliasson's globally established reputation as master journeyman and flatlander[22] *par excellence* has made his voluntary self-entombment all the more special. This anchoritic practice is regarded as one of the purest, most severely withdrawn, seemingly penitential, and incalcuable acts of *virtus*. In the months leading up to the ceremony of enclosure (Studio-Eliasson's "grave" is on permanent display in Haus 2, Berlin), Studio-Eliasson's professional-personal oeuvre was interpreted as an extended network, or flow of relations, emitting from the workshop. As Caroline Jones commented, the itinerant assemblage of masters, Journeymen, and apprentices (plus, lest we forget, the extended animal, vegetable and mineral entourage) resulted in "multiple modes of production—outsourcing, collaborating, prototyping, fabricat-

---

[22] PETROVSKY'S MARGINALIA: . . . "Flatlander": post-work terminology describing creative cognitariats who pursue remunerable interests within nonhierarchical managerial structures. The computer game development company Valve coined the term "Flatland". Valve employees received a desk on wheels which they could physically push around the building until they found a project (or people) that interested them. There were no managers, no set work hours (play and work are regarded as identical), salaries were determined by employees with their peers, and no one resigned because any "outside" conflicts (health, family, desire to travel, change of interests, etc.) could be negotiated and brought "inside" the corporate fold as remunerable activities. See: www.valvesoftware.com/company/Valve_Handbook_LowRes.pdf.

ing, experimenting, representing, exhibiting, publishing—all of which fuse[d] at the level of knowledge production".[23] The "artworks" leaving the studio, she further expounded, concretised as nodal extensions of the Studio-Eliasson assemblage itself—as "dispersed social-technical-spatial entities" that translate codified knowledge into tacit experience "in the culture-laden body of a viewer".[24] Studio-Eliasson, thus, was an attempt to generate and embody a hypereconomic assemblage of practices, to become a hub that dissolved distinctions between production, transfer, consumption and virtus.

At the time of Studio-Eliasson's enclosure, the Journeyman, in all of its guises (the economic migrant, the exile, the fundamentalist vagrant, the tourist, the precarious worker, the residency artist, the hacker, *compagnon*) was fast becoming the dominant archetype within the deterritorialised flows of neomedieval cultural production. Journeymen and flatlanders honed and recycled their subject positions "by harmonizing their codes with other codes, by making their singularity resonate with a history and with problems born of other cultures."[25] As a "semionaut", the Journeyman's transubstantial corpus exists "exclusively in the dynamic form of its wandering and the contours of the circuit it describes".[26] The neomedieval artist-entrepreneur is "always at sea".

Considering its endlessly cosmic dispersal of subjectivity, it is tempting to interpret The Eliasson's corporeal bracketing as a result of some kind of schizoid break—an immense psychic fatigue brought on by a perpetual surfing and tramping through a cultural rain that never lets up. Is The Eliasson simply looking for a permanent place to hang Adam's Kirtle, a finite shelter (as the becoming-corpse) from the

---

[23] Jones, "The Server/User Mode", 324.

[24] Jones, "The Server/User Mode", 323–324.

[25] Nicholas Bourriaud, *The Radicant*, trans. James Gussen and Lili Porten (New York: Lukas and Sternberg 2009), 30.

[26] Bourriaud, *The Radicant*, 55.

infinite, synapse-zapping intrusions of a hyper-scrutinized and hyper-scrutinizing reality?[27] The same question could be applied to the phenomenon at large. Is the anchoritic tradition a politico-aesthetic reaction to the "participatory panopticon"[28] or an attempt to crawl beneath the "ubiquitous sensors" that constituted "Privacy 2.0"?[29] We could, perhaps, look to the anchorites of our reactivated "middle" for suggestions.

As medieval historian Michelle M. Sauer argued, in the thirteenth century, when the position of anchorite was highly coveted, life was conducted with "no expectations of privacy. Every function of daily life—including sexual relations—was, at least in some sense, a shared experience".[30] In the medieval household, occupants cohabited within a quasi-domestic and bustling flow of human and non-human entities, from farm animals and harvested crops to children, neighbours, lodgers and all the equipment of day-to-day labour. Anchorholds, by contrast, were "small, private, regulated, and empty—all scarce commodities in the Middle Ages".[31] In this light, the anchorhold seemingly offers respite from a vociferously probing and intrusive world of biotically peeping eyeballs and digitally sensing sensors.[32]

---

[27] PETROVSKY'S MARGINALIA: . . . "Adams Kirtle": an Eschatological term referring to the flesh of Adam which he adorns as clothing until it may be discarded in the eventual ascent to the Godside.

[28] Jamais Cascio, "The Rise of the Participatory Panopticon", *World Changing*, 2005. Available online: www.worldchanging.com/archives/002651.html.

[29] Jonathan L. Zittrain, *The Future of the Internet—And How to Stop It* (New Haven: Yale University Press, 2009), 205.

[30] Michelle M. Sauer, "Representing the Negative: Positing the Lesbian Void in Medieval English Anchoritism", *thirdspace: a journal of feminist theory & culture* 3.2 (2004): par. 3. Available online: www.thirdspace.ca/journal/article/view/sauer/178.

[31] Sauer, "Representing the Negative," par. 2.

[32] PETROVSKY'S MARGINALIA: . . . this is obviously far too reductive. Why retrospectively install such proto-individuation upon the thirteenth-century subject? Why suggest that solitude and privacy

Yet, as Robert Hasenfratz noted, many anchorites "withdrew" from the world in full knowledge that they would, paradoxically, find themselves fully at the center of parish life. As he infers from *Ancrene Wisse*[33], the recluse's appointed servants or handmaidens not only attended to their daily needs, but, more crucially, acted as mediators with the outside world. These verbal messengers enabled the development of widespread anchoritic communication networks and, in some cases, the parish anchorhold acted "as a sort of bank, post office, school house, shop, and newspaper-services which today are provided mainly by public and quasi-public institutions".[34] In conjunction with these routine services, many anchorites became spiritual celebrities attracting pilgrims from afar, providing a link between this world and the next.[35] The medieval anchorite, then, did not so much cut itself off from the world as offer itself up to the world as an embodied intersection, a one-stop-shop, between the commonplace and the extraordinary; the terrestrial concerns of everyday life and the Empyrean sublime. The anchorite today functions as a pontifex[36]—a constructer of bridges transversing worlds.

Ask any Vieille Ville calèche driver as they trundle past the Notre-Dame thekary[37] and they will tell you: The Eliasson

---

were becoming prized within an otherwise communal and hybridist (not-yet-modern-enough) medieval world?

[33] PETROVSKY'S MARGINALIA: the essential early thirteenth-century "guide" for anchoresses.

[34] Robert Hasenfratz, "Introduction", *Ancrene Wisse*, ed. Robert Hasenfratz (Kalamazoo, MI: Medieval Institute Publications, 2000), par. 13. Available online: www.lib.rochester.edu/camelot/teams/awintro.htm.

[35] Hasenfratz, "Introduction," *Ancrene Wisse*, pars.13–14.

[36] PETROVSKY'S MARGINALIA: . . . Latin: 'bridge-maker', from *pons*, 'bridge' and *fex*, 'to make'.

[37] PETROVSKY'S MARGINALIA: . . . Thekary: term coined by New York anchorhold attendant Greggery Peccary after the artist Paul Thek with particular reference to his lost masterwork *The Tomb*

is a hypereconomic commodity, a person-object incubated via the discourses of Studio-Eliasson and maintained by the veneration of the community. The locals know this to be true. Studio-Eliasson's transfiguration into the Notre-Dame anchorite integrated Studio-Eliasson's relations of hypereconomic circulation into a single person-object: The Eliasson. Does this integration signify a quelling of the hypereconomic tide, a final anchoring in safe habour? To the faithful, Eliasson's is not the abjuration of hyper-linked (and radically de-privatised) subject positions at all, but an attempt to amplify such relations through a folding-in or condensation of the "culture-laden body" of the former Studio-Eliasson assemblage, into a single point of radiating intensity.

The Eliasson's corporeal fusion with the ecclesiastic stone of the Notre-Dame Basilica creates a super-dense compound of affective material. Pilgrims marvel at its intensely elevated *virtus*, an immense gravitational pull that can be felt by passing within fifty feet of the thekary, drawing forth the luminous detritus of *émeute*. Its astonishing years of unbroken silence (not even its two masked "attendants" have betrayed it) have discharged a pandemic of speculative "The Eliasson"-themed discourses, tinged with apocalyptic neurosis. What is it doing? Has it sublimed unto the Empyrean? Crossed to another dimension? Is it Jesus? A terrorist in a cell? Will it explode? Its mighty flexing of ascetic muscle has been likened to the "bizarre athleticism of the 'fasting-artist' type . . . an athleticism of becoming that reveals only forces that are not its own".[38] The Eliasson's entombed and inde-

---

(1967). The work, popularly referred to as *Death of a Hippie*, consisted of a pale pink wooden structure, within which lay a full-size, wax effigy of the artist (including human hair and nails) surrounded by personal effects arranged for use in the afterlife. As the popular title indicates, the work was often interpreted as a lamentation on the failure of 1960s countercultural idealism.

[38] Giles Deleuze and Félix Guattari, *What is Philosophy*? trans. Hugh Tomlinson and Graham Burchell (London: Verso,1994), 172.

terminate flesh forms a "bloc of sensations"[39] held in place, not by "bone or skeletal structure", but by a "house or framework".[40]

The Thekary of The Eliasson is "but the most shut-up house [that] opens onto a universe".[41] Not so alien, then, to the Studio-Eliasson oeuvre of old, this anchorhold does not shelter its semionaut from the cosmic forces of infinite code, but draws the universe, tight-beamed, in through its tiny portal. This is no all-consuming black hole. This thekary has two portals, one unto the world and a hagioscope that offers itself unto the sanctum of Notre-Dame, enabling lines of flight to go from house-territory to town-cosmos, from the finite to the infinite. Talk about core!

[39] Deleuze and Guattari, *What Is Philosophy?*, 167.
[40] Deleuze and Guattari, *What Is Philosophy?*, 179.
[41] Deleuze and Guattari, *What Is Philosophy?*, 180.

Me-Machine for Throwing Shit at the Moon

Wonder was [in the middle ages], associated with paradox, co-incidence of opposites; one finds mira (wondrous) again and again in the texts alongside mixta (mixed or composite things), a word that evokes the hybrids and monsters also found in the literature of entertainment.[42]

Supposedly this SE hole in the Sunnyside district is where the current global anchorite craze started. In fact, the anchorhold itself is certainly of more recent genesis than that in Notre-Dame, and, unlike the former, purposefully engenders a surprising degree of community interaction. Built by local artisans way back in 1992, and not populated for many decades after its completion,[43] the archorhold is protected by 1-

---

[42] Caroline Walker Bynum, "AHA Presidential Address: Wonder", January 3, 1996, par. 8. Available online: http://www.historians. org/about-aha-and-membership/aha-history-and-archives/presidential-addresses/caroline-walker-bynum.

[43] PETROVSKY'S MARGINALIA: Although the cell was specially commissioned for anchoritic practice no suitably committed recluse could be found then. Volunteers lasted between one day and two months until the project was simultaneously criticised as 'hopelessly

hour fire resistance-rated construction and an automatic sprinkler system in accordance with Oregon State Fire Code. Arrangements were made for the anchorhold to be strictly monitored 24/7 for health and safety purposes. To this day, a server from the Waffle Window takes regular written requests from its anchorite through the ambient temple's peephole for more tea lights, Tibetan prayer flags, pine nut kernels, fried chicken 'n' waffles, kombucha, etc. The anchorite logs the interactions faithfully in its Ex Libris Anonymous hand-made vintage book journal.

The flattered local community of Portland, Oregon have certainly kept their promise to venerate their anchorite! The Sacamano's tangible "contact relics" populate the community (of people and things) with thousands of transfigured host objects, each one infused with the somatic effects of the donor's distributed body. The corpus mysticum of the original body "spilled over into the vitality, the animation or ensouledness, of every body in which these multiplying phenomena occur",[44] the neighbourhood absorbs, redistributes and recycles this mad multiplicity of meticulously inscribed part-human hybrids.

While a well-kept secret on the growing PDX thekary circuit, Portland's first anchorite only came to wider international attention through Antonio Gambini's overhyped *Journey to the West*. It was while standing in line to witness the sensual enormity of a Farm Fusion from the Waffle Window on SE Hawthorne Blvd—two simply must become one within this gastromantic entanglement—that Gambini observed, directly across the street, a barred portal set into a turquoise painted wall three inches above the sidewalk. Upon crossing to inspect, a golden light emanated from inside. And so,

---

antiquated' and 'ahead of its time'. Just like Virtual Reality, the project was shelved until the next suitable epistemic shift brought it in line with global market trends.

[44] Karmen Mackendrick, "The Multipliable Body", *postmedieval: a journal of medieval cultural studies* 1.1/2 (2010): 113.

Gambini "discovered" Portland's anchorite, an experience which, as every schoolchild knows, the *compagnon* found to be the second most profound and transforming of his magnificent journey:

> Through the peephole of the cell I spied a magnificent Me-Machine, its tangible user interface offering rich affordances and fully immersive ambient interactions with the sensorium. In the middle of the Me-Machine, a treadmill was lavishly decorated in the mid-century neobaroque fashion, including the standard Willard altar with crystal and incense of Lycean myrrh set up with all manner of glimmering protrusions and frivolously eclectic attachments. The entire contents of the cell—including the small bunk, refrigerator, chamber pot, steel tub and The Sacamano itself—were painted gold to enable awesome surface-to-surface conductivity. The faint odour of Lycean myrrh piggybacked a more potent fragrance of stale sweat out into the street. Once you've seen it, you can't imagine any other form of anchorhold!
>
> The golden anchorite—tightly muscled yet waiflike and of indeterminate gender—mounts the Me-Machine at its steepest elevation and begins to walk in place. "Stop reducing everything!" screams The Sacamano. As the speed is dialled up and the recluse breaks into a jog, a projection appears on the wall depicting a monastically robed and bearded figure standing cross-armed atop what appears to be a mountain of discarded consumables. The projection is arranged just so that a second smaller window (the "hagioscope") corresponds to the area where the Vintage Store Keeper's head would normally appear.[45] From this aperture, small objects are

---

[45] PETROVSKY'S MARGINALIA: The Vintage Store Keeper projected on the screen appears to be a reference to the virtual-somatic religion of Mercerism in Philip K. Dick's 1968 novel *Do Androids Dream of Electric Sheep?* In this religion worshipers grip the handles of

ejected, striking The Sacamano at various points in the body. As The Sacamano slowly increases pace, so too does the velocity of the projectiles until the pain of impact appears to become intolerable and the anchorite slows down to a walk. During this respite, the Sacamano's perspiring body can be observed through the increasingly translucent layers of body paint. It is covered in bruises and tiny scars. After a few neck rolls, power shrugs, and motivational fist-pumps, it picks up pace and the auto-flagellation continues.

I stepped back at this point, my body-sleeve emoting tweet-clouds of concern. I stumbled over something, falling backwards. At my feet a gold painted cooler. In this box I was invited to leave an object—perhaps the remains or wrapper of my Farm Fusion—which, as I had just witnessed, would be put to good use. Anyway, I hope this gives you some idea of the program.[46]

The informal title of this anchoritic ritual—*Me-Machine for Throwing Shit at the Moon*—allegedly derives from The Sacamano's flippant retort to a local reporter from *Proto-Bitch* magazine who asked what it was busy constructing in the SE Hawthorne basement. Given The Sacamano's former reputation as a content curator and master relic-er, the remark was widely interpreted as sarcastic commentary on the anthropocentric folly of scientific attempts to subjugate a profoundly indifferent universe. Though there may be partial truth here, it seemed apparent from Gambini's vivid description of the early years that Sacamano's anchorhold was home to the first, and foremost, fully immersive, ambient

---

Empathy Boxes that are linked up to form a noosphere. Participants join in the suffering of Wilbur Mercer, a man who takes an endless walk up a mountain while stones are thrown at him, the pain of which the users also endure.

[46] Antonio Gambini, *Journey to the West* (undated), Project Guthenberg: http://www.gutenberg.org.

body-contact "relic-ing" device, or "Me-Machine".

One of Willard's most popular boutique products, the Me-Machine, was Sherlocked to enable the user to cancel all personal gift-debt obligations by becoming a relational hub for expanded para-human networks. The Me-Machine stood in contradistinction to the unpopular Man-Machines of the industrial era. Rather than instrumentalise the body as if it were a cog in a network of commoditised labour relations, the Me-Machine concerned free exchanges of desire. The Me-Machine was not focused so much on tailoring and silvercasting experiences to niche markets that already existed (this kind of mass customisation failed to become a growth sector), but rather with stimulating supply and demand for clusters of experience. The Me-Machine fed a bazaar,[47] a raucous commercial labyrinth within which there was no vantage point but wherein users would develop a cacophony of new itches to scratch.

Once immersed in the Me-Machine interface, the users' "bespoke" desires were "bundled", cracked, taken-apart, reassembled, resurrected, cooked, remixed, recycled and networked into a singular marketable commodity. The anchoritic user of the Me-Machine ceased to be a human subject, transfiguring into a person-object, and thus a conduit or node within the common terrain of the Me-Machine's sonorous metaverse. The Me-Machine's singularity played itself like an instrument. Unique timbre, assonance, and dissonance were produced by tangential interference between "bundles" drifting with its field. Thus the adoption of the Me-Machine was a bilateral development—the Me-Machine created new users just as these new users created new "bundles" for the Me-Machine. At an exorbitantly high price, the Me-Machine promised a fully integrated, ambient, sensorial continuum, a temporary reliquary characterised only by

---

[47] See Eric S. Raymond, *The Cathedral & the Bazaar: Musings on Linux and Open Source by an Accidental Revolutionary*, rev. edn. (Sebastopol, CA: O'Reilly Media, 2008).

its *middle-ness*.

The ambient withdrawal from conventional "terrestrial" consumerism offered by the Me-Machine, paradoxically, again, redistributed its anchorite as pontifex for a metaversal sublime. Ambience, in its association with "background noise" or "room temperature", is most readily allied with the captivating immersive atmosphere of the bazaar and with the lack of "perspective" it offers us. To get a clear picture of things, one free of static, such ambience is the snow that needs to be identified and discounted, an interloper to be calibrated out of the experiment. It is in this sense that Paul Virilio rallied against "soronity" and its "prosecution of silence".[48] For Virilio, silence is voiceless in the Me-Machine's mash-ups, babble, and chatter. This creates an impossible bind in which mutism signifies only consent to the omnipresent clamour of the souk. The choice to remain thoughtfully silent has been taken away by the increasing volume of noise, a buzz amplified by the unfurled long-tail of the Me-Machine. The anchoritic tradition imposed by the Me-Machine ensures that people, spaces and things can longer be considered mute; everything is vacuumed into its semantic web of perpetual interference. Soronity is the Me-Machine's black hole, and the louder it gets, the more attractive its magnetism; it has no respite.

After a pre-selected period of time, the Me-Machine normally disconnects its user, allowing them to return to the terrestrial business of perpetually renegotiating their neoliberal agency. By walling itself inside a retrofitted Me-Machine, The Sacamano became a permanent fixture of Willard's global product line, a unique, bespoke, person-object of equivalent status with all other objects. At the same time, The Sacramano became the local-product par excellence, the SE Hawthorne anchorhold venerated as the smallest of small-batch ateliers. Thus Gambini learned the secrets of the

---

[48] Paul Virilio, *Art and Fear*, trans. Julie Rose (London: Continuum, 2003), 39.

mass distribution of the artisanal.

Before returning to Les Cours Mont-Royal to luncheon triumphantly with RÉSO's grand masters, Gambini took a little time out to wander the Federal Work Programme-paved sidewalks of PDX, admiring the ambundant rose trees of the luscious Sunnyside 'burbs and the wild Doug Firs that peppered the reclaimed commons of Laurelhurst Park. En route he sampled the delights of PDX's neomedieval makers, marvelling at the hand-crafted "golden share-boxes" enveloping the gossamer thin MacBooks that decorated brewpubs and artisanal-cafes in Burnside. Inside his share box, which came free with a tall mochachino, he found an exquisite wooden relic, digitally-inscribed at ADX Portland with the motto: *Half tide dock, Mănăstirea Humorului, Pittsburgh and Susquehanna Railroad, Royalty Theatre, Glasgow, Basic Education High School, thN Lng folk 2go, Albert de Rochas, Periapical abscess, Vanlandi, Scamp grouper, Katsura Atrina rigida, Cardigan, Salvador Capín, STS-42, Aalst, Lázaro Cárdenas, Michoacán, 1917–18, List of MTR station codes, John de Brantingham, Zheng Zhi*[49]—the perfect souvenier of his journey to the west.

In what sense, if any, is The Sacamano anchorite still relevant? One of the world's fastest growing anchoritic sites, it has all the right ingredients for an unforgettable pilgrimage. The contact relic-ing aspect of the neomedieval anchoritic tradition is unbeatable in its recognition and celebration of the emancipatory potential and marked proliferation of non-modern quasi-objects throughout the cyborgian[50] and no-

---

[49] Contact-Relic inscription generated by Ian Bogost's Latour Litanizer: http://www.bogost.com/blog/latour_litanizer.shtml.

[50] See Donna, J. Haraway, *Simians, Cyborgs and Women: The Reinvention of Nature* (New York: Routledge, 1991), 181: "Taking responsibility for the social relations of science and technology means refusing an anti-science metaphysics, a demonology of technology, and so means embracing the skillful task of reconstructing the boundaries of daily life, in partial connection with others, in communication with all of our parts. It is not just that science and technolo-

madological life-world of global capitalism. Quasi-objects[51] are objects that are neither natural objects nor social subjects, but monstrous composites circulating in (and crucially as) networks of translation and mediation. Part semiotic, part biological, part human, part mineral, part computer, part myth, quasi-objects shape human practices by drawing people into amorphous relations with non-human actants or agents. A scale-free hypereconomic artisanal facility, quasi-objects are simultaneously fabricated, circulated and consumed within the anchorhold's Me-Machine.

In *We Have Never Been Modern*, Bruno Latour argued that the constitution of modernity arose from an epistemic purification that detached the knowledge of people (culture and politics) from the knowledge of things (nature and sci-

---

gy are possible means of great human satisfaction, as well as a matrix of complex dominations. Cyborg imagery can suggest a way out of the maze of dualisms in which we have explained our bodies and our tools to ourselves."

[51] Bruno Latour is following the work of Michel Serres: "A ball is not an ordinary object, for it is what it is only if a subject holds it. Over there, on the ground, it is nothing; it is stupid; it has no meaning, no function, and no value. Ball isn't played alone. Those who do, those who hog the ball, are bad players and are soon excluded from the game. They are said to be selfish. The collective game doesn't need persons, people out for themselves. Let us consider the one who holds it. If he makes it move around him, he is awkward, a bad player. The ball isn't therefore the body; the exact contrary is true: the body is the object of the ball; the subject moves around this sun. Skill with the ball is recognized in the player who follows the ball and serves it instead of making it follow him and using it. It is the subject of the body, subject of bodies, and like a subject of subjects. Playing is nothing else but making oneself the attribute of the ball as a substance. The laws are written for it, defined relative to it, and we bend to these laws. Skill with the ball supposes a Ptolemaic revolution of which few theoreticians are capable, since they are accustomed to being subjects in a Copernican world where objects are slaves": *The Parasite*, trans. Lawrence R. Schehr (Minneapolis: University of Minnesota Press, 2007), 225–226.

ence), placing them at either extremity of a subject/object pole. Over time, the average citizens, bound up in this matrix of imposed dualisms, found their naive belief systems being "denounce[d], and debunk[ed] and ridicule[d]"[52] by social scientists guarding the ontological integrity of both poles. On the one side, when people believed objects to have intrinsic meaning, the social scientist taught them about fetishisation, that "Gods, money, fashion and art offer only a surface for the projection of our social needs and interests".[53] On the flipside, when people believed themselves to be free as human subjects, the social scientist (now allied with the natural scientist) endeavoured to show how the power of biology, language, and economics "determines, informs and moulds the soft and pliable wills of the poor humans". Latour concludes that, in "the first denunciation objects count for nothing," while in the second "they are so powerful that they shape the human society . . . . Objects, things, consumer goods, works of art are either too weak or too strong".[54]

Latour does not argue that objective forces and social constructions are mere fabrications, but that modernity, in order to clearly define itself against non-modern cultures past and present, rendered unthinkable (while at the same time accelerating) a "middle kingdom" of hybrid nature-culture assemblages, "frozen embryos, expert systems, digital machines, sensor-equipped robots, hybrid corn, data banks, psychotropic drugs, whales fitted with radar sounding devices, gene synthesizers, audience analyzers, and so on," where "everything happens".[55]

Paradoxically, it was the intensive differentiation, sorting and classification (humanity/non-humanity and the crossed

---

[52] Bruno Latour, *We Have Never Been Modern*, trans. Catherine Porter (Cambridge, MA: Harvard University Press, 1993), 53.
[53] Latour, *We Have Never Been Modern*, 52.
[54] Latour, *We Have Never Been Modern*, 53.
[55] Latour, *We Have Never Been Modern*, 37, 49.

out ~~God~~) of the modernist project that enabled the global expansion of hybrid networks that "continue to multiply as an effect of this separate treatment".[56] It was in the vast un-differentiated middle kingdom of quasi-objects and quasi-subjects that the neomedieval aesthetic first took root in the cult of neo-dada relics, the becoming-other of the post-human nomad, and now, in the revival and global adoption of the "full-fat" anchoritic practice—a final return to the scat-tered, unbounded excesses of pre-modern, loosey goosey embodiment, and to the "deeply weird multiplicities" and monstrous fusions of persons, things and Gods.[57]

And it was here, dear Journeymen, that we unearthed, dusted down, and held aloft the enchanted objects denied to us by the negative dialecticians and "signifier enthusi-asts"[58] who sought to protect us from their alienating, reify-ing, and objectifying allure. As Latour lamented,

> Haven't we shed enough tears over the disenchantment of the world? Haven't we frightened ourselves enough with the poor European who is thrust into a cold soulless cosmos, wandering on an inert planet in a world devoid of meaning? Haven't we shivered enough before the spectacle of the mechanized proletarian who is subject to the absolute domination of a mechanized capitalism and a Kafkaesque bureaucracy, abandoned smack in the middle of language games, lost in cement and formica? Haven't we felt sorry enough for the consumer who leaves the driver's seat of his car only to move to the sofa in the TV room where he is manipulated by the powers of the media and the postindustrialized society?![59]

---

[56] Latour, *We Have Never Been Modern*, 13.

[57] MacKendrick, "The Multipliable Body," 110.

[58] Gilles Deleuze and Félix Guattari, *A Thousand Plateaus: Capitalism and Schizophrenia*, trans. Brian Massumi (London: Continuum International Publishing Group, 2004), 74.

[59] Latour, *We Have Never Been Modern*, 115.

For Jane Bennett these narratives of disenchantment had to be disassembled since they contributed to the very conditions they portrayed. The delineation of the nature/culture poles as "orders no longer capable of inspiring deep attachment inflects the self as a creature of loss and thus discourages discernment of the marvelous vitality of bodies human and nonhuman, natural and artifactual".[60] Following Latour, she argued that "sites of enchantment" permeated the landscape of modernity and exist today in "the discovery of sophisticated modes of communication among nonhumans, the strange agency of physical systems at far-from-equilibrium states, and the animation of objects by video technologies—an animation whose effects are not fully captured by the idea of 'commodity fetishism'".[61] To be enchanted, she wrote, is to be "struck and shaken by the extraordinary that lives in amid the familiar and the everyday".[62]

And it is the very same magical refrains that continue to adorn every one of The Sacamano's golden graspable user-interface contact-relics. When night falls, the Portland anchorhold is host to a thrilling heterotopic configuration of objects not of its own making—generating interminable litanies of illicit subject-object encounters.

---

[60] Jane Bennett, *The Enchantment of Modern Life: Attachments, Crossings, Ethics* (Princeton: Princeton University Press, 2001), 4.

[61] Bennett, *The Enchantment of Modern Life*, 4.

[62] Bennett, *The Enchantment of Modern Life*, 3–4.

THE LONDON STONE

The world is neither a grey matrix of objective elements, nor raw material for a sexy human drama projected onto gravel and sludge. Instead, it is filled with points of reality woven together only loosely: an archipelago of oracles or bombs that explode from concealment only to generate new sequestered temples.[63]

Let's hear it for pavements! My urban cousins, the unsung heroes stopping humans everywhere from walking in the road or the dirt.[64]

What's in a name? Anyone who has had the great fortune to visit Charing Cross Station in London will fondly remember the branch of WH Smiths located directly across from the Cannon Street entrance.[65] The history of the branch goes

---

[63] Graham Harman, "On Vicarious Causation", *Collapse* II (2007): 211.

[64] The London Stone, *Twitter:* twitter.com/thelondonstone.

[65] PETROVSKY'S MARGINALIA: WH Smiths were assembling an

way back to 1981. Alas the newsagent chain has gone, raptured during the early phase of the Greater Recession. For the anchoritic pilgrim willing to travel the distance, the eviscerated retail outlet's true charms lie beneath. The mundane topography of Charing Cross makes it easy to get to, except by boat. Walking offers an excellent overview of the territory prior to planning a longer, more intimate visit.

Observe carefully an extruding stone fascia with a glass panel protected by a decorative steel portcullis. A brass plaque on the sloping roof confirms that this is the house of the London Stone[66]—a mythic chunk of limestone of unknown purpose and origin, now reclaimed as an alien anchorhold by the Fraternity of Tiny Ontologists [FTO][67]. During the weeks that Eliasson's enclosure ceremony caused a media storm, the FTO quietly announced that the London Stone had been elected worshipful master of their brotherhood and invited everyone to a street party to retroactively celebrate its entombment. This would be the first and final work of the FTO who, as far as anyone can gather, have followed WH Smiths into the ether.

Locals visit the stone regularly throughout the summer (and sometimes in winter, too) as they pass by on their way to a local cob kiosk. The stony anchorite stares blankly, infinitely withdrawing behind its stony kirtle. What is it doing, this rudely solid thing? "Well", as the FTO might have said, "it is stoning!" "But what is it?" the Journeyman might ask. The Tiny Ontologists have left a tiny answer: "It *is*." This may sound annoyingly reductive, but the FTO are telling us the opposite. The London Stone cannot be reduced to any of its

---

excellent marinaded sesame carrot grilled sandwich.

[66] PETROVSKY'S MARGINALIA: Yeah, I read about this on Jeffery Cohen's blog: www.inthemedievalmiddle.com/2013/02/a-door-into-stone.html.

[67] PETROVSKY'S MARGINALIA: Almost certainly homage to Ian Bogost's brand of Object-Oriented-Ontology. In *Alien Phenomenology* he proposed a "tiny ontology": tiny enough to be one word written on the front of a baseball cap—"is".

perceived qualities. For some it is crystallised CaCO3, and for others it is a druid "index stone", a prehistoric fetish stone, a psycho-geographical place-mar-ker, a talismanic protector of the city or the stone that posts tweets on the daily life of Cannon Street. Yet these are just human percep-tions—what is the London Stone to the pavement below it, the steel bars that protect it, or the building that entombs it? It is all of these relations and none. It is this very inexhausti-bility that makes it real, and that points to a deeply weird inner reality, a molten core, that is more than the sum of its external relations.

In his January 2010 blog entry, "Onticology–A Manifesto for Object-Oriented Ontology," Levi Bryant sketched out the heretical propositions of a nascent philosophical movement broadly referred to at the time as Speculative Realism. Alt-hough differing considerably in their ontological perspec-tives, the cohort were loosely united in their opposition to what Quentin Meillassoux had termed "correlationism"—the tendency of post-Kantian philosophy to limit its enquiry to the mutual interplay of human thought and objective reality. Provocatively declaring the year 1781 a fateful watershed marking the devastating Copernican Revolution of Immanuel Kant's *Critique of Pure Reason*, Bryant forwarded the SR position that Western philosophy had persisted in a "univer-salised transcendental anthropology" that was cyclically in-vestigating the various mechanisms by which human cogni-tion structures the world. In other words, the category of the human continued to dominate a species-narcissistic ontolo-gy in which objects in the world are reduced to mere propo-sitions by human beings. Against this asymmetry, Specula-tive Realism—or in one of its more prominent variants, Ob-ject Oriented Ontology—stated not only that objects exist, fully independent of human observation or cognition, but that the human subject is just one particular type of object amongst others.[68]

---

[68] Levi Bryant, "Onticology–A Manifesto for Object-Oriented Ontol-

As rumour has it, the FTO was founded anonymously by ex-members of the Cybernetic Culture Research Group—a radical collective of para-academic researchers who enthusiastically combined philosophy, techno-science, natural science, medieval mysticism, science fiction, numerology, and complexity theory with late 1960s Anglo-French gastronomic alchemy in an effort to explode the insular and overly self-reflexive fiefdom of academic humanism. The shift from this deleuzoguattarian schizo-nomadic praxis towards object-oriented, speculatively pragmatic medievalism was clearly inspired by the strange phenomenology of Graham Harman who, in 2010, proclaimed:

Against the model of philosophy as a rubber stamp for common sense and archival sobriety, I would propose that philosophy's sole mission is weird realism. Philosophy must be realist because its mandate is to unlock the structure of the world itself; it must be weird because reality is weird. "Continental science fiction", and "continental horror", must be transformed from insults into a research program.[69]

Harman's realism rejected philosophy's human-world coupling by stating that the whole of reality is constructed from objects alone. By objects he meant "any reality with an autonomous life deeper than its qualities, and deeper than its relations with other things"[70], and thus including molecules, solar systems, Gandalf,[71] The Eliasson, Canada, hallucinations, iPhones, psychoanalysis, farm animals, scientists, lab equipment, draftsmen, lighting technicians, art historians,

---

ogy", *Larval Subjects*, January 12, 2010, pars. 3–6: larvalsubjects. wordpress.com/2010/01/12/object-oriented-ontology-a-manifesto-part-i/.

[69] Graham Harman, "On the Horror of Phenomenology: Lovecraft and Husserl", Collapse IV (2008): 334.

[70] Harman, "On the Horror of Phenomenology", 346.

[71] PETROVSKY'S MARGINALIA: Bike mechanic at Abraham's?

house plants, construction materials (from sub-atomic parti-cles to entire solar bodies), carpenters, hydroponic gardens and sustainable foodstuffs, actors (theatrical), state-of-the-art lighting/heating apparatus, visionary pedagogues, alchemi-cal compounds, critical theorists, chefs, archivists, black-smiths, professional psychics, electricians, medievalists, com-puter frameworks, organic compost systems, documentari-ans, solariums, artisans, sofa-beds, poets, electricians, object philosophers, air conditioners, humidors and baby-sitters, lumps of rock, a minute of time, and hammers. Furthermore, reality is fundamentally weird because its objects withdraw from each other. To explain this Harman developed Heide-gger's "tool analysis", in which he proposed that when we are using a hammer we only perceive it through its function or "equipmentality". It is only when the hammer is broken that we see its materiality ("wood", "metal") as previously hidden dimensions of its being. Harman universalises this proposition to the point where all objects can only make contact through "sensual profiles". When fire burns cotton, for example, it does not make contact with all the properties of cotton (texture, smell, price, etc.), but merely its flamma-bility. Likewise "dogs do not make contact with the full reali-ty of bones, and neither do locusts with cornstalks, viruses with cells, rocks with windows, nor planets with moons".[72] The real London Stone (as the FTO would have it) can only be what it is—it hides behind its relations to neighbouring objects (we Journeymen included) who can only speculate what it might be.

And yet, despite its withdrawal, the London Stone (this 'alien' anchorite) still engages with other objects in the world. The more it withdraws, the stronger the gravitational force or allure that warps the trajectory of passing objects, drawing them into mutually speculative relations that in turn generate new sensual profiles. But how, exactly, do ancho-rites collide and relate when they are so entombed with their

---

[72] Harman, "On Vicarious Causation", 189.

hidden cores? In Harman's theory of "vicarious causation", objects interact through an intermediary, third object called a "sensual vicar". As a Christian vicar provides a pontifex between God and humans (as does the anchorite), so sensual vicars act as mediators between real objects. Sensual objects, Harman explains, exist on the interior of real objects. They are how real objects perceive other objects—for example, the real object of "fire" does not directly encounter a real object "cotton", but a sensual object "cotton", which for fire would be "fuel" or "flammability". The anchorite thus translated is the vicarious link between the finitude of the sensual realm and the infinitely withdrawn mysterium of the real. This brings us back to the earlier proposition that the anchorite does not withdraw from the world so much as open up to it. As Timothy Morton writes,

> Withdrawal isn't a violent sealing off. Nor is withdrawal some void or vague darkness. Withdrawal just is the unspeakable unicity of this lamp, this paperweight, this plastic portable telephone, this praying mantis, this frog, this Mars faintly red in the night sky, this cul-de-sac, this garbage can. An open secret.[73]

The Fraternity of Tiny Ontologists existed for a tiny amount of time to anoint a tiny alien anchorite in a tiny anchorhold, but the implications were far from tiny. When Graham Harman proposed that causality (object-object relations) takes place in the sensual realm, he was claiming aesthetics as first philosophy. Aesthetics, he argued, had hitherto served as the "impoverished dancing-girl of philosophy—admired for her charms, but no gentleman would marry her".[74] Since Kant, aesthetics had enjoyed a prominent role as an onto-

---

[73] Timothy Morton, *Realist Magic: Objects, Ontology, Causality* (Ann Arbor: Open Humanities Press/MPublishing, 2013), par. 5. Available online: openhumanitiespress.org/realist-magic.html.
[74] Harman, "On Vicarious Causation", 216.

logical dating agency, matching up human subjects with their objective surroundings. And now, staring in puzzlement at the tiny, stony anchorite in its tiny stony anchorhold can we not wonder, as did Timothy Morton, if the aesthetic dimension is not the "vast nonlocal mesh"[75] that pulls all of reality into its causal relations? According to Morton,

Aesthetic events are not limited to interactions between humans or between humans and painted canvases or between humans and sentences in dramas. They happen when a saw bites into a fresh piece of plywood. They happen when a worm oozes out of some wet soil. They happen when a massive object emits gravity waves. When you make or study art you are not exploring some kind of candy on the surface of a machine. You are making or studying causality. The aesthetic dimension is the causal dimension. It still astonishes me to write this.[76]

---

[75] Morton, *Realist Magic*, par. 14.
[76] Morton, *Realist Magic*, par.15.

Departure and/or Arrival

> *Aesthetics is not a discipline dealing with art and artworks, but a kind of, what I call, distribution of the sensible. I mean a way of mapping the visible, a cartography of the visible, the intelligible and also of the possible.*[77]

In looking back at the rise of neomedieval aesthetics and the anchoritic tradition, the Journeyman may recall the absence (or at least indifference) to "art" in the enveloping discourse. Discussions making claims and counter-claims for the "artistic" status of emergent neomedieval practice materialised of course, but were quickly engulfed in the tsunami of Western non-humanism. It was as if a certain fatigue had taken hold regarding the constant bickering over art's precise ontological status. At the height of the global economic paradigm of "cognitive" or "creative" capitalism, the attributes and practices that once defined the field of artistic production—virtuoso individualism, self-determined flexibility (always at work, always at play), creative autonomy and highly networked mobility—were increasingly perceived as synonymous with those of the nomadic creative class of Flatlanders, knowledge workers who supposedly contributed to the alienating neoliberal agenda of appropriating and marketing subjective experience. A general atmosphere of accusation had mobilised around the field of art. As Liam Gillick put it, artisans were increasingly perceived as "people who behave, communicate, and innovate in the same manner as those who spend their days trying to capitalize every moment and exchange of daily life. They offer no alternative to this".[78] In

---

[77] Jacques Rancière, "Our Police Order: What Can be Said, Seen, and Done", *Eurozine* (2006): www.eurozine.com/articles/2006-08-11-lieranciere-en.html.

[78] Liam Gillick, "The Good of Work", in Julieta Aranda, Brian K. Wood, and Anton Vidokle, eds., *Are You Working Too Much? Post-Fordism, Precarity, and the Labor of Art* (Berlin: Sternberg Press, 2011), 61 [60–73].

a perplexing contrast to this accusation, the immaterial labour of artists, taken *en masse*, seemed to constitute what post-operaist theorists had proposed as the "communism of capitalism"[79]—a cognitive multitude capable of re-appropriating the production of common goods (including fragile human subjectivities) from within the system of capitalist accumulation. In this sense, artisans faced not just an accusation, but a call-to-arms. They were imbricated as a creative core within the culture industries and as such had a responsibility (yet again) to "redirect their anger towards commodification, market domination and the capitalistic system".[80]

As if this immobilising double-bind weren't enough, the age-old arguments over art's innately transgressive power to mobilise against the ravishes of global capitalism were becoming tiresomely bifurcated over the apparently insoluble divide between "art" and "life". As Jacques Rancière noted, the "two great politics of aesthetics" were to be observed at work

in the sublime nudity of the abstract work championed by the philosopher and in the propositions for new and interactive types of relationship proposed by the artist and today's exhibition curator. On the one hand, there is a project for aesthetic revolution in which art, by effacing its difference as art, becomes a form of life. On the other, there is the resistant figure of the work in which political promise is negatively preserved . . . through the separation between artistic form and other forms of life.[81]

To reflect again on Latour's thesis, what we are witness-

[79] Paolo Virno, *A Grammar of the Multitude: For an Analysis of Contemporary Forms of Life*, trans. Isabella Bertoletti, James Cascaito, and Andrea Casson (New York: Semiotext(e), 2004), 17.

[80] David Harvey, "The Art of Rent: Globalisation, Monopoly and the Commodification of Culture", *Socialist Register 2002: A World of Contradictions* 38: 108.

[81] Jacques Rancière, *Aesthetics and its Discontents*, trans. Steven Corcoran (Cambridge: Polity, 2009), 36.

ing is an endlessly dialectical battle between "strong objects" and "strong subjects". In the "strong objects" corner autonomous artworks (evoking the unrepresentable sublime) are weaponized against their nasty cousins, the "commodity form". In the "strong subjects" camp (evoking micro-utopias of communal living), the social artwork is embodied by "emancipated" participants, now fully armoured against the corporate overlords. Neither approach fully escapes the specialist (and hierarchical) ghetto of artistic production and the subject/object apartheid is played out ad nauseam.

The only possible telos for this dialectic was the categorical dissolution of "art" altogether, which was (in the annals of modern art) always an intolerable (and now discursively exhausted) proposition since it confounded dialectical thought as self-negating and essentially cyclical. But, while Rancière was coming to the conclusion that the aesthetic regime of art functioned through the very suspension of "opposed logics" and "paradoxical constraints",[82] another group of heretical thinkers had sneaked in through the backdoor of the Enlightenment divide and re-emerged on a different path entirely.

Amidst all this dialectical hair-pulling, "neomedieval aesthetics" and the new anchoritic tradition quietly emerged and embarked upon practices that recognised no qualitative difference between extraordinary and commonplace aesthetic experience. An essentially bi-rational form of "speculative pragmatism" evolved from a haphazard re-activation of the pre-modern mysterium that had never been fully expunged from the "spaces brutally lit by alien reason".[83] The liturgical mash-ups and common oddities that litter the pathways of the neomedieval traveller have been brought to light by what Ben Woodward called the "weirding of philosophy"—an attempt to think outside the "dead loop of the human skull" and to "recognize not only the non-priority of

---

[82] Rancière, *Aesthetics and Its Discontents*, 44.
[83] Michel de Certeau, *The Practice of Everyday Life*, trans. Steven Rendall (Berkeley: University of California Press, 1984), 104.

human thought, but that thought never belongs to the brain that thinks it; thought comes from somewhere else".[84]

Take your tour of the bittersweet anchorholds discussed in this guide—if it's summer, bring a plastic bag and a bathing suit. Reinvigorate your sense of wonder at the bizarre hypereconomy of sensual relations and aesthetic transfigurations manifest throughout the middle kingdom of the great subject/object divide. Consider the anchorite who heroically straddles the ontological dyke that we Journeymen must constantly leap—never settling on one side or the other. Now try it yourself! When your legs start to tremble, your britches tear asunder, and your groin aches to high heaven, wonder at the anchorite who, with mighty yoga skills and limbs of steel, adopts this position forever with the ascetic grace of a lobster clinging steadfastly to the rim of a steaming pot.

---

[84] Ben Woodard, "Mad Speculation and Absolute Inhumanism: Lovecraft, Ligotti, and the Weirding of Philosophy", *continent.* 1.1 (2010): 13 [3–13].

∽

xyzzy: Contemporary Art Before and After Britain

Pru Forrest
Newcastle Art Gallery, New South Wales

We are looking backwards
We are running backwards
Running through time into the past
Taking retro to its logical conclusion

The Mighty Boosh, Series 3, Episode 3, BBC 3 (UK, 2007)

PART I. NEOMEDIEVAL ARTWORLDS

It has long been common curatorial practice to assume that the international art world of the early 21st century was an exemplar of globalisation, that contemporary art was a global currency, a *lingua franca* that knew no boundaries. Recent historical revisionism suggests, however, that the contemporary art world's patchwork striation of space was a perfect exemplar of geopolitical neomedievalism in practice. The global art system provided but one example in which there were competing legitimate organising principles for the cultural arena, in which individuals were legal members of a transnational community while also having legal responsibilities to the territory in which they resided. Indeed, *fin de siecle* neomedieval theories of international relations may be pertinent when considering art's global infrastructure in this period—which, as a highly opaque unregulated economy, was remarkably similar to the disconnected ungoverned spaces of medieval Europe.

According to Alexandr Petrovsky,[1] to consider any artworld as a system of international relations structured in neomedievalist terms—with actors performing the roles of artisan (artist), vassal or overlord—it would need to conform with the following neo-feudal petitions:

1. Art scenes are relatively small, territorialised, fiefdoms.

2. Successful artists operate as hired mercenaries, often simultaneously representing the competing interests of different fiefdoms.[2]

3. As managers of fiefdoms, critics, artistic directors, curators and dealers act as the artworld's vassals. Vassals are reciprocally indebted to one another.

4. Vassals pledge fealty to overlords in the international art market: patrons and collectors, national arts councils and international arts bodies.

5. The private market pursues a monarchial form of order, while public sector arts councils are more ecclesias-

---

[1] See Alexandr Petrovsky, *Transfiguration is Commonplace*, MBA thesis, University of the Mall of America Online.
[2] Contemporary artists were not "serfs", since they were not wholly part of a manorial system.

tical in their outlook.

6. While the private/monarchial and public/ecclesiastical are competing forms of authority, they are mutually constitutive overlords.[3]

7. The overlords of the artworld have no absolute supranational authority and must share power. They may, nevertheless, command a great deal of influence in determining which forms of vassalage prevail.

In the early 21st century, contemporary art was still being produced in distinctive communities of place ("art scenes") that collectively formed a global community of practice ("artworld"). Contemporary art did not, as yet, constitute a medievalist manorial economy, since local art scenes were not, and did not attempt to become, "self-sufficient" ecologies. While contemporary art was often, through necessity, a bespoke locally manufactured product, it was one ultimately intended for free trade and wide distribution throughout the global artworld.

While an "emerging" artist's resources were relatively scarce and their mobility limited, the fabrication of artworks could not be affordably outsourced. Productivity was therefore most frequently resourced within and supported by local fiefdoms. Provincial resourcing strengthened the social ties and debt-bonds of local art scenes, forming modern confraternities through creating distinctive communities of place. The fiefdom in which an artist lived and worked, the reputation of the generative context, served not only to validate the authenticity of their work but also routinely invested in its production.[4] The manufacture of works of art, at least in

---

[3] Of course the private/public division is a post-medieval imaginary.

[4] As a community of place, an art scene generated events, objects, and sites for veneration. It also patronised local artistic production by gifting administrative confraternities in the not-for-profit sector. This differed from contemporaneous maker economies, wherein compo-

the research and development phase, was largely reliant on public subsidy and gift economics. As these economies were democratically accountable they had to concern issues of representation and cultural sovereignty.[5] Art subsidised by such economies could not escape the cultural politics of the fiefdom. Public subsidy and gift economies were debt-bonds that tied artistic loyalties and proclivities to localised "art scenes" and were, ultimately, responsible for ongoing constructions of "regional" and "national" schools of contemporary art.[6] It is, therefore, constructive to consider what remained of the public system of patronage for art in terms debated in contemporary neomedieval studies of international relations.

Public patronage of contemporary art continued to answer to the peculiar political requirements of the sovereign state as well as to the aesthetic convictions of the international artworld. It thus embraced polarised demands—subsidiarity and supranationalism, the vernacular and the global, cultural monasticism and creative economics—operating with a neomedieval foresight that was incomprehensible to most sovereign states. Since tax-raising powers and lottery revenues[7] remained at the behest of sovereign states, public grant-awarding bodies were unambiguously regional and national rather than international.

The twilight years of the United Kingdom of Great Britain and Northern Ireland (UK) provide a good case study of the artworld's neomedievalism in practice. Four sovereign Arts Councils in the UK exclusively supported the work of artists

---

nents were ordered and shipped from anywhere in the world then assembled before being redistributed as modified commodities.

[5] Such as the social production of space and processes of territorialisation.

[6] If this were not the case, then art scenes would simply be nodes in an international network of makers; a community of practice without any community of place.

[7] An example of a public-private partnership that allowed private enterprises to profit while raising taxes for public works.

living in its constituent nations—Scotland, England, Wales and Northern Ireland[8]—developing distinctive national imaginaries at the expense of a unitary contemporary British, European or global art. The dissolution of the Arts Council of Great Britain (ACGB) in 1994 significantly limited the patronage of a "British" macro-national imaginary *within* the UK, Balkanising public patronage for the arts. In Britain and Northern Ireland, there was no "UK" as far as the administration of culture was concerned, cultural policy was entirely devolved from Westminster to national parliaments in Belfast, Edinburgh, and Cardiff. Such cultural devolution had existed in the UK since the 1960s, pre-empting political devolution by over three decades.

The UK's regional and national Arts Councils helped to create the economic conditions in which vernacular artistic microclimates flourished. England, Scotland, Wales, and Northern Ireland each had independent means to build a distinctive and appropriate infrastructure and a sustainable independent art scene. The Arts Councils were autonomous and answered to their respective parliaments[9] and thus to different political ideologies and distinct national imaginaries. There was a quasi-federal system in play here. England, for example, not only had its own Arts Council, but had regionally devolved bodies relating, approximately, to its Regions and their population density. Since artists were patronised exclusively by their national or regional arts council, choosing the most appropriate region to work in was a crucially strategic decision in establishing a practice.

---

[8] The Scottish Arts Council was founded in 1967, The Arts Council of Wales in 1994, the Arts Council of Northern Ireland in 1962, and the Arts Council of England in 1994. ACGB finally disbanded in 1994, the same year that ACE emerged. Until 1994, the ACGB was the *de facto* Arts Council of England, a good example of Great Britain and England being mistaken for the same entity.

[9] Creative Scotland to Holyrood, Arts Council of Wales to Cardiff, Arts Council of Northern Ireland to Stormount and ACE to Westminster.

These structures were echoed internationally. For example, at the Venice Biennale, the official British Pavilion in the Giardini was augmented by separate Scottish, Welsh, and Northern Irish Pavilions as part of the Biennale's "collateral events" programme. There was no English Pavilion (since England was a stateless nation); rather there had been unofficial independent representation from Sheffield, Manchester and the London Borough of Peckham, which boasted no less than two "pavilions" in 2009. The independent national and civic pavilions overlapped with, and deliberately challenged, the authority of the official UK representation. This cultural turn in territorialisation was a way of responding to neoliberal globalisation, wherein the state was no longer the dominant site of capitalist reproduction.

We should note that—while the Scottish, Welsh and Northern Irish Pavilions offered more, albeit alternative, forms of national sovereignty—the civic pavilions appeared to transcend "national identity" altogether. The self-promotion of creative city-states, burghs, and neighbourhoods as cultural and economic dynamos was a neomedieval phenomenon. In a cultural economy that was globally networked, the discourses of "national culture" were increasingly being subordinated to a pursuit of cultural capital that was at once local and global. In this sense, the collateral events of Venice exploited the patronage of the (intra-)national to draw the attention of the international artworld to local art scenes. The Balkanisation of the Venice Biennale, then, was indicative of the uneven distribution of cultural capital between the world's "creative cities". The "national" discourses in Venice that attempted to interject between local communities of place and the global community of artistic practice were a small price to pay for invaluable public patronage.[10]

---

[10] Access to public funding was highly regulated in an ecumenical sense. Artists who successfully established local and national support and/or achieved market recognition were far more likely to

Neomedievalism is a useful lens through which to reconsider the allegedly *international* character of such contemporary art biennials. With less than 50% of the world's nations represented at the Venice Biennale, it could not convincingly claim to be internationalist—conversely, it represented contemporary art's neo-feudal gangsterism. Venice was a snapshot of how a global community of practice received local art scenes and of how, in turn, those scenes transformed the values of the international artworld. Run by a small South London gallery, the Peckham Pavilion had more global visibility than many of the African states that could not afford to participate. This striation of space, however, could have some advantages. For those that could afford it, unofficial representation was one way that aspiring city-states, intra-nations, and diasporic ethnic groups found a global voice. International art events were, therefore, both a shop window for the creative economies of imperial sovereign states and a means by which those extant forms of territorialisation might be challenged and renegotiated.

In medievalist terms, the more established contemporary artists became, the more mercenary they became—working as hired hands, deploying their fealty in the service of multiple overlords. As they established their reputation beyond their fiedom, artists were increasingly mobile and capable of exploiting entitlements in different regions. Since post-medieval art resisted incorporation as a trade and failed to industrialise, contemporary artists seeking patronage had to frequently shift loyalties between the cultural agencies of sovereign states, non-state actors, and the global marketplaces. Although legally bound by the strictures of the state, the contemporary artist became itinerant to exploit entitlements offered by different regions, moving on once a particular obligation had been fulfilled and available financial re-

---

attract international public-sector patronage. This built unity and cooperation in relationships and actions within the public sector of the international art world.

sources exhausted.[11]

The export of "national art" was fraught with territorial ambiguities. Unlike international sporting events that required competitors to prove their citizenship, artists could choose to represent any nation (or city) participating in an international exhibition. Generally an artist's current place of residency determined which state would invite them to take part, but this was not an essential requirement. The English artist Liam Gillick's participation in the German Pavilion of the 2009 Venice Biennale was neomedieval in this sense. Gillick operated as an artistic mercenary, offering his services to the Federal German Republic in return for their patronage. We can also find instances of deterritorialised nations taking part in the Venice Biennale by establishing pavilions that implied forms of ethnicity that transcended modern states, most notably the Roma Pavilion. We also need to consider intra-nationalisms that were always overshadowed by the international state system. The Olympics Games, for example, did not permit intra-national or inter-ethnic competition. In the artworld there was a distinctly more fluid, neomedieval conception of territorial polity.

Many artisans in the '00s participated in the reinvigorated pre-industrial economy of international art fairs wherein objects were valued more highly than experiences.[12] As more wealth was concentrated in the hands of fewer people, vassalage was responsible for the circulation of new relics and for

---

[11] While they may have encountered more opportunities to travel and remain abroad than most citizens, artists' international movements and work entitlements were nevertheless restricted by tight immigration regulations.

[12] This is in contradistinction to the wider experience economy of post-industrialism that attempted to market subjective experience as an immaterial cultural form. The commercial sector of the artworld in the early 21st century was operating in reverse gear, returning to a pre-industrial system of manufacturing unique, high-value objects.

the widespread retreat into cultural monasticism.[13] Vassalage was key to enabling, or denying, mobility. Curatorial celebrations of cultural supranationalism found at international biennials not only served to mask the centrifugal forces of vassalage that dominated the art world in the '00s— *they were a product of vassalage.*

The social and geographical mobility of some artists did not change the fact that borders and financial constraints still existed for citizens who could not afford their own fantasy island. Artists were not merely subject to the educational policies of their own sovereign states. The regulation (or lack of regulation) of the art market in many states impacted upon intellectual property and regional licensing agreements. Artistic mobility (like artistic licence *per se*) was as illusive as it was fraught with complexity. Although the artworld remained an unregulated institution, it operated a hierarchal system of vassalage involving numerous state and non-state actors.

Many of the dominant organs of contemporary "British" Art were not "national". For example, while the state-funded TATE organisation purported to be British, in territorial terms, it was not; TATE operated exclusively in England. As such, TATE cannot be considered to have been "British" in the geographical sense.[14] TATE adopted national (TATE Britain), global (TATE Modern) and vernacular (TATE St. Ives/Liverpool) identities in different locales to make the brand relevant, improving the corporation's image. As TATE's franchise grew, it became a post-national global brand competing with comparable international art museums such as the Guggenheim and MoMA. Its mission was no longer correlated with the small potatoes of British statecraft or English nationalism; rather, it was a global leisure destina-

---

[13] The snowballing dealer-collector system that was encouraged in the deregulated global financial sector enabled the privatisation of contemporary art.

[14] In contrast, the BBC had branches throughout Britain and Northern Ireland and so can be considered to have been UK-wide.

tion. TATE's ultimate fealty, therefore, was to a supranational artworld rather than to the nation state that supported its activities.

Like the global playground of the world's wealthiest 1%, the art market of the early 21st century echoed the culture of Europe's transnational medieval aristocratic elite. The artworld was a global economy that networked internationally through a busy calendar of temporary international art fairs and biennials. Appearing to occupy a non-territorial space, actors operated in a transnational market that was perpetually mobile and constantly renegotiating recognition and authority. The art market was monarchical in a medievalist sense, since it was not geographically restricted by sovereign jurisdiction.[15] The constitutive power of the market's itinerant network was hierarchal rather than distributed. While access to information—especially in the physical form of fairs and biennials—was negotiable through the prior acquisition of sufficient cultural and social capital in civil society, it was equally a commodity to be bought, sold, or inherited. Either way, this chivalric code ensured that access to the art market's information-based economy was strictly limited.

When compared with the social production of value that supported grassroots movements such as crowd-funding, the speculation of the contemporary art market was fiscally conservative. Collectors were more likely to invest in objects than intellectual property, viewing art as the contemporary equivalent of gold bullion. This conservatism favoured the production of "unique" artisanal material objects to be conserved and maintained rather than open processes and projects that might be fabricated and reproduced. The art market was relatively risk averse, investing in work that had al-

---

[15] Although the local and national facilitated the generation of cultural capital, there were no significant local or national markets in contemporary art. High prices were achieved only in the global international marketplace. Key actors in the art market were loyal only unto their overlord peers. Being place-less, they did not suffer from pangs of disloyalty to communities of place.

ready been "relic-ed" and was therefore more likely to increase in value. Vassals in the public and not-for-profit sector
were engaged in more ecumenical matters, generating theories and establishing contemporary art's transnational values.
They were in the ecclesiastical business of "relic-ing" artistic
practices, providing a hub that embodied the artworld's relations.

While contemporary art was commonly perceived to be a
speculative commodity, floated freely in the market, it was
more frequently manufactured to order through a public
system of patronage, one that imagined itself as an alternative to brute market forces.[16] The art market could not generate cultural capital autonomously since it was a system of
distribution and consumption with no means of production.
The market only provided a career for artists that had already established a practice and an audience through other
means. The patronage of "emerging artists", therefore, emerged either from the state, as a form of self-subsidy, or a
mixture of both.

Without a private system of workshops or guilds, the
private sector depended on public subsidy to formally edu-
cate artists and provide them with tertiary support through
the awarding of grants and loans. From this perspective,
production was outsourced to a no-cost mixture of state and
philanthropic organisations that operated in an ecclesiastical
fashion. In this sense, the art market relied on vassals not
only to perform the task of identifying and advocating significant new work but of giving artists access to expensive land-
bound resources. Such vassals were mainly employed in, or
volunteered in, the state or not-for-profit sectors, the workshops in which contemporary artistic research and development took place.

---

[16] In *Art Scenes: The Social Scripts of the Artworld* (New York: Jorge
Pinto Books, 2012), artist Pablo Helguera pointed out that the market did not represent the values of the artworld as a whole, especially given that so much of the world was denied access to the international art market.

Only sanctioned relics accrued the social and cultural capital that made them valuable in the market. So, while the monarchical private sector could influence the production of art by providing financial incentives to encourage artists to participate in the art market, it could not dictate the direction of the artworld as a whole.[17] The regulatory bodies that existed at a national level, however, had far greater influence, since they could determine which forms of cultural vassalage would be supported in the state sector. These public overlords, then, had powers to excommunicate insubordinate vassals and with them the artists they espoused.

The private and public sectors were not mutually exclusive; on the contrary, they clearly overlapped and interlocked in a neomedieval fashion.[18] This was all the more evident following the world financial crisis of the late '00s, when the public sector was substantially curbed to subsidise the cost of bank welfare. State support for culture, along with enlightened, democratically elected civic authority was systematically replaced by shadowy and unaccountable "private-public partnerships".[19] As the state withered, the public

---

[17] The private sector would not benefit from controlling the means of production since the mutable category of "emerging art" was essential for moving large sums of money around.

[18] The cosy relationship between the private and the public sector led to many conflicts of interest wherein public money was used to pay for the production of works of art clearly destined for the market with no return to taxpayers. This ambiguous overlapping was quintessentially neomedieval, recalling the lack of division between public and private space in medieval societies. As vassals, art dealers and public sector artistic directors were mutually constitutive members of the same class.

[19] For example, as a replacement for the Scottish Arts Council and Scottish Screen, Creative Scotland—a quango (Quasi-Autonomous Non-Governmental Organisation) that bundled the arts together with business development and the tourist industry—offered an approach to government of the arts in Scotland that was at once paternalistic (the long-standing principle of arm's length having being abolished) and neoliberal (viewing the arts primarily as eco-

sector was required to speak the language of economics and justify its decisions in market terms. The skeletal public sector looked to what was being supported by the market as a barometer of what forms of vassalage it should "invest" in. The process of veneration became circular, the public sector acting more explicitly in partnership with the market in the belief that it would make it more efficient and "sustainable", while the market continued to rely on the emaciated public sector to provide it with blessings and free resources.

The metaphorical medievalism of contemporary art extended into other areas of practice. For example, we might consider contemporary artistic nomadism as a form of pilgrimage, the workshop model of production as a re-articulation of the guild system.

The growth of state-funded art institutions and international expos in the early 21st century should alert us to the fact that the international Westphalian system was still very much alive in contemporary art. Domestic systems of artistic patronage largely remained obligated to the Westphalian system of absolute state authority. Artists seeking public support were subject to the political whims of local and national governments—to how fiefdoms decided, variably, to support the cultures of naturalised citizens and foreign nationals. While artists were no different from any other citizens in this respect, the nature of their profession encouraged them to exploit subsidies at home and abroad. Contemporary artists had little to gain by remaining static, and acts of pilgrimage, tactically, were a means to an end.

The most common form of contemporary artistic pilgrimage involved the *laissez- faire* migration to sanctified sites of production. Since artists began their careers in time-rich cash-poor economies, they were attracted to citadels that promised a low cost of living and relatively few employment restrictions. Artistic confraternities emerged in "creative" cities that provided a temporary path of least resistance, a

---

nomic drivers of culture industry).

supportive community of place and access to the artworld's global community of practice. The required conditions for an "art mecca" to emerge were not generated by artists. While there had been a concerted attempt to socially engineer creative climates in '90s Britain, they were far more likely to emerge where catastrophic economic mismanagement, political instability, and rapidly changing demographics depressed property values.

This form of pilgrimage was cyclical. Being a bulwark of the cultural economy, the influx of artists into an urban neighbourhood, invariably, increased the value of property and drove up the cost of living. Artists either had to establish a market for their work or move on to a more affordable environment. Given the striation of the artworld into artisans/vassals/overlords, not all artists who moved to a supportive community of place stood to profit enough to sustain a living from selling their own work. Since marketisation was the job of vassals rather than artists, most artists were driven back into pilgrimage, passing through in pursuit of their practice.

Another form of pilgrimage concerned the growth of art residencies, one of the most transparent ways that artists found public sector support to conduct research and development. The itinerant residency circuit came with strings attached. Residencies allied to the cultural economy of place-making operated an implicitly medievalist form of patronage, commissioning a pilgrimage that would enable communion between artist and site. As a pilgrim, the contemporary artist was a stranger who may offer fresh insight. Rather than providing a Euclidian means of navigating or controlling territories, the contemporary artist was a freelance postmodern geographer, offering fluid conceptions of space comparable to pre-modern cartography, moral and sensual palimpsests of non-synchronous person-objects and object-events.[20]

---

[20] See David Woodward, "Reality, Symbolism, Time and Space in

In the early 21st century, such residencies often privileged environmental, social, and historical research that promised to "other" the local, finding the miraculous in the overfamiliar. Of course social, environmental and historical pre-moderns can play an important role in the artistic re-imagining of the present. However, the mere act of inviting artists to temporarily relocate and work in a less familiar environment was considered to be an effective way of adding value and a sense of uniqueness to a place, transforming spaces into potentially popular sites of pilgrimage. Contemporary art residencies did not produce relics or perform miracles to anoint holy sites. The sites simply needed to be activated to allow their cultural potential to be narrated. In ritualising space, residencies promised to perform a neomedieval role in the experience economy.[21]

Residencies flourished in places where there was a civic desire to encourage cultural exchange and enhance the host's reputation for internationalism. Since they were so heavily invested in cultural authenticity, residencies were implicated in the promotion of the vernacular through a vernacular dialogue. In practice, there were a number of factors that made this promised dialogue of vernaculars very difficult to achieve. Contemporary art spoke an ecclesiastical *linga franca* that regulated standards in the field transnationally. The ecumenical tropes of site-sensitivity and fieldwork that were active in the residency circuit, for example, formed part of this *linga franca*. The fact that contemporary art was considered a global culture made it a homogenising force in opposition to the vernacular.

The misconception that contemporary art was an international "visual language" that needed no "translation" actively encouraged the mobilisation of artistic labour in the inter-

---

Medieval World Maps", *Annals of the Association of America's Geographers* 75.4 (December 1985): 510–521.

[21] Biennials performed a similar role curatorially, ritualising extant sites for bi-annual pilgrimage.

national arena. In the neo-realist world of international relations, artists (and athletes) were idealised diplomats and
ambassadors, roles they were often happy to play. At this
level, a few artists found themselves engaged in a form of
cultural diplomacy, representing the values of their nation on
a world stage. While internationalism was greatly esteemed
in this international arts sector, reciprocal and multilateral
partnerships between arts organisations were notoriously
difficult to maintain in most practices. Contemporary art did
not have a free trade licence. Artists and works of art moving
between states were subject to the same customs regulations and tariffs as everyone, and everything, else. If a sovereign state decided to tighten the restrictions on its borders,
the reciprocal impact was felt internationally. A tension,
then, was evident in the effect of sovereign states exercising
their cultural authority, something that that enabled artistic
pilgrimage while determining its terms and conditions. As
national subjects and foreign nationals, artists were subject
to these conflicting and overlapping demands.

Contemporary art's neomedieval infrastructure was also
influenced by non-state actors in the private sector. The
global art market had long afforded speculative forms of
production, embracing the modern idea that contemporary
art was not produced to commission, as it had been in the
middle ages, but was, rather, a product to be floated freely
on the market. The market played a pivotal role in affirming
post-medieval imaginaries of artistic autonomy and their
attendant divisions of creative labour.[22] Artistic autonomy
was the primary way in which the liberal subject embodied
the perceived anarchy of the international system of sover-

---

[22] From the perspective of production, contemporary art continued
to be egocentric, promulgating the post-medieval concept of the
artist as the sole progenitor of their work, manufacturing personalised ontologies, and constructing reputations around sovereign
subjects. Artists who worked as auteurs could not be considered to
follow medievalist means of production.

eign states.[23]

While the market manufactured an artistic subject unbound by supra-artistic authority, in practice, this required a neo-feudal distribution of roles: that artists produce, dealers, curators and critics distribute, and collectors consume. Herein lay its neomedievalism. The market required modern artistic subjects, but to establish the illusion of their autonomy, it relied on the maintenance of clearly delineated neo-feudal roles: on the art world's mercenaries, vassals, and overlords.

In practice, such divisions of labour maintained themselves so long as contemporary art continued to operate as a guild economy. While contemporary artistic practice was established and supported through networks of local confraternities, it was difficult to establish vertically integrated manufacturing and vertical monopolies throughout the artworld. Indeed, the appeal of confraternties was such that, at the turn of the 21st century, the local workshop model grew in popularity. This was particularly prevalent among artists seeking to participate in a collaborative commons. Workshops were perceived as a means of bundling skills and resources, of hollowing out the ego from art practice, of shifting the emphasis from actors to networks. Both the gallery and the studio were thus reinterpreted as stages upon which social alchemy would be performed.

The workshop, in effect, was a pontifex, building bridges between contemporary art and the practices of everyday life by engineering interactions between participating social subjects. From this optimistic perspective, contemporary art would break free of its specialist enclave and work towards a non-hierarchical production of micro-utopias, transient instances of the commons that would resist recuperation

---

[23] From a neo-realist perspective, the anarchic artistic subject was the embodiment of the anarchism of the Westphalian state system, a self-possessive individual who did not recognise supranational authority. This is a distinctly post-medieval archetype, the ascendancy of the sovereign self-accompanying the rise of the sovereign state.

through their stealthy impermanence. Within this deflated ontology of contemporary art, the artist's role was that of the "sociable expert",[24] a workshop leader who made the translation of tacit knowledge his principle craft.

Simultaneously, the workshop model was adopted by market-oriented artists who needed to keep apace with the ever increasing demand for their work.[25] While they were led by the brand-building artisans (the "antisocial expert"[26]), entrepreneurial workshops did not replicate medievalist practices of indenture or apprenticeship wherein less experienced artisans learn their craft by following the lead of a master. They were, effectively, small-scale manufacturing concerns designed to manage the extant division of artistic labour more efficiently. Although they increased the speed and scope of fabrication, it would be inaccurate to describe them as industrial—they resembled, at best, a medieval form of small scale artisanal production aimed exclusively at plutocrats.[27]

The booming international market relied appreciably on a plutocracy that invested heavily in contemporary art. The

---

[24] "The danger to others posed by people driven by excellence crystallizes in the figure of the expert. He or she appears in two guises, sociable or antisocial. A well-crafted institution will favour the sociable expert; the isolated expert sends a warning signal that the organisation is in trouble": Richard Sennett, *The Craftsman* (London: Penguin, 2008), 246.

[25] ". . . post-studio practices initially seemed like a bracing challenge to the old-fashioned figure of the lone artist in the studio. These alternative approaches have nonetheless opened onto the reestablishment of workshop-type enterprises designed to sustain both high production volume and the logistics of international artistic careers": Martha Buskirk, "Introduction", in *Creative Enterprise: Contemporary Art between Museum and Marketplace* (New York: Continuum, 2012), 3.

[26] Sennett, *The Craftsman*, 246.

[27] Contemporary artists operated on a much smaller scale than makers, garage geeks who fabricated and modified existing commodities as a profitable hobby.

character and wealth of the plutocracy began to change rapidly in the early 21st century. A visible divide was growing between the geekocracy, the digital entrepreneurs that had become among the wealthiest individuals in the world, and the contemporary art market. Silicon Alley was not investing in contemporary art—it did not buy the work of emerging artists, was not a philanthropic supporter of the arts, and did not even appear to value the arts as a form of capital. Writing in the *New York Times*, Alice Gregory speculated on the reasons for this:

> There are all sorts of plausible explanations: the tech industry is relatively new (especially in New York); its members are young, busy and most did not plod through four years' worth of liberal arts syllabuses.[28]

A laboratory culture spawned in universities, the tech world was not so dissimilar from the workshop commons model that had arisen amidst contemporary artistic confraternities. It identified itself as iconoclastic culture of self-learning rather than a practice of canonical rote learning.[29] Tech valued transparency: it grew up in public. As Gregory noted, entrepreneurs who had made their fortunes from start-ups disliked the secretive approach of the art market,

---

[28] Alice Gregory, "Does Anyone Here Speak Art and Tech?", *The New York Times*, April 3, 2013 (Fashion & Style): http://www.nytimes.com/2013/04/04/fashion/art-and-techology-a-clash-of-cultures.html.

[29] It's important to stress here that this was the utopian self-image of the tech industry. The reality was more complex and less virtuous. For example, companies such as Google and Facebook were not open; rather, they were Fordist in their aims (if not in their methods) to monopolise their markets. The main revenue streams of tech companies that offered "free" services came from data mining and consumer profiling, providing bespoke information to specialist marketers and government security agencies. In this sense, the web primarily served the narrowcasting of more conventional proprietorial markets such as commerce and manufacturing.

its hidden and fixed prices, its preoccupation with vetting consumer's social and cultural capital, and the closed experience of viewing art in a private white cube.[30] The tech world, in contrast, imagined itself as a culture of sharing, of open sources, and creative commons. Given their antipathy towards the anti-social expertise of market-oriented workshops and the proprietary black-boxing of objects, the economic shift from real to virtual estate-based fortunes heralded the immanent collapse of the art market. Since the art market's consecration and monopolising of the charismatic monad was rejected by this culture, it had to adapt to connect with its new tech overlords, or risk being completely disenfranchised. It was not a case of simply appealing to the new rich as patrons, but of adopting their culture of production and distribution.

To overcome its disconnect with the new economic elite, the art market of the early 21st century could not simply faciliate a similar adaptiveness. We need to seriously consider the values at stake in such a bargain. The culture of the electronic nouveau riche was one that preceded their economic rise, and it constituted its core value system. To compromise those values risked ostricisation from the tech community and thus economic ruin. Similarly, contemporary artists had, since the late 1960s, developed networks of their own that were independent from, and often in contradistinction to, the art market. Why would these artists compromise their own hard-won values to ensure the future of an art market that was, largely, indifferent towards them? The model of patronage that assumed artists must compete to provide luxury goods for a tiny coterie of plutocratic overlords was,

---

[30] "To those used to start-up culture, with its utopian transparency and meritocratic ideals, the art world's barriers to entry are discouraging and confusing. Parties are exclusive. Works are not always sold to those with the most money. Images are often not online. Invoicing can take months. There is, to borrow a term from the lexicon of tech culture, a preponderance of inconvenient 'friction'": Gregory, "Does Anyone Here Speak Art and Tech?"

historically, a relatively recent one. There was no reason to assume that it could or should continue indefinitely.

The value of sharing was a culture that generated a new economy. For contemporary art to adapt to these conditions it had to become entrepreneurial—it had to generate a long-tail economy of its own. The aspects of the artworld that were in alignment with the start-up culture of tech were already prevalent in its artist-led and not for profit organisations.

PART II. THE ROUGH MUSIC

No longer automatically conceived as a relatively primitive staging post en route to some higher telos or more sophisticated stage of human understanding and self-realization, that which has gone before can be revisited not only as a source of instruction on the present, but also as existing in some kind of intellectual and developmental parity with it. In the light of the contemporary crisis of scientific rationality, pre-scientific narratives or forms of understanding can from this point of view be invested with new insights; older ways of thinking may be charged with correcting the mistakes or deficiencies of contemporary prejudice; categorizations and conceptual divisions that in the perspective of a classic liberal humanism were deemed perverse or fantastical or simply confused offer themselves as potential sources of a . . . "posthuman" enlightenment.[31]

Since the 1980s—a time when historical gestures were routinely discredited as a renewed form of authoritarianism—contemporary artists have avoided appearing to be overly concerned with the past, fixing their eyes firmly on the present. We might consider project-based work, site-sensitivity, time-based art, and the social turn to be, means by which artistic practice *contemporised* itself. Being contemporary concerned flow, the cyclical movement from cultural relevance to irrelevance, maintaining the hectic pace of drifting

---

[31] Kate Soper, "The postmedieval Project: Promise and Paradox", *postmedieval: a journal of medieval cultural studies* 1.1/2 (2010): 256.

from one project to another. Mobility, contingency and adaptibility became prized qualities in contemporary art.

Perpetual presentism did not concern itself with epoch-spanning perspectives, with a longer now. Neomedievalism held the promise of a *longue durée*, speculation on pre-modern futures providing an antidote to the pathologically short-term mentality of the modern sovereign subject. The late '00s were "ravaged by a pervasive medieval nostalgia".[32] *Altermodern*, the 2009 Tate Triennial, constructed its own little medievalisms, featuring a range of works engaging with neo-paganism (Olivia Plender), shamanism (Marcus Coates), and carnivàle (Marvin Gaye Chetwynd).[33] *Altermodern* reflected a concern with the medievalisms evident in other exhibitions and projects across the UK at the end of the noughties, including *Disclosures II: The Middle Ages*, *Laxton* (part of *Histories of the Present* produced by Nottingham Contemporary), *The Long Dark* (2009, curated by Michelle Cotton at International 3, Manchester and Hatton Gallery, Newcastle-upon-Tyne), *The Dark Monarch* (2009, Tate St. Ives, Cornwall), Torsten Lauschmann's solo exhibition *The Darker Ages* (2009, Mary Mary, Glasgow), and Alex Pollard and Clare Stephenson's *Four Fatrasies* (2010, Pump House Gallery, London).

Among UK-based artists schooled in the histories of modernisms, there was a high degree of self-awareness that retreat into irrationalism and fantasy was *expected* to emerge at points of "crisis" in modernity, such as the global financial crash of 2008. *The Long Dark* explicitly related this fissure to John Ruskin and the neo-Gothic of 19th-century

---

[32] Umberto Eco, "The Return of the Middle Ages", *Travels in Hyperreality*, trans. William Weaver (London: Picador, 1987), 66.

[33] While *Altermodern*'s thesis stressed the role of the artist as "homo viator", a contemporary journeyman drifting through space and time, it was not overtly neomedievalist. Indeed, the exhibition manifesto, written by curator Nicolas Borrriaud, eulogised and universalised mobility in ways that were challenged by neomedievalist International Relations theory.

industrial England—*The Dark Monarch* to its neo-romantic progeny in the early 20th century. The fact that the pre-Raphaelite and neo-Romantic episodes formed canonical medievalist chapters in the history of English art was crucial in establishing the imaginary "national character" of modernism in England. This narrative distinguished English modernism as reactionary and primitivist; rather than embrace modernity, it sought escape through a return to the modern world's preconditions. *The Long Dark* and *The Dark Monarch*, in their different ways, correlated the eccentric modernity of the sovereign English subject with territorial and cultural sovereignty.[34] In both cases, medievalisms formed a foil to modernity, arming English modernists with pre-fabricated, pre-modern alternatives to the UK's military-industrial imperialism. The scholastic and second-hand nature of these 21st-century medievalisms signalled their neomedievalism: "not a dream of the Middle Ages, but a dream of someone else's medievalism. It is medievalism doubled upon itself".[35] Medievalism within the canon of English art, therefore, was as much a product of modernity as it was a cultural response to it.[36] Equally, the simulacral

---

[34] I write "English" rather than "British" here as English art existed before (and after) the formation of the UK. Since the UK did not unify until 1707, there was no "British" medieval art. The medieval-modern in the UK was therefore characterised by the invention of distinctive pre-British medievalisms in Scotland, Wales, England, and the province of Ulster. For an account of the Scottish medieval-modern, see Tom Normand's *The Modern Scot: Modernism and Nationalism in Scottish Art, 1928–1955* (Aldershot: Ashgate, 2000).

[35] Amy S. Kaufman, "Medieval Unmoored: Through a (Cracked) Glass, Darkly", *Studies in Medievalism: XIX: Defining Neomedievalism(s)* (Cambridge: D.S.Brewer, 2010), 4.

[36] In this '00s, medievalisms came to be regarded as situational, changing and shifting into multiple forms in accordance with the perspective of the person applying the concept. See Elizabeth Emery, "Medievalism and the Middle Ages," *Studies in Medievalism XVII: Defining Medievalism(s)* (Cambridge: D.S.Brewer, 2009), 77–91.

neomedievalism[37] of the early 21st century was the symptom of a longer-running tension between the advocates of modern rationalism and pre-modern syncretism, a competition that was a product of post-medieval renaissance and enlightenment. When this tension manifested itself in cultural production, it reflected competition for power in contemporary society.

Taking its lead from medieval nonsense poetry, Pollard and Stephenson's *Four Fatrasies* was a collaborative installation that filtered the "Dark Ages" through Victorian medievalist sensibilities. Stephenson's sculptural guardians formed a medievalist tableau to Pollard's bespoke Italian sports shoes and afforested paintings (many of which featured Robin Hood-style vagabonds). This textural brogueing of the preindustrial, pre-Enlightenment, and early modern was one that always remained self-consciously contemporary in perspective: "If medievalism can be said to work within a framework of distance (reverential or otherwise), then neomedievalism obliterates distance in an intensified combination of love and loathing, its desire for the past torn asunder between denial of history and a longing for return."[38] *Four Fatrasies'* bricolage of neomedieval argots, its use of peculiarly "English" folk morphologies was as much an established vernacular of English modernism as it was an absurd riposte to the techocratic drift towards dis-integrated European transnationalism.[39]

Such artists were particularly prone to the hauntological tendencies found within popular medievalisms, to their invocations of ambient or unseen terrors and hidden phantas-

---

[37] See M.J. Toswell, "The Simulacrum of Neomedievalism", *Studies in Medievalism: XIX: Defining Neomedievalism(s)* (Cambridge: D.S.Brewer, 2010), 44–57.

[38] Kaufman, "Medieval Unmoored", 2.

[39] European transnationalism questioned the basis of statehood and ethnic imaginaries by separating the practices and processes of cultural production from the geographies of recognised macro-states.

magorical cultural anachronisms within the present. Plender's focus fell on historical pressure points before and after
science—fusions of science and spiritualism. In particular, it
involved a revisitation of the pseudo-spiritual movements of
Romanticism and early mystical modernisms. Rosicrucianism,
neo-paganism, and theosophy also offered the kind of curious, conspiratorial early modernist aesthetic of faith and
redemption that attracted the contemporary neo-medieval
mind. This followed a dominant tendency to question the
logic and presumptions of Western Enlightenment,
bookending early modernism's similar concern regarding the
limits of Enlightenment.

Plender's focus on the Modern Spiritualist Movement
(1848-) and the British youth organisation *Kindred of the
Kibbo Kift* (2006),[40] for example, was rooted in the fact they
were modern medievalisms invented and promoted by charismatic individuals. The complex syncretism of the Modern
Spiritualist Movement offered a distinctive, and popular,
example of the constant re-invention of medievalist folklore.
Kibbo Kift's woodcrafting and its invocation of Native American, Norse and Saxon rituals, legends, clans and tribes was
a rich example of the pre-modern consciousness that swept
through modern co-operative scouting.[41] The Kibbo Kift was
a notable medieval-modern that was not uncommon in the
heroic phase of modernism. Their neomedieval mourning of
historical authenticity was precisely what Plender foregrounded. Plender's work was as a whole was characterised
by an engagement with the *para* and the *pseudo*, with the
inventiveness that abounds when we leave the calm charted
waters of modernity. Hearsay, myth, legend were all readily
in the service of *para*- and *pseudo*-historical movements that
arose in response to modernity. Where modernist spiritual-

---

[40] Kibbo Kift was active from 1920 until 1951.

[41] As part of the Co-operative Movement, the Kibbo Kift promoted
pacifism and an international utopianism in lineage with William
Morris and John Ruskin's medieval-modern Christian Socialism.

ism re-enchanted the world, and neo-pagan scouts communed directly with their pre-modern forebears, Plender evoked the cooler stance of the melancholic researcher, keeping an observational distance.[42]

Plender's work concerned how modernist forms of post-secularism were manifested and replicated in the present. As in the 20th century, early 21st-century futurity was dominated by technocentrism. However, as we have seen, the canon of English modernism fostered a futurity that castigated this position, *looking backwards* to alternative, allegedly less-technologically interventionist future-pasts. Kibbo Kift's hand-made Saxon cloaks, archery and mumming were precursors to the 21st century's alternative medicines and organic foods. While the late middle ages were a time of great technological advance, popular medievalisms admonished the pre-modern era as a time of social and technological equilibrium. The trope of medieval stasis was a boon to social and political movements seeking some form of (mythical) stability in a rapidly changing world.[43] Medieval stasis was one modern medievalism that underwrote contemporary culture.[44] Plender, then, was not concerned with a comparative analysis of contemporary and medieval cultures, or with the dis-

---

[42] Plender's research on the Kibbo Kift, for example, was undertaken on a residency at the rural retreat Grizdale Arts, near Lake Coniston, Cumbria, England in 2004. This formed part of Grizdale's "Year of Romantic Detachment" and culminated in an exhibition at PS1 in New York. In neomedievalist terms, it is significant that Coniston in the Lake District was a favourite retreat of John Ruskin and often considered to be the birthplace of English Romanticism.

[43] Neomedieval theories of International Relations are predicated on the fact that the middle ages were dynamic.

[44] "Medieval stasis" was, arguably, a medievalism generated in the middle ages itself. For example, the feudal system generated a legal system that defended fealty in perpetuity. This generated a medieval account of the future in which all social and economic relations were guaranteed forever by feudalism. Where modern futurity became increasingly fixated with change, pre-modern futurity was preoccupied with stasis.

covery of primary medieval sources; rather, she was working with medievalisms as her primary materials. Studies of medievalisms formed part of Plender's rich tapestry of media. She transformed these materials through performative praxis. As such, we might consider aspects of Plender's work to be *neomedievalist* in the sense of simultaneously being the study of, and a contribution to, medievalisms.

Did such neomedievalism constitute an intervention into the culture of contemporary medievalisms? Was it a form of institutional critique akin to that promulgated in the art of "The Long Nineties"?[45] The theatrical and fictional nature of Plender's work would preclude an overt social turn as prosaic and dogmatic. The social turn certainly remained evident, but only as a proxy, a given context that need only be implied. Plender's work drew attention to the fact that new medievalisms were constantly being fabricated, and had been since the middle ages.[46] For Plender, it was a question of opening up this field of study as a futurist practice.[47] Contemporary artists were attracted to the speculative and fantastical aspects of medievalisms. They were involved in speculation themselves, and so in the production of neomedievalisms.

While performances such as *In Search of the New Republic (or the tables turned)* (Serpentine Gallery, London 2006) were rigorously researched, Plender's work imparted an air of professional amateurism, the illusion of the culturally authentic.[48] In occupying this expanding cultural territory, it did not help to distinguish between the professional and the

---

[45] Lars Bang Larsen, "The Long Nineties", *frieze*, Issue 144 (January-February 2012).

[46] Perpetrating this view was also the aim of Leslie Workman in establishing the journal *Studies in Medievalism* in 1979.

[47] Hedley Bull's new medievalism, equally, was pure speculation, a future scenario that he held out little hope for.

[48] We need to remember that artists were not medievalists. They were appropriating studies of medievalisms. As such, we can think of them as scholar-fans, or professional amateurs.

amateur; to do so would be to vastly underestimate fans' intelligence (not to mention their economic potential):

> Pro-Ams are a new social hybrid. Their activities are not adequately captured by the traditional definitions of work and leisure, professional and amateur, consumption and production. We use a variety of terms many derogatory, none satisfactory—to describe what people do with their serious leisure time: nerds, geeks, anoraks, enthusiasts, hackers, men in their sheds. Our research suggests the best way to cover all the activities covered by these terms is to call the people involved Pro-Ams.[49]

Marvin Gaye Chetwynd's work exemplified a sprightliness and candour reminiscent of community and amateur dramatics. Costumes were home-spun, the choreography jerrybuilt and customarily botched. The participants in the Chetwynd Mime Troup were friends. There was the perennial threat of interactivity, of the audience being invited to play a part. The stock medievalism used to describe Chetwynd's actions and tableaux was "carnivalesque". This is fitting in one sense. Rather than drawing sustenance from the good taste and sensibilities of serious culture, Chetwynd's paintings, collages, objets d'art and performances were energised dedications to the cult of ugliness. Yet not everything within the realms of pop grotesquery was admitted for reprocessing. Nor was the spontaneity which was generally associated with her performances entirely what it seemed. Chetwynd was careful to borrow from choice cuts of intermediary sources, most of which were themselves already deliberate forms of self-critical distortion. There was a knowing sense of the carnivalesque as always being authorised, of going through the motions, and of temporarily acting out transgression.

---

[49] Charles Leadbeater and Paul Miller, *The Pro-Am Revolution: How Enthusiasts are Changing our Economy and Society* (London: Demos, 2004), 20.

The Pro-Am cultural communities and economies that Chetwynd drew upon were, perhaps, more diverse and eclectic than Plender's subjects, including *Star Wars* fans, Hulksters, Glam Goth Meat Loafers and Live Action Role Players. Never groupies, dedicated fans worked as Pro-Ams in their respective fields—writing their own scripts, filling in back stories, making story-things, and producing critical coverage of the objects of their desires. The relationship between artists and their (human) resources can all too often compare with that between colonial anthropologists and the "natives". Rather than maintain a detached view, Chetwynd took matters into her own hands, collaborating with her troupe to make costumes and props, to paint scenery, to script and perform in her own productions. Yet, as a neomedievalising scholar-fan, Chetwynd wasn't as concerned with being as truthful to detail as fan-scholars often could be.[50] In *Star Wars*—a performance based on one of the most prolific medievalist franchises in modern times—Jabba the Hutt's language Huttese was very carefully assembled from the ancient Incan dialect, Quechua. Star Wars fan-scholars have spent almost many years perfecting this *lingua franca* by studying the movies in great detail. Going straight for effect, Chetwynd's Jabba spoke fluent Persian.

Chetwynd was no autodidact; before studying Fine Art at the Slade and Royal College of Art, she read History and Anthropology at University College London. Her interests and methods seemed to lie somewhere between art, history, and anthropology. There was a sense that some of Chetwynd's happenings might be loose anthropological experiments. They recall also the populist history-in-action documentaries that were the staple fare of British television. Chetwynd's interest in Spartiatism and carnivàle emerged

---

[50] For a discussion of the distinction between "scholar-fans" and "fan-scholars", see Matt Hills, *Fan Cultures* (London: Routledge, 2002).

from anthropology and the sociology of popular culture.[51] An embrace of medievalist forms of carnivàle was particularly evident in her use of troupes of mummers in seminal performances such as *Debt, A Medieval Play* (2005).[52]

It would be wrong to castigate Chetwynd's self-sufficient folkmote as a manifestation of a "new irrationalism". Her art was allusive and analogous. Although they may have been informed by history and anthropology in equal measure, the acts performed by her troupe were not consumed by rehearsing the past; they concerned the present. They were a proxy battle between a homogenising technocracy and its discontents (represented by the radical characters of darker ages). While "medieval" was often abused as a byword for negative clichés associated with the Middle Ages—creationism, paleoconservatism, torture, gang lords—Chetwynd's neomedievalism provided a focus on more liberal associations with the early 21st century: subsidiarity, Latin transnationalism, close community bonds, social participation, the commons and heightened sensuality. The "liveness" of Chetwynd's performances allowed this version of the folktale to be both liberated and retold repeatedly.

Plender and Chetwynd shared a fascination with medievalist resources that was visually explicit in their work. In a similar fashion to the oral-formulaic composition of the folk tradition, we can think of their neomedievalism as concurrently illustrating and performing. Cultural neomedievalism, in this sense, was a recalibration and reactivation of premodern assemblages, broken down, outmoded or faulty machines fixed and adapted by the practitioner and applied to contemporary use. The practice of "mumming" was a key case in point. Since mumming formed part of the Kibbo Kift's rituals, it appeared *ready-made* in Plender's lectures

---

[51] In particular, Mikhail Baktin and Greil Marcus.

[52] *Debt*, to paraphrase Chetwynd, was a play that would perhaps be of interest to an audience in 2005. It makes sense to consider it in relation to the debt economy of contemporary art, an economy heavily reliant on gift-bonds.

and guided tours. Mumming also informed much of the Chetwynd Mime Troupe's theatrics. Mumming is a medieval-ism in so far as there are no transcripts of the mumming plays said to have been performed in medieval England. Our knowledge of mumming, therefore, is part of a folk tradition, one known only through new acts of performance. Mumming may be medieval in origin, but it is a contemporary living event. The fact that mumming is an overtly social and confrontational art form lent itself to contemporary artistic practice. Mummers reverse the normative modes of behaviour, adopting inversions of speech, gender and social roles, placing the audience on the defensive. Mummers are not professional actors—instead, they are amateurs, ordinary citizens transforming into temporary avatars by adopting home-spun disguises.

We can find significant uses of mumming throughout the art of the '00s. For example, Tatham & O'Sullivan's mumming troupe *Slapstick Mystics with Sticks* performed *Thou Art That!* (Great Western Road, Glasgow, 2001). *The Slapstick Mystics with Sticks* transformed into a series of performances, notably at Frieze Art Fair in London (15-18 October 2004), before becoming a short novella. Mumming was also central to the performances of Plastique Fantastique. For example, *Plastique Fantastique Ribbon Dance Ritual to Call Forth the Pre-Industrial Modern* ("The Event", Birmingham, 2007), while resembling a pagan calendar custom, verged on a form of *Charivari* or "rough music", a raucous vigilantism in which the regeneration of Birmingham's Bull Ring shopping complex, including its obligatory Anthony Gormley sculpture, was made subject to a light roughhousing by the mummers. The mobbing was invoked as a discordant liturgical form:

What is a Pre-Industrial Modern? Well, well, well, well might you ask exactly just-such-a-question, for it is not as straight forward as it might at first appear (indeed, it is a very queer, a very wonky thing). For certainly—and this is our understanding [All: this is our understanding]—there are apparent so-called pre-industrial moderns that are little more than impostors, fakes, shadows of the Spectacle, more of the same . . . we are talking about those despicable commodities clothed in the new. We spit on them. [All spit][53]

Again, it is the second-order nature of such practices that transforms them from medievalisms into neomedieval ciphers, toolkits for practice. This was wholly consistent with the celebration of contemporary art's extradisciplinarity, the search for tropisms that enabled self-learning and the acquisition of (relatively) new competences. Rather than perfect a singular genre or form, contemporary artists mined disciplines and practices that they felt might inform their work. This was certainly evident in the wilful amateurism of neomedievalist contemporary art, a playfulness born of the autodidactic nature of the inquiry. Extradisciplinarity was the *sine qua non* of contemporary art. It would be disingenuous to claim that neomedievalism, or any interdisciplinary work, was "innovative" or pushed beyond the boundaries of contemporary artistic practice in this sense. Since it was so ecstatically undisciplined, the art of the early 21st century had few boundaries to push beyond. Nevertheless the question remains. Why were contemporary artists so drawn to the neomedieval?

As subject matter, medievalisms offered malleable alterior presents remote (or obscure) enough to liberate this kind of performative, ludic research. As a method, neomedievalism provided an ever expanding tropism, a novel point of entry into an inexhaustible range of contemporary subjects. Neomedievalism's elasticated atemporal looping and folding opened a longer perspective on artistic practice—premodern conditions providing insight into postmodern condi-

---

[53] Plastique Fantastique, *What is a Pre-Industrial Modern? The Gawkin Must be Made!*: www.plastiquefantastique.org/performance 02.html.

tions. Neomedievalism was a means of circumventing the late modernist industry, reading the present as simultaneously embodying conflicting elements of what has preceded it: modernism and the pre-modern. Much contemporary art embodied the pre-modern, thus, in its disaffection with the modernist auteur and in its embrace of collectivist and collaborative practices. At the same time, a significant sector of contemporary art continued the practice of preindustrial, artisanal modes of production, distribution and consumption. Produced and consumed in very small quantities, contemporary art was never modern in the industrial sense.

We can easily list ways in which the British Isles in the early 21st century mirrored their medieval pasts: a thousand years in which ordinary people suffered from global warming, economic meltdown, and a pandemic that killed half the population. It was also increasingly clear that Europe's modern experiment with sovereign nation states was in deep crisis, returning neomedieval subsidiarity and supranational authority to the continent. Such analogies were neomedieval practices, adaptive responses to a connected world in which space and time were being compressed. Such neomedieval practices were part of a broader imaginative process of exposure to otherness—folding in and getting out. Advocates of an alternative consciousness that would be better informed by the positive aspects of the pre-industrial, pre-Enlightenment, and early modern were always self-consciously postmodern in perspective. Embarking on an extra-disciplinary pilgrimage, artists travelled far beyond the negations of modernism and its limited analysis of modernity. Neomedievalism was but one suppressed alterity that postmodernism released into the wild.

This was particularly pressing during a period in which technologically advanced post-industrialism was in such deep crisis. Artists based in the UK were canonically ordained to lose their rational minds in challenging the diluted positivism that was the experience economy. But neomedievalism did not have to equate with an embrace of the irrational, nor was it predisposed to recycle the past as a way of celebrating the tyranny of the present. The neo-feudalism generated in this narrative was one—with its emphasis on a complex mixture of individual autonomy and multiple loyalties—that fused with neomedievalist readings of globalisation. Of course, the fascination with the other had to extend beyond "British" and European medievalisms. It also had to engage with simultaneity—with the fact that there were many moderns and thus many pre-moderns and post-moderns. Neomedievalism, then, was a lens through which contemporary artists identified and justified the present in the past and through which they narrated this past in terms of how they imagined their futures. It has no logical conclusion.

∽

Chapter 5

When Transfiguration Became Commonplace

Pru Forrest
Newcastle Art Gallery, New South Wales

I love looking at what HSN and others have to offer in avatar vestments, but when it comes time to buy, I prefer in-app vestments that are one-of-a-kind and hand-coded. The hand-coded items are creative and made with care because someone's heart and soul has been put into designing and creating the piece. Plus, great customer service isn't handed out like it used to be by retailers. But when you buy directly from the artisan, you get personalised service.

a priest avatar to Bob Sacamento, HSN website

Host refers to a process whereby objects become persons and persons become objects. The concept of "host" describes how cultural production may be understood as an array of "vessels" that collect, reassemble and transmit collective meaning. These vessels (human and non-human) are not strictly subject to the rigid hierarchical classification (such as art/non-art) prescribed by "promoters of technical rationalities and financial profitabilities"

but rather, following Michel de Certeau (1984, 107), they oper-
ate within the tactically sublimated realms of the practice of eve-
ryday life.

Alexandr Petrovsky, *Transfiguration is Commonplace*[1]

PART 1. FRANKLIN MINT SCHOOL OF LEADERSHIP

Alexandr Petrovsky's passion for inspiration, creativity and innovation was evident in his long and distinguished career as a developer, content curator, and entrepreneurial provocateur, pioneering new developments in the field of hy-

---

[1] Alexandr Petrovsky, *Transfiguration is Commonplace*, MBA thesis, University of the Mall of America Online.

pereconomic promotions. Of course, in his prime, Petrovksy was an avid collector and "arranger" of celebrity Cryostickers. This collection—which served as a springboard to Petrovsky's visionary hybrid of content and brand curation—is researched and archived by a dedicated team of interns drawn from his contributor community. Free&d-ing tirelessly at the Petrovsky Foundation of the Lay's Stax Museum of Fine Arts in his hometown of St. Petersburg, Florida, the interns maintain a vast mnemosyne of fin-de-siecle Cryostick-based culture, a must-see for any pilgrim on the Petrovsky trail.

Towards the end of his life, Petrovsky, more aware than ever of his own mortality, returned to re-examine the roots of his practice, his early relic-ing as an apprentice under the master content curator Bob Sacamano at the Willard Corporation. *When Transfiguration Became Commonplace* (Newcastle Art Gallery, New South Wales), is the first exhibition to explore this facet of Petrovsky's ascendancy. It does so *via negativa*. Examples of Petrovksy's relic-ing are notably absent from the exhibition. Petrovsky's freesearch and development is implied, inferred in the handiwork of Brandeum's peers, forebears, and disciples. The vast exhibition is ambitious in scale, conflating examples of proto and post-Petrovskian "Sherlocking" and "relic-ing", to give a fuller sense of the importance of these largely forgotten practices.

The legendary anchorite Sacamano holds a central place in this reassessment. In recent years, Sacamano's entrepreneurship has become increasingly central to understanding the richness of Petrovksy's early practice as a developer. Sacamano claimed, erroneously, to have coined the term "relic-ing", a phrase he used to describe his business studies teaching, undertaken while hosting on the Home Shopping Network (HSN) in the Tampa Bay area. When Sacamano first joined HSN, the television channel was still serving as one of the main forums for authenticating and trading domestic commodities. All this was to change as the great economic catastrophe generated a fatal combination of hyperinflation and relentless breaches of the security of financial information. As the restricted economy was replaced with what George Bataille once termed the "general economy", hypereconomics flourished. The denationalisation of fiat currencies and an assemblage of "alternative" forms of trading, such as barter and gift economies, Local Exchange Trading Systems (LETS), virtual currencies, *hawala*, and *furta sacra* would soon emerge as competing means to address these concerns. Petrovsky led the way in exploiting and developing the emerging hypereconomy.

Petrovsky first encountered Sacamano while enrolled in the "20-Minute MBA in Content Curating" at the University of the Mall of America Online. Sacamano, a visiting associate professor at the University's Franklin Mint School of Leadership in Les Cours Mont-Royal, ran an accredited MOOC (Massive Online Open Course) on "Neomedieval Entrepreneurialism" based in PATH. His controversial business ideas were predicated on a medievalist reading of the escalating economic crisis:

> Neomedievalism embraces the spectral traces or "uncertain knowledges" of its historical past as part of an ever-morphing, force-feedback simulation (or permanent rehearsal) of coming events. The longing for a future assembled from a bricolage of pre-modern components embeds itself deeper with every advance in the technologies of representation. The fantasy endeavours to supplant the Real through ever more immersive verisimilitudes.[2]

His maverick pre-modern approach contrasted dramatically with the then dominant Franklin Mint School of Leadership's emphasis on *futura*, promoting dated mantras such as "the

---

[2] Bob Sacamano, MOOC course descriptor, "Neomedieval Entrepreneurialism", Franklin School of Leadership, University of the Mall of America Online, PATH.

long tail", "black swans", "the tipping point", "the war for talent", and "corporate responsibility".[3] The economic crisis was prompting new security questions, questions to which only Sacamano had the answers. The answers came in the shape of two closely related practices: "Sherlocking" and "relic-ing".

Sherlocking was predicated on the commonly held assumption that culture was permeated by socioeconomic discourse at every conceivable level—from conception through production to distribution and consumption—just as socioeconomic discourses were pervaded by cultural debates. A modicum of artistic autonomy, nevertheless, lived on in mythical form, embodied in the online gift-economy. Transmogrified from its hippie roots by how-to knowledge, knowledge made freely available by the new wave indie media and hip-capitalism of the 1970s and '80s, the online gift economy offered services that few others in the corporatised cultural sector could provide.

"Freeconomics" was widely presumed to be at the root of the immediacy that helped to generate cultural capital.[4] The "indies" at the forefront of cultural developments tended to be those that found the most creative ways to exploit freeconomics. To generate and maintain 'free' resources, the indies observed a strict, albeit unwritten, moral code:

- There shall be no commodities, only gifts and counter-gifts.
- No lurkers. To receive, you must give.
- Gifts must be bestowed upon the commons or exchanged peer-to-peer within your network.
- Gifts may be exchanged for social prestige, but not for profit.

---

[3] See John Micklethwait and Adrian Wooldridge, *The Witch Doctors: Making Sense of the Management Gurus* (New York: Times Books, 1996).

[4] See Chris Anderson, *Free: The Future of a Radical Price*, New York: Hyperion, 2009.

We can draw a number of observations from this. Firstly, in a general sense, gifts, rather than money, provided the indies with the means of defining and maintaining social relations and status. Secondly, all forms of gift giving were reciprocal: to receive something *committed* you to counter-gifting *within your own network*. There was, therefore, a localised system of establishing value among peers within a specific community of practice. Thirdly, provided that you gifted your output to the commons you were free to use the open resources of the commons. Thus, distinct communities of practice[5] were reciprocally tied to one another via a commonwealth of networks.

The reciprocal nature of the gift in this code of conduct meant that participants were obligated to the indie commonwealth, since to take part in this culture meant partaking of the fruits of the commons. On entering a reciprocal relationship with the commons, participants were forever subordinated to it. The commonwealth provided a *largesse* greater than any individual could return to it in the form of a counter-gift. The commons' gift was agonistic, a potlatch, a "non-extinguishable debt".[6] This helped to generate an "immediacy of return" in the form of rapidly increasing the cultural capital of the indies. While governance of the indies varied widely in practice, most indies provided open access to their projects and developments via committee and open membership-based organisation. Elected committees kept ledgers of gifts and counter-gifts to ensure that reciprocity was honoured and that the commons was sustainably "farmed" via regular donations.

While corporations could exploit the commons as "free" research and development (free&d)—they could not offer the flexibility, collegiate culture and loyal communitarian res-

---

[5] See Etienne Wenger, *Communities of Practice: Learning, Meaning and Identity* (Cambridge: Cambridge University Press, 1998).
[6] Florin Curta, "Merovingian and Carolingian Gift Giving", *Speculum* 81 (2006): 676 [671–699].

ponses of the indies since they were corporatised rather than socially democratised. Indies were personalised—as very small organisations they had no choice other than to erode the roles of producer, distributor and consumer. This allowed them to fully develop the implications of the cultural turn to the symbolic realm of work and the economy, generating a "consensus of authenticity".

Indies were "authentic"—an illusion of sorts created by the fact that they made labour more transparent and collective and less diffused and departmentalised than it had been in larger cultural corporations. The indies' consensus of authenticity ensured that they were patronised in ways that many cultural enterprises would loved to have been. They were rewarded via the increasing levels of contribution people volunteered, perhaps, initially, as an interested visitor or, in time, as services, goods, time, and labour donated freely. Cultural capital was dependent on the veneration of a community, and this veneration was construed socially. The more the community gifted to the indies, the more venerated and powerful the commons became.

The power of the open network seemed to attest that, for many fundamental forms of research, cooperation could prove preferable to competition. While it may have been cooperative, the gift economy was far from uncompetitive. There was intense competition for status exercised through lavish peer-to-peer gift exchange. Competition for power raged through the generation of gift "debt" obligations between members as well as between the indies themselves. The complex co-oper-tition that generated the cultural capital of the indies was driven by spiritual trade with the higher power of the commons. Whatever form of gift exchange they participated in, indie members made donations *pro anima* towards the singularity[7] in anticipation of the day when they would become one with technology. The highest

---

[7] Raymond Kurzweil, *The Singularity Is Near: When Humans Transcend Biology* (New York: Viking Penguin, 2005).

ethical gesture of gifting "proprietorial" knowledge selflessly to the greater good of the commons offered participants "divine compensation in the form of salvation",[8] not only from commerce *but from their corporeal bodies*. This is what made indie media more "valuable" than the proprietorial media they sought to supersede. Since reputation was socially constructed, indie media—the code, the ideas and the social capital generated in the open source movement—was considered to be "embodied". It carried the *virtus* of the community.[9] Indie media were, effectively, person-objects.

The indies themselves were a means of socially incubating person-objects via social networks. For Sacamano, this phenomenon closely resembled the pre-modern practice of "relic-ing". Petrovsky's endnotes recall how Sacamano required his students to play *Age of Empires II: Age of Kings* (1999) to gain a deeper understand how medieval[10] monasteries, monarchies, and townships relied upon a communal set of beliefs revolving around an established cult of sainthood. For a cult to be constructed and bound to a particular geographic region, the saint (after being "discovered" or "invented") must be physically present in the form of their relics. To maintain the veneration of a community (and the vital influx of pilgrims) a consensus of authenticity had to be upheld through repeated displays of thaumaturgic powers.[11]

---

[8] Curta, "Merovingian and Carolingian Gift Giving," 674.

[9] "The simplest answer to the first question is that a relic is a physical object that is understood to carry the *virtus* of a saint or Christ, literally the virtue but more accurately the power of the holy person. It could be a bone or bones, some other portion of the body, or merely some object that has been sanctified by having come into contact with a sacred person": Cynthia Hahn, "What Do Reliquaries Do for Relics?" *Numen* 57.3 (2010): 290.

[10] "Not a period term at all, but an open-ended theme": Leslie J. Workman, quoted in Kathleen Verduin, "The Founding and the Founder: Medievalism and the Legacy of Leslie J. Workman", *Studies in Medievalism* XVII (2009): 19.

[11] Such as revelations, cures, and the cursing of enemies.

The regularity and quality of such posthumous displays brought enormous benefits in revenue and a competitive edge over neighboring regions with less effective relics or no relics at all.[12] A person-object then, could not be considered solely in terms of its "thing-ness" alone, but must rather be considered as a relational hub or conduit within a network of inter-human subjectivities.

Developing his comparative study of *Age of Empires II*, Sacamano argued that the indies functioned in a similar way to medieval townships, with indie media acting out the role of relics bestowed as gifts upon the community. The fortunes of the indies in the larger commons were based upon the veneration, influence, and fame of their fastidiously crafted social media. Sacamano argued that it was not possible to liberate such person-objects into capital, that indie media could not meaningfully be incorporated as a commodity to be bought and sold like any other.[13] Indie media were, in material terms, something less than mere dust. By definition, they were the products of cults.[14] So, indie media

---

[12] See Patrick Geary, "Sacred Commodities: The Circulation of Medieval Relics", in Arjun Appadurai, ed., *The Social Life of Things: Commodities in Cultural Perspective* (Cambridge: Cambridge University Press, 1986), 174–176.

[13] Cynthia Hahn speculated on the relational qualities of medieval relics and their reliquaries (as a compound unit) that contribute to their "omnipresent persistence" as duel transmitters of aesthetic and social meaning. A relic removed from context, Hahn argued, has no intrinsic worth. Even within a taxonomy of the commonplace, a relic is less than abject. It was only through the Christian process of "relic-ing" that transfiguration occurred. This involved an elaborate series of clerical investigations and public trials to establish the "truth" of the object in question before veneration in the final ritual of "elevation". See Cynthia Hahn, "Objects of Devotion and Desire: Relics, Reliquaries, Relation, and Response", in *Objects of Devotion and Desire: Medieval Relic to Contemporary Art* (New York: Bertha & Karl Leubsdorf Art Gallery, 2011), 8–19.

[14] Subcultures of shared interests that transformed into sophisticated communities of practice with unique rituals, proclivities and motiva-

also had no intrinsic value—its value was relational.[15] It was held in esteem by specific participatory communities—but not necessarily by the whole commonwealth.[16] The value of an open source was something primarily bestowed by a benevolent community in recognition of its own benevolence. The indie's rituals of elevation were acts of authentication performed by moderators that had the approval of each community of practice.[17] These rituals confirmed a commitment to the pontifex[18] of a particular media since this enabled the community to devote more of their time to cooperative development in the expectation that their good deeds perhaps would, in *futura*, be noticed by other indies in the wider commons. The devotion of the indies to their media was motivated by competition with other indies for willing volunteers. Simultaneously, their unified belief in the commons as a shared resource bound the indies to one another. And so, communities that worked hard to venerate their pontifex would rapidly grow both in reputation and in numbers.

From these observations, Sacamano drew a few important conclusions:

- Indie media were highly affective accumulations of embodied human relations (person-objects).
- The value of indie media was indexically related to the moral virtue of its free circulation.

---

tions.

[15] The relational nature of the gift within the indies was the basis of the "situational" nature of value in the hypereconomy that emerged from the indies.

[16] " . . . 'authenticity' meant less identification with a particular saint's body than efficacy in terms of communal needs": Geary, Sacred Commodities, 181.

[17] For example, forum mods, elected committee members of not-for profit collectives, etc.

[18] The pontifex was a common "bridge", a basic kernel that allowed different user groups to cooperate in the development of a media.

- Indie media were collectively manifested, elevated (relic-ed), and supported by their cult (community of practice) in order to venerate the commons.
- Indie cults were hosted by their overlord, the commons of open source sainthood.
- The gift of the commons was agonistic, and since it could not be counter-gifted it was, effectively, an eternal debt.

These factors made Sacamano's goals of appropriation and commerce difficult, to say the least. Theft was not an option, as to remove indie media from its host cult would destroy it. Indie media would have to remain in circulation within its venerating community to convince wider congregations that it was authentic. This did not, however, prevent merchants from establishing a context within the commons in which "relic-ing" could take place. Sacamano argued that entrepreneurs should therefore host their own platforms—benevolent communities that would encourage the flourishing of cultural capital, for only having cultivated themselves could the fruits of indie cults be harvested. Sacamano's platform would provide a framework for participation-based development and social networking that emerged from the culture it incorporated. It would reward the creative sector's sweat-equity labour market by providing it with a host, a "free" platform in which creative services that had attracted a critical mass of prosumers would be forever enshrined.[19]

---

[19] In developing the indie reciprocal economy of gift/countergift, Sacamano aimed to establish a modern form of serfdom, playing the role of Seigneur. Medieval serfs were in a gift-bond with their overlords. Seigneurs allowed serfs to use their land in return for the bestowal of gifts at defined times each year. Since land was not incommesurate with the gifts that serfs could offer (the produce of their labour), the gift-bond was, in effect, a debt in perpetuity. In hosting indies, Sacamano, likewise, established a gift-bond (a "Sherlock") in perpetuity, legally enshrining the host's terms and conditions as "A Pledge of Fealty to the Overlord Willard".

For Sacamano, "Sherlocking" was not theft but, rather, a pious act of hospitality. Sherlocking was the greatest gift.[20] Indeed, the gifting of reliquaries, of platforms for participation, was wholly consistent with the "co-opetitive" culture of reciprocity that generated indie's authenticity of consensus. Sacamano ventured that a benevolent community would happily reciprocate his offer, agreeing to the terms and conditions of entry into his community of practice in return for providing their venerable labour as relic-ers. In this way he would secure the consent of indie media's holy bodies.

Sacamano defended Sherlocking as his moral obligation to safeguard indie media by hosting it in his proprietorial framework, performing "good-works" in return for "good-works". In return, Sherlocked indies were only obliged to bestow gifts upon the Willard Corporation "every year on seven different occasions: Easter, haymaking, harvest time, grape harvest time, Christmas, Shrovetide, and Mid-Lent!"[21] These gifts were defined in relation to the proprietorial platforms in which Willard's Sherlocked indies operated. In general, Willard took a 30% share of any intellectual property developed within its host reliquaries. Such a stake would allow Willard to take the best ideas and develop them independently into their own commodities without breaking the indie's strict taboos on commerce. Sacamano performed the role of curate, taking care of the soul of the indie media by providing it with an improved ecosystem, a more generative context.[22] Sherlocking, for Sacamano, enabled these indie

---

[20] Sacamano here drew inspiration from "furta sacra", the cult of the "holy theft" of saints' relics, and the stories of their movement between reliquaries.

[21] Jean-Claude Schmitt, "Appropriating the Future", in J. A. Burrow and Ian P. Wei, eds., *Medieval Futures: Attitudes to the Future in the Middle Ages* (Woodbridge: Boydell Press, 2000), 7.

[22] "This is a political discourse with its roots in the predominant Anglo-American critique of community and common property, dating back to the fourteenth century: that the 'sloth, idleness, and misery' of serfs in feudal England represented the biggest obstacle

relics to become whole; to join the body of his reliquary offered true transcendence through the mass veneration of a far greater congregation. Sherlocking was the benevolent exploitation of freeconomics, crowdsourcing, open source, and not-for profit knowledge for profit. For Sacamano, it was simply a case of choosing the right indie media cult to Sherlock. This was a job for the legions of interns and employees working for Sacamano's business empire, Willard: Technology for Enchantment™.

PART 2. WILLARD: TECHNOLOGY FOR ENCHANTMENT™

Since their origins in the early 1970s, the culture of MMORPGs[23] had been relentlessly medievalist. As Eddo Stern observed, the relation between medieval fantasy and computer gaming began as early as 1972 when US Department of Defence researcher William Crowther was inspired by his love of the pen-and-paper role playing game *Dungeons and Dragons* to develop the seminal text-based game *Colossal Cave Adventure* (1976). In doing so, Crowther had

---

to the productivity of agriculture": Michael Goldman, "Customs in Common: The Epistemic World of the Commons Scholars", *Theory and Society* 26.1 (February 1997): 4.

[23] Massively Multiplayer Online Role-Playing Games.

unwittingly inaugurated the "beige age of swords and cir-
cuitry"[24] and the definitive narrative genre for what would
later develop into socially-networked gaming environments
know as MUDs[25], and finally as the fully fledged open-world
MMORPG that then operated on a global scale.[26] Stern hu-
morously, and presciently, speculated that the *Dungeons
and Dragons*-obsessed, "socially awkward 'geeks'"[27] of the
1960s and '70s—a period that witnessed a great resurgence
of fantasy genre publishing—would become the pioneers of
the 21st century's online technologies and economies. Ste-
reotyping aside, the art of "questing" in networked real-time
strategy games such as *Tribal Nations of The Scorpion*, *War-
hammer*, the *Protectorate of the Me-Machine Islands*, *Polare
Directorate*, *Medieval: Total War*, and *Runescape* was undertaken by the largest communities on the internet, with *World
of Warcraft* alone hitting a subscriber base of 12 million in
2010, making its community larger than many sovereign
states. The dominant MMORPGs of the early 21st century
were co-constructed by benevolent communities of practice,
minecrafters who regularly participated in the veneration of
their constructed worlds.

As with Europe's great gothic cathedrals, open world
MMORPGs were built by numerous anonymous hands, minecrafters all ascribing to a common, albeit unwritten, typology. This

---

[24] Eddo Stern, "A Touch of Medieval: Narrative, Magic and Com-
puter Technology in Massively Multiplayer Computer Role-Playing
Games", in Frans Mäyrä, ed., *Computer Games and Digital Cultures
Conference Proceedings* (Tampere, Finland: Tampere University
Press, 2002), 258.

[25] Multi-User Dungeons.

[26] Romantic medievalisms were not at all limited to the role-playing
game genre. For example, in the mid-1980s, Nintendo's platformer
Mario kicked-off the greatest franchise in gaming history, reviving
the video gaming industry after it collapsed in 1983. The choice of
back-story was no coincidence. Mario must rescue a princess from
an evil dragon residing in a medieval castle.

[27] Stern, "A Touch of Medieval", 259.

collective production of reverentia made minecrafters particularly susceptible to liturgical displays of belief, to facilitating fantastical revelations, sacrifices, cures and curses. As an accursed share, reverentia were connected to less "saintly" indulgences, such as increasingly outrageous displays of flaming, trolling, and avatar-on-avatar violence. Since these forms of destructiveness and anti-social behaviour were ubiquitous online, the influx of new minecrafters into a MMORPG was directly proportionate to the magnetism of its post-secular experiences. Sacamano's teachings from *Age of Empires II* told his followers that mighty MMORPGs thrived or collapsed on the quality of their reliquaries.

Unlike other luxury trade items such as gadolinium, lutetium, terbium, and dysprosium, these person-objects held an indeterminate and fluctuating value, impossible to calculate in purely monetary terms. In fact, their value exceeded their base immateriality to an extraordinary degree—not just through the high level of codemanship applied to their (often spectacular) skins, nor purely through their reported transubstantiate powers, but rather via their ability to establish and hold in place inter-regional networks of power and control. This was allied to a transnational model of production and distribution that approached "neomedievalism" creatively, as a heuristic device allowing corporations to re-conceptualise sovereign statehood as an "historically unique anomaly which had a beginning and will also have an end".[28] This real-time strategy revelation was the basis of Willard's legions of interns and employees, and it would generate a relic-ing rush as boomers and speculators—including the impressionable young Petrovsky—scrambled to reach these promised lands. Three major open world MMORPGs battled for minecrafters in this period: the newly post-Communist Tribal Nations of The Scorpion, the Protectorate of the Me-Machine Islands, and the Polare Directorate. While the mar-

---

[28] Joerg Friedrichs, "The Meaning of New Medievalism", *European Journal of International Relations* 7.4 (2001): 481.

ket in MMORPGs was a lucrative one, the geopolitics of these MMORPGs was complex and unwieldy, based, as it was, on then current neomedieval propaganda concerning US International Relations.[29]

The deep divisions within Tribal Nations of the Scorpion is a case in point. The Grand Duchy—a conspiracy of Kings, governors, numerous legates, journalists, knighted Irishmen and spies—established itself amidst the many fissures in Tribal Nations' plasma pantonality. Taking their lead from the work of children, medieval carpenters and guerrilla gardeners, this micro-nation spearheaded the emergence of green anarchism that swept across MMORPG communities. The Grand Duchy made confederate claims of sovereignty from Tribal Nations that were not entirely preposterous, despite what the chatrooms said to defy the champions of organisation and ownership. Their claims upset the precarious balance of the Tribal Nations. The Grand Duchy led a call to order the disorder of the system and drive out the chaotic influence of the accident in solidarity with the Duchy diaspora that had migrated to the Southernmost fringes of the Protectorate of the Me-Machine Islands, which was, then, one of the few remaining autonomous MMORPGs.

It wasn't possible just parachute into a MMORPG and set up an in-game marketplace for trading relics. As part of a family of indies, MMORPG communities had their own vernacular systems of value; any interloper would have to spend a great deal of game-time establishing and securing their social capital on a MMORPG's own geo-political terms. Besides, as we have seen, it wasn't possible to *sell* relics . . . a gift-economy had to be established in which to appropriately venerate and bestow them.

Peer-to-peer investment in Willard financed the explora-

---

[29] International Relations neomedievalism, despite the apocalyptic language adopted by some contributors, did not suggest an actual return to a new "dark age" but instead utilised the past to shake up modern ontological assumptions about the inevitability and immutability of the nation-state system.

tion, enclosure, and militarisation of MMORPG space. Playing the role of speculators and pioneers, Willard's interns and employees established a system of licensed burghs by preaching the Tragedy of the Commons to ambitious minecrafters with the most remarkable skills. Together, these parties of experienced minecrafters established incentivised pre-industrial enterprise zones, manors designed to attract professional avatars such as Lindensmiths, Master Relic-ers, and their apprentices. These professionals would not be involved with modding Willard's creations, rather, they would craft the "product" that Willard intended to Sherlock.

These gated communities of practice were be "protected" by Willard's mercenaries: "The Tong". The Tong would ensure that all makers seeking to work in the pre-industrial zones were suitably skilled and that they were incorporated (Shanghaied) into the Willard Compagnon of Minecrafters. In return for their safe burgage, Willard's subjects would pledge fealty to the corporation's standard terms and conditions of indenture in addition to agreeing to the suspension of *habeas corpus* operational in the larger, more volatile, MMORPG world. Crucially, they agreed to the regular "gifting" of relics to the Willard corporation as a token of their gratitude to their Tong Seigneurs at Easter, haymaking, harvest time, grape harvest time, Christmas, Shrovetide, and Mid-Lent *in perpetuity*. Williardburghs, therefore, became vital in-game centres for the production and distribution of relics. Mesmerised by "aesthetic awe bordering on the religious",[30] the MMORPG citizens who lived beyond the walls of Willard's city-states self-policed and participated in the licensing and "black-boxing" of relics.

PART 3. MAGISTRA VITAE

To gain some work placement credits in his MBA, Petrovsky

---

[30] Alfred Gell, "The Technology of Enchantment and the Enchantment of Technology", in J. Coote and A. Shelton, eds., *Anthropology, Art and Aesthetics* (Oxford: Clarendon, 1992), 40.

applied to free&d for Willard: Technology for Enchantment™—
Sacamano's monopolistic relic-ing brand. Following a "neomedieval office" model developed by soft capitalists the
Valve Corporation, Willard ran a "flatland" organisational
structure. There were no bosses, no line managers. Free&d-
ers chose which projects they wanted to work on and hoped
that their relentless innovation and application would eventually land them with paid employment. While, to investors
in the outside world, Willard ostensibly operated like any
other corporation, internally the flatland office was a mael-
strom of overlapping and shifting loyalties as cabals fought it
out for the best project interns.

. . . people don't join projects because they're told to. Instead, you'll decide what to work on after asking yourself the right questions . . . . Employees vote on projects with their feet (or desk wheels). Strong projects are ones in which people can see demonstrated value; they staff up easily. This means there are any number of internal recruiting efforts constantly under way.[31]

Petrovsky's placement was at the Weiden + Kennedy Building in downtown Portland, Oregon. Aspiring neophytes entered through a battered cabin class door marked "Rose City Room" guarded by a giant beaver, and started to negotiate the building's convoluted intern guidance system. According to data mined from Petrovsky's smart phone, this had been arranged in the circuitous route of Chartres Cathedral's floor labyrinth. It is now estimated that there were at least forty thousand interns ensconced in this maze of typical and standardised retractable post and belt crowd control mechanism. The uniform glare of 1,734 florescent

---

[31] VALVE, "How Do I Pick My Projects?", in *Valve Handbook for New Employees* (Seattle, Washington), 8. It may be pertinent to note here that certain anchoritic tendencies blighted Valve's post-Fordist utopia. Insiders reported high instances of social withdrawal ranging from protracted periods of time spent in washroom cubicles to bouts of faux monasticism where employees (initially as a kind of joke referring to the overt medievalism of online game culture) began to hand-write code by candlelight in makeshift scriptoriums. One of the first employees ever to "quit" Valve is reported to have spent nearly all of her time in the flatland's gym. She allegedly told a *Wired* magazine reporter, "The treadmill offered me a kind of meditative respite. It reminded me of a summer job where I worked on an assembly line building cell-phones. I watched TV in the evenings (studying too, of course) and slept at night. Sometimes, closing my eyes on the treadmill, I would imagine myself as a chunk of molded plastic trundling along the conveyor belt. Kind of self-enclosed, you know, unconcerned and happy going nowhere." For many of its indentured workers and interns, the flatland was an infinite hell of punitive creativity.

strip lights bore down inexorably upon the brows of the interned as they shuffled along the line like extras in *Dawn of the Dead*, eventually reaching a branch in the queue. It wasn't obvious which way would be the quickest. Taking the wrong route ran you all the way around the Rose City Room and back to the entrance, forcing you to retrace your steps! Finally, after just over a week, Petrovsky was able to board Willard's titanic "Sandbox".

The Sandbox provided prospective interns with everything they needed to rehearse and pitch projects in which Willard might show interest. Petrovsky, effectively, was on trial, closely monitored on CCTV by Willard's elite team of recruiters. Petrovsky had raised some sponsorship towards his internship registration fee through RocketHub's crowd-funding site. His biggest benefactor was ITV, the new owners of NBC who were profoundly aroused by his pitch for a populist genre mashup of cooking, medievalism and time travel. Petrovksy pitched TV food pundit and anchorite Greg Wallace on a voyage that would take him from mid 21st-century Norway to medieval England where he would co-host a new historical cooking programme, *Magistra Vitae*. Inserting the xyzzy command, Wallace would travel cabin class, the film crew monitoring his every move in the ship's hull as he mixed with vagabonds and serfs. The pilot would be important for teasers in between the ads for Hellman's Mayo and Cheese Strings.

In the Sandbox, Petrovsky set to work animating *Magistra Vitae*'s opening titles in CGI. The sequence opened inside the lapel pocket of Wallace's Alexander McQueen jacket, which sported a pop-up travel version of the "ITV Peace and Reconciliation Cuboid". Wallace fumbled to grab the cuboid, a completely opaque block of black glass, as it slithered between his olive-oiled fingers. Sensing his greasy fingerprints, it mumbled into action. Wallace beamed his winning smile and sucked down hard on a lime, pulling in his cheeks. The startup instruction beamed out from the cube onto the hammock dangling above him, the light refracting off of his freshly shaven head to startle a neighbourly rat.

Petrovsky imagined the ITV P&RC as a four-sided beamer capable of projecting images (1,000 megawatt) from each of its facades. Each screen could be configured to display an ITV online game.[32] *Magistra Vitae* would function as a product placement opportunity for this lucrative online game. The CGI titles made it look simpler than a deconstructed chicken pie. Wallace clicked the link with his forefinger and was soon online. The ITV games page popped up on the hammock. Wallace's four games of choice were:

1. Family Fortunes
2. Catchphrase
3. The Price is Right
4. Bullseye

Petrovsky's business plan sold the ITV P&RC as "this summer's beach craze". Members of the public would be invited to interact with the games and, hopefully, win cash prizes. Currently ITV online charged 0.14 Bitcoins (BTC) for 50 credits, which was around 0.00278 BTC per game. To secure a cut from in-sourcing the ITV games, Petrovsky invented an exclusive in-game currency based on the "medieval England" theme of *Magistra Vitae*. He would charge a groat per game, four days wages for a farmer, or the price of a quail's egg in late 14th-century England. Those who had no money could indenture their cooking skills or barter food for a punt on the ITV P&RC. The camera crew, meanwhile, would cut an authentic slice of dark age veg talk for the series.

As content-curator-in-chief of the *Magistra Vitae* project, Petrovsky would effectively be charging his "medieval" clients the real terms equivalent of 0.00694 BTC per game (=140.13 North Korean Won), bringing in a cool profit of 0.00416 BTC per game, enabling the ITV P&RC to pay for

---

[32] Please visit http://www.itv.com/Games/default.html and make your selection.

itself. Of course, if the participants did well, they could win a cash prize of up to 2.08217 BTC, paid by ITV online each week. "That money, the money they win, that would be safe", Petrovsky imagined Greg saying to camera. In the pilot episode, the cuboid would be placed in the heart of York, just outside the Shambles. It would be open to view 24 hours per day during the period of lent in 1377.

Petrovsky had taken time to configure a sound hyper-economic financial model. While the cuboid was the size of a small jar of truffles, it produced only images. Sound was to be produced through Binatone Bluetooth enabled speakers that ran on solar power. Wallace, the time traveling coster-monger, would buy them from Ca$h Convertors and sell them back to Ca$h Convertors when the cuboid's residency was over. Some of profits from selling the games to the vill-eins would cover Wallace's hefty Michelin restaurant tab and the interest on the speakers from the pawnbrokers. The cu-boid's projection screens would be assembled by the ground force of the Korean People's Army who would pro-vide the scaffolding and canvas in return for having a re-cruitment ad shown on the cuboid during the ad breaks. The internet connection would be provided by KCC Europe, led by Jan Holterman in Berlin in collaboration with the North Korean government's neomedieval investment committee.[33]

---

[33] Tentative comparisons between the multiple loyalties of Western European Christendom and both the increasing power-overlaps between sovereign states and the transnational market economy began as early as 1962 with the classic realist, Arnold Wolfers, pro-posing a kind of "new medievalism", a move "toward complexities that blur the dividing line between domestic and foreign policy": *Discord and Collaboration: Essays on International Politics* (Balti-more: The Johns Hopkins Press, 1962), 241–242. A novel devel-opment in international relations in the early 21st century involved the world's largest single currency unions—NAFTA and PR China—working in collaboration with global corporations to encourage separatist movements in rival economic unions of "medieval" nation states, most notably the European Union. This often meant surrep-titiously supporting "medievalising" tendencies in foreign cultures

The connection would be established through a satellite link from North Korea to servers located in Heiligkreuzkirche (Church of the Holy Cross) in Schwäbisch Gmünd. In return KCC Europe would be offered first refusal on all other ITV online gaming cuboid ventures in the Democratic People's Republic of Korea.

PART 4. LINDOW MAN

Magistra Vitae clearly impressed Petrovksy's masters and soon he was invited upstairs to cruise the Willard office as an official intern. He had heard rumours about "The Tong", a cabal of heavy-shippers busy dreaming up schemes to Sherlock high-street clothes, shoes, skins, shapes, and various types of accessories for avatars as well as blue-chip military, devotional, and liturgical objects for MMORPGs.

While avatar accessories and blue-chip objects were downloadable, they were licensed, or "leased", from Willard to the gamer for periods of 12 or 24 months at a time. Tribal Nations of The Scorpion, Protectorate of the Me-Machine Islands, and Polare Directorate would not authenticate jailbroken relics or relics relic-ed by non-compagnon members. Of course, minecrafters could simply have established alternative open source gaming worlds, but, thanks to Willard's

---

and politics. Once independent, small nations would either establish a weak currency of their own (and thus could be new sources of cheap labour), denationalise money completely or align their reserves with one or other of the hegemonic reserve currencies: the Dollar and the Yuan. Those who lived in the soverign states of the reserve currencies were destined to gain a greater share of the world's wealth. Such neomedieval foreign policy was informed by a reading of Janet L. Abu-Lughod's analysis of the collapse of global trade, "Restructuring the Thirteenth Century World System", in *Before and After European Hegemony: The World System A.D. 1250-1350* (New York: Oxford, 1989), where she writes, "Of crucial importance is the fact that the 'Fall of the East' preceded the 'Rise of the West,' and it was this devolution of the preexisting system that facilitated Europe's easy conquest" (361).

aggressive Sherlocking, the economy of the licensed MMORPGs had become too powerful to make this attractive. Besides, there were other factors to consider. To jailbreak or counterfeit a relic reduced it to mere modifiable code. Petrovsky was certain that his code would be an attractive proposition to The Tong—beautifully crafted, certainly, but the possibility of enchantment lay in the richly variegated surfaces generated by the code, not in the code itself.

Despite operating a flatland offline, the online Willard corporation was involved in a complex process of veneration. Not only did Willard's relic-ing cabals manufacture relics, they furtively established their "authenticity" with whispering campaigns funded by a combination of social micropayments and *hawala*. Effectively, the relic-ing cabals transfigured Willard's products and secured its fortunes by remunerating influential minecrafters to worship its relics by recuperating social micropayment sites. Social micro-payments had started as a way of supporting good deeds—giving credit to openly online services and resources or sponsoring avatars who gave up drinking for a month. Tax-deductible charitable donations could be made to a large network of influential MMORPG avatars in virtual currencies. Willard would make regular donations to social entrepreneur avatars to secure their favour and ensure that their products were placed. Although the avatars would have no legal obligation to their donor, if they failed to carry out their wishes, payments would unceremoniously cease. The charities were thus held in a reciprocal gift-bond with their corporate benefactors.

Commercial relic-ers such as Petrovsky held multiple accounts with the main MMORPGs and regularly took part in the gameplay as participant observers—sometimes playing "free-burghers" to surreptitiously abet Willard's trade in influence or acting as The Tong seigneurs running various protection rackets. Petrovsky's avatar "Lindow Man" was a mainstay on Protectorate of the Me-Machine Islands where he made rank of "Provost" on the board of a major social enterprise, "Caves of Angry Shockhead". Attempting to flesh out all the side-stories into the bargain, Provost Lindow Man spent almost a year as a mole developing the business plan of a splinter group of Duchy who were calling for the formation of a People's Grand Duchy Republic of the Unfortunate Islands. Playing the consummate high-net-worth Duchy, Lindow Man led a coven of plotters from amidst the topiary of the Caves of Angry Shockhead in the Pays de Champagne-Terre-Blanche to democratise their economic opportunities. This infamous "Grand Plot" involved a process of gradual arboreal Cornwalisation, orchestrating territoire and vaguely maintaining some internal consistency as "agents for social change".

Lindow Man's high standing in "Me-Machine" regularly brought Petrovksy into contact with Willard's cabal of virtual currency traders, wealthy avatars who grew rich from taking commission before making micro-payments to MMORPG avatars in rival gaming platforms. Seeing a short-term opportunity to make some money, he moved his desk away from the relic-ers and began working with the virtual trading project cabal.

Legally speaking, such a profession should not have existed. MMORPGs were still obliged by offline customs authorities to internally police orders for high amounts of virtual currency as well as avatars with extraordinary order transactions. Unless they were earned through in-game labour, much of which was performed by political prisoners in Chinese labour-camps, the authentication and movement of virtual currencies online required the professional skills of Lindensmiths.[34] Additionally, there were no legal means to

---

[34] The Lindensmith's role was to verify the authenticity of virtual currency and issue it with the Public Key Certificate required before it could be traded into hard currency by online brokers. The Lindensmith would sanctify the currency by performing a ritual developed in the Caves of Angry Shockhead involving the laying on of hands while reciting the NASM assembly code for a boot sector that prints

make transactions directly between the accounts of rival MMORPGs. A virtual currency had to first be exchanged into an offline currency—where it was subject to duty—before being exchanged into another virtual currency.[35] As hard currencies plummeted in value, this became a very risky business. The virtual currency traders circumvented this problem by using *hawala*—"which relies not on wire transfers and other recorded transactions, but rather on in-person deposits that reach their intended recipients through untraceable faxes, emails, and cell phones that are then shredded, deleted or discarded".[36] *Hawala* transactions allowed currency transfers to be made across incompatible platforms and offline taxation to be circumvented.

Although much of the open world MMORPGs preferred to operate gift and barter economies, fostering collaboration and reciprocity, the blurring of the line between gifts and commodities took hold of MMORPGs as the offline world developed an urgent need to establish a stable global-reserve currency that was geographically independent. In

---

"Real Money" in PURE. The role was comparable to the traditional Goldmith's job of inspecting the "Corrupt, shaved, and false coins that assailed the medieval economy": Richard Sennett, *The Craftsman* (New Haven: Yale University Press, 2008), 61. Lindensmiths were members of the International Compagnon of Lindensmiths, a professional body that closely monitored their activity.

[35] "All of the other virtual currency dealers require players to make real money transactions outside of the game and then log back into the game to receive their purchases. Even then, the goods must be delivered in such a way so that the game moderators do not suspect foul play. In this regard, the virtual currency exchange is more akin to the black market than it is to the Federal Reserve. As a result, statistics for the exchange of virtual goods are imperfect at best, and no one can really know how much trading is going on": Jordan Hicks, "Virtual Currency Exchange," *What MMORPG?*, June 6, 2011: http://www.whatmmorpg.com/articles/virtual-currency-exchange.php.

[36] Bruce Holsinger, "Follow the Money", in *Neomedievalism, Neoconservatism and the War on Terror* (Chicago: Prickly Paradigm, 2007), 24–25.

their desperation, many chose to believe that a virtual currency would be more likely to hold its value within the virtual realm at a time when offline currencies were extremely volatile. [37] As national credit ratings dropped and investors lost faith in hard currencies, once "alternative" currencies and means of exchange flourished. The fact that MMORPG currencies were denationalised made them a more viable proposition; to many they even offered the promise of an end to currency speculation and attendant hyperinflation. MMORPG banks also had the salient advantage of being a product of the mass participation and "situational utility"[38] of the hypereconomy. The fact that each run on off-line banks saw swarms of panicked savers moved their investments into the MMORPG hypereconomy only helped to strengthen this impression.

PART 5. HYPERECONOMICS

. . . a 'hyper-economic' system combines flows of globally aggregated scalar information on prices with mechanisms for sharing knowledge about situational utilities of groups of resources.[39]

The seeming stability of the virtual currencies came as a result of minecrafters pioneering their own hybrid value sys-

---

[37] For example, following England, Wales, and Northern Ireland's exit from the European Union, the run on Sterling forced the Bank of England to adopt Smurfberries (SfB) as the nation's currency. England's treasury became the *de jure* property of Petrovsky's Caves of Angry Shockhead Investment Group, an elite cabal of avatars based in Me-Machine Islands.

[38] Alexander Chislenko and Madan Ramakrishnan, "Hyper-Economy: Combining Price and Utility Communication in Multi-Agent Systems", paper presented at "ISAS '98: Intelligent Systems and Semiotics", IEEE International Symposium on Intelligent Control/Computational Intelligence in Robotics and Automation/Intelligent Systems and Semiotics, Gaithersburg, Maryland, 1998.

[39] Chislenko and Ramakrishnan, "Hyper-Economy".

tem. In the early days of open world MMORPGs, minecraft-ers gradually switched their investments from hard curren-cies to virtual currencies. They did this partly for ideological reasons, and partly to advance their game progression in an online open world. Ideologically speaking, minecrafters saw hard currencies as a dated and corrupt concept. Such cur-rencies were underwritten by offline sovereign states with the purpose of consolidating their power over the users of the currency and with the express aim of aiding and abetting the economic exploitation of self-interested individuals who did not participate in the "real economy". In contrast, virtual currencies were the product of an emerging hypereconomy of *prosumers*.[40] While prosumers, like the indies, utilised the commons to nurture their communities of interest, they were not committed to "natural economies" such as barter or gift-bondage.[41] Nor were they morally opposed to finance-based trade. On the contrary, prosumers actively pursued an as-semblage of economic practices that dissolved production (Bataille's superabundance of energy, the erotic, the sacred), transfer (sale, exchange, gift, theft), and consumption (re-view, adaptation, redistribution) into *integrated* and *calcula-ble* acts of hypereconomic circulation.

Following indie's "No Lurkers" code, the hypereconomy was not split into producers and consumers: everyone was required to be a producer-consumer. Those who did not produce could not consume (and vice-versa). Although hy-pereconomic practices existed off and online, hypereconom-ic currencies developed in the virtual realm where they could be more easily calibrated in relation to *virtus*. Online hyper-economic systems developed the unquantifiable relational

---

[40] Alvin Toffler first introduced this phrase in "The Prosumer Ethic", in *The Third Wave* (New York: William Morrow & Company, 1980), 403.

[41] "At no time in the Middle Ages was the European economy strict-ly speaking a 'natural economy', in which barter and self-sufficiency characterized the production, exchange, and consumption of com-modities": Geary, "Sacred Commodities", 170.

value of indie media as a "situational" concept of value *that might be quantified*. A handful of trusted hypereconomic accounting systems established the *virtus* of a given economy. Virtual currency was, thus, widely regarded to be a "virtuous currency" in contrast with that circulating in "corrupt" offline banks.

The hypereconomy exploited advanced information technology to combine information on prices with complex data on *virtus*, producing a richer index of value to inform more efficient trade in goods and services. In the hypereconomy, *virtus* was shorthand for symbolic or cultural capital, which, as we have seen, was a notoriously difficult quality to index as it was bestowed socially rather than via a "direct transfer of resources or observations of natural agents' activities".[42] The hypereconomy emerged in the 1990s as an attempt to quantify (and thus to subjugate) social capital as "situational" knowledge: user-generated knowledge produced by prosumers for prosumers. In the booming Experience Economy[43] of the 1990s, the *virtus*-value of goods and services would go up and down depending on the collective experience of their communities of users. Whether it be a free-range egg, a cordless power drill, a cluster of spa services, or an avatar's high heels, the hypereconomic commodity was a relational hub in a network of inter-human subjectivities. Since its esoteric value was maintained by the veneration of the community, the situational nature of a hypereconomic commodity made it a "commodified-relic". If the hypereconomic commodity was a person-object incubated via online peer reviews, community discussion boards, and word-of-mouth, then it followed that the discourses that enveloped them were a form of relic-ing.

Willard's involvement in the emerging funny money mar-

---

[42] Chislenko and Ramakrishnan, "Hyper-Economy", 2.

[43] See Gerhard Schulze, *Erlebnisgesellschaft: Kultursoziologie der Gegenwart* (Frankfurt: Campus Verlag, 1992), and Joseph Pine and James Gilmore, *The Experience Economy* (Boston: Harvard Business School Press, 1999).

kets was underwritten by its trade as an agency "collecting individual experiences and forming aggregated situational and general utility estimates".[44] Willard applied unique situational information, gathered through its embedded interns, to lead trade in virtual currencies. It was able to use this information to become the first corporation to sell and profit from indulgences.[45] As the Willard Corporation became more deeply immersed in the hypereconomy's rapidly expanding markets, it began to hold most of its assets in virtual liquidity. Although it was a limited company registered in the Tampa Bay Area, Willard largely avoided paying US$ taxes to Florida's Department of Revenue by making all of its transactions exclusively in L$ denominations.[46] As the holder of some two trillion in linden dollar-denominated savings, Willard's investors had reason to be concerned about the long-term strength of the L$. To spread its risk, Willard also held liquid reserves of Me-Machine XIII Platinum, Bitcoins, WoWGold, Dark Age of Camelot Platinum, Tribal Nations of

---

[44] Chislenko and Ramakrishnan, "Hyper-Economy", 4.

[45] Since it was possible to exchange hard cash for virtual currencies, it was, effectively, possible to purchase and trade in "indulgences", hypereconomic bonds that came preloaded with *virtus*. Holding virtual currency did not immediately generate *virtus*, but it could be used to support philanthropic actions that would, thus raising standing in the hypereconomy. Raising your user approval rating could, for example, be "bought" by purchasing enough sprites for minecrafters to raise a new barn for their community. Conversely, the generation of *virtus* could translate into virtual currency. Willard's loyal interns worked tirelessly as minecrafters to generate *virtus* and raise the corporation's approval rating. The virtual investments they generated formed hypereconomic bonds for Willard to trade as indulgences.

[46] The USA continued to use the 2001 Patriot Act to restrict the laundering of its nationalised US$ currency into virtual currencies. Laundering in virtual currencies, such as Bitcoin and Liberty Reserve, involved hackers wiring money from a fiat currency to a virtual currency, then exchanging it back again into hard cash, making its origins almost impossible to trace.

The Scorpion Groats, and Smurfberries, allowing it to lead trade in currencies on the funny money markets.[47] Willard's decision to start paying its employees and investors exclusively in Linden Dollars—the virtual currency that, in spite of showing 12% inflation, was rapidly becoming the most stable on the planet—was a seismic leap in the history of capital investment, money, and credit.

Offline, the Clauswitzian-Westphalian system (CW) of territorial sovereignty and nation building began to give way to something that mirrored the multiple, asymmetric layers of authority found in MMORPGs, with each "nation-state" sharing and devolving significant elements of governance. The popular success of neomedieval sovereigntism meant that there were more micronation-states in the world than at any time since the mid-17th century. Their public sectors emaciated from soaring debt-to-GDP ratios, excluded from larger monetary unions, and unable to foster strong fiat currencies of their own, many newly sovereign micronation-states took the nuclear option of privatising money, allowing their citizens to "make their dealings in a currency they trust".[48] The abolition of legal tender initially generated anxiety, overwhelming people with different means to make everyday transactions. While foreign fiat currencies remained cheap and inflationary, the time-banking mercantilism promulgated by LETS became the most trusted form of currency, securing the wealth of regions. Mass generation of *virtus* through LETS rapidly established manorial economies characterised by highly localised neofeudal divisions of labour. The greater the number of manorial economies pursuing endogenous LETS there were, the more intra-national imbalances grew between autonomous merchant towns, further

---

[47] Commission was taken by virtual currency traders, who would take a cut of 3% per transaction in virtual currencies only, none of which was subject to taxation or to restrictions on the laundering of nationalised currencies.

[48] Frederich Hayek, *Choice in Currency: A Way to Stop Inflation* (London: Institute of Economic Affairs, 1976), 19.

eroding one-nation statehood. In place of the CW system arose a disintegrated patchwork of fiefdoms banking in time and, in many cases, attempting to provide their own forms of social assistance.

Since LETS was designed to restrict the transnational movement of capital, and since there were no trustworthy fiat currencies, virtual currencies became the primary means of deterritorialising capital. Those who resented the economic disparities and market restrictions of "village economics" sought an easy way out of LETS by participating in the transnational funny money markets. While LETS offered a steady route to community prosperity, virtual currencies promised something of the neoliberal era's unbounded wealth and mobility. For many, labouring locally in the LETS communities was far less enticing than minecrafting online.

The more reliant the world became on denationalised currencies, the more transnationals like the Willard Corporation became involved in leveraging global policy with its vast reserves of digital money and virtual estate. As non-state actors such as Willard began to monopolise offline transnational relations, the remaining large nation-states belatedly focused their attentions on the stewardship of on-line territories.[49] Bidding wars erupted between rival conglomerations of private and state operatives over the "aggregated symbolic constructs"[50] of virtual estate. Large corporations and state treasuries competed to exchange cheap fiat currencies for strong L$, hoping to make the L$ a likely candidate for a single global currency to efface the atomised LETS. Those nation-states still seeking to maintain their fiat currencies began to devote an increasing amount of federal investment in "online security", the development of virtual military strategy. The effect of this was to increase the value of online

---

[49] Some nation-states sought to legalise the booming trade between fiat and virtual currencies in a late effort to tax and control it. See Park Si-soo, "Ruling to Boost Sale of Cyber Money", *The Korea Times*, January 10, 2010.

[50] Chislenko and Ramakrishnan, "Hyper-Economy", 4.

territory creating the rapid expansion of burghs and a steep rise in the prices of virtual goods and services. Roleplaying online to minecraft indulgences for Sherlockers such as Willard, or as mercenaries acting on behalf of nation-states, became far more lucrative than working in the restricted local and national economies off-line. As a corollary of their wide adoption and growth among many who had hitherto never ventured online to roleplay, MMORPGs became increasingly closed worlds.

PART 6: BRANDEUM

Thorns whisper perfidious penance as bats unleash sanguine fangs. Foolish mortals secrete perfidious abattoirs as oblivion engulfs the spectral requiem. Darkness ascends silver deception while pyres collapse from Elysian arterial spray. Prayers unleash nocturnal torment and entangle our bloody souls.[51]

From careful analysis of his Wikipedia entry, we can see that Petrovksy's internship officially ended after eleven-and-a-half months, just before Willard would have been obliged to give him a permanent contract. To encourage his free&d, Willard started to pay Petrovsky in micro-payments of untaxable L$. As well as a loyalty reward, Sacamano gave Petrovksy a stake in the fabrication side of Willard: access to treatable code, but without files, only with the vendor's full permission, to whom Petrovsky was obliged to put permissions ("No Copy, No Transfer", as this licence was commonly known.) Without the exclusive templates for treatable relics and skins, Petrovsky was lucky to make a profit of more than 60.000L$ a month from relic-ing. Despite operating a developmental flatland, Sacamano still controlled the means of distribution, the context into which the virtual relics shipped. As such, Petrovksy and fellow relic-ers constantly risked being Sherlocked on any innovations they made. The pressing question for the budding entrepreneur was, how do you

---

[51] Petrovsky's draft for Brandeum's corporate vision.

make making make a living? This became the million linden dollar question that Petrovsky set out to answer in his MBA thesis "Transfiguration is Commonplace".

Encouraged by Sacamano, Petrovksy returned to *What Do Reliquaries Do for Relics?*, a classic MBA MOOC set text. Here, Hahn argued that medieval relics were

> considered part of the still-living world and thus able to reproduce themselves. They are able to do this in terms of contact relics—oil, perfume or cloths that are allowed to touch the body and gain a measure of sanctity—but they also "reproduce" more immediately. They make gifts of themselves."[52]

While virtual relics were designed to reproduce easily, they could not encounter the offline bodies of minecrafters. Petrovsky wrote:

> The "knowledge production" of the relic-object was, then, validated through the addition of a second material element—the reliquary. It is at this point of "enframement" that the relic would conjoin with its container. The reliquary comes to define the elevated relic by paradoxically masking (in precious materials) the very social relations that brought it (and continue to bring it) into being. In this sense it becomes the material body of the relic and by extension the body of the saint. In this sense the reliquary can be understood as compound object with the physically abhorrent matter inside (a piece of cloth, a bone, parchment or skin) retaining a base connection to the commonplace, making its objecthood secondary to the relational power now transmitted through the aesthetic encasement. This function is particularly apparent in reliquaries that conceal their contents (as opposed to a

---

[52] Cynthia Hahn, "What Do Reliquaries Do for Relics?" *Numen* 57.3 (2010): 295.

philatory which allow a partial view inside) and are never intended to be opened. Removing the core from the realm of the visual emphasises a sacral power not meant for human eyes.[53]

For Petrovsky, the difficulty with Willard's licensing model and over-reliance on Sherlocking remained that the ready accessibility of the relic's code could breed incredulity. The virtual relic, somehow, had to be concealed in a reliquary of its own. But how do you conceal and deny access to a relic that is fundamentally codified and infinitely reproducible? It was in thinking about the symbiotic relationship between the relic and reliquary that Petrovksy hit upon an idea of "Brandeum", a hybridised wearable computer technology that combined romanticised nostalgia for a tween cult with commercial bioinformatics.[54] Wearable Brandeum pendants would host the code of the most exclusive blue-chip virtual relics available, but would be unreadable and impenetrable. To attempt to open the pendant would result in destroying the host device and thus its code. To become part of the body of the gamer, the host device had to transubstantiate—it had to be a person-object in its own right. Petrovsky had the perfect wetware in mind.

As a ten-year-old, Petrovksy received a lapel sticker containing DNA extracted from the corpse of his dead grandmother. Such cheap pendants, pioneered by Cryostick, a team of entrepreneurs from Canada's *Dragon's Den*, were handed out like candy at major brand funeral homes, unwittingly spawning a craze among tweens. Kids were transfixed by the macabre cult of swap-meets that revolved around the cyrostickers. Seizing the opportunity, Cryostick had the bright idea of licensing the DNA of dead and living celebrities, transforming it into mass-produced stickers, and bun-

---

[53] Petrovsky, *Transfiguration is Commonplace.*
[54] The most valuable pendants were worn low around gamer's necks, hiding them from would-be thieves.

dling them with packets of potato chips. Although the tween cult lasted only just over a year, bankrupting Cryostick, a large number of adult collectors, notably the MMORPG demographic, ensured that the secondary and black markets remained very healthy for Cryostickers. Petrovksy, as we know, was one of the most avid collectors.

While Petrovksy free&ded for Willard, developments in bioinformatics had dramatically reduced the price of DNA writers, portable storage devices that could burn data onto strands of DNA. Ceasing the opportunity, Petrovksy used his meagre profits from Willard to trade in celebrity Cyrosticker DNA. Meanwhile, at Willard, he took the lead with his project: "Brandeum". The Brandeum cabal soon attracted a team of young interns who worked hard at costing and outsourcing the production of wearable relics to Chinese labour camps. Brandeum traded aggressively as a developer for minecrafters who wanted unique wearable computing. Within a month, Brandeum had launched a range of pendants and virtual reality goggles designed to host Willard's blue-chip relics.[55] As a collector himself, Petrovksy was perfectly placed to exploit the Cyrostickers nostalgia among minecrafters of his own age, creating miniature marvels hermetically-sealed in finest gadolinium. In a split-profit deal, Sacamano would sell Brandeum's products on HSN as talismans for devotees of Tribal Nations of The Scorpion, Protectorate of the Me-Machine Islands and Polare Directorate, offering his faithful congregation "automated semantic signalling, higher levels of complexity, efficiency and adaptability, global cognition and advanced system self-consciousness."

---

[55] On establishing the Brandeum cabal, Petrovksy was offered a paid position by Willard. Had he turned this offer down, would he have retained full control of the project's intellectual property?

REFERENCES

CHAPTER 1 — L'AMÉRIQUE SOUTERRAINE

[null]

CHAPTER 2 — IMPERIUM ET SACERDOTIUM

The New Middle Ages. TV series. United Kingdom: BBC 2, 1994.

Alsayyad, N. and A. Roy. "Medieval Modernity: On Citizenship and Urbanism in a Global Era". *Space & Polity* 10.1 (2006):1–20.

Anderson, J. "The Shifting Stage of Politics: New Medieval and Postmodern Territorialities?" *Environment and Planning D* 14 (1996):133–154.

Berzins, C. and P. Cullen. "Terrorism and Neo-Medievalism". In N. Winn, ed., *Neo-medievalism and Civil Wars*. London: Routledge, 2004.

Bull, H. *The Anarchical Society: A Study of Order in World Politics*. London: Macmillan, 1977.

Buzan, B. "From International System to International Society: Structural Realism and Regime Theory Meet the English School". *International Organization* 47.3 (1993): 327–352.

Castells, M. *The Rise of the Network Society*. Vol. I of *The Information Age: Economy, Society and Culture*. Massachusetts: Blackwell Publishing, 1996.

Cerny, P.G. "The New Security Dilemma Revisited: Neomedievalism and the Limits of Hegemony". Paper presented at International Studies Association conference, March 18-21, Montréal, Québec, 2004.

Deets, S. "The Hungarian Status Law and the Specter of Neo-Medievalism in Europe". Paper presented at International Studies Association conference, March 18-21, Montréal, Québec, 2004.

Dror, Y. *Crazy States: A Counterconventional Strategic Problem*. London: Heath/Lexington Books, 1971.

Editorial. "Marois Should Have Known Scottish Trip Would Flop". *Montreal Gazette*, January 30, 2013.

Falk, R. "State of Siege: Will Globalization Win Out?" *International Affairs* (Royal Institute of International Affairs 1944-) 73.1 (1997): 123–136.

Friedrichs, J. "The Meaning of New Medievalism". *European Journal of International Relations* 74.4 (2001): 475–501.

Hassner, P. *Violence and Peace: From the Atomic Bomb to Ethnic Cleansing*. Budapest: Central European University Press, 1997.

Hobbes, T. *Leviathan: Or the Matter, Forme, and Power of a Commonwealth Ecclesiasticall and Civil*, ed. M. Oakeshott. New York: Simon and Schuster; 2008.

Holsinger, B.W. "Medieval Studies, Postcolonial Studies, and the Genealogies of Critique." *Speculum* 77.4 (2002): 1195–1227.

Holsinger, B.W. *Neomedievalism, Neoconservatism, and the War on Terror*. Chicago: Prickly Paradigm Press, 2007.

Holsinger, B.W. "Empire, Apocalypse, and the 9/11 Premodern". *Critical Inquiry* 34.3 (2008): 468–490.

Holsinger, B.W. "Medievalization Theory: From Tocqueville to the Cold War". *American Literary History* 22.4 (2010): 893–912.

Huntington, S.P. *The Clash of Civilizations and the Remaking of World Order*. New York: Simón & Schuster, 1996.

Kaplan, R.D. "The Coming Anarchy". *The Atlantic* 273.2 (1994): 44–76.

Kobrin, S.J. "Back to the Future: Neomedievalism and the Postmodern Digital World Economy". *Journal of International Affairs* 51 (Spring 1998): 361–386.

Linklater, A. *Critical Theory and World Politics: Citizenship, Sovereignty and Humanity*. New York: Routledge, 2007.

Matthews, D. "From Mediaeval to Mediaevalism: A New Semantic History". *The Review of English Studies* 62.257 (2011): 695–715.

Mikkeli, H. *Europe As an Idea and an Identity*. Basingstoke: Palgrave Macmillan, 1998.

Morgenthau, H.J. *Politics Among Nations: The Struggle for Power and Peace*. New York: Alfred A. Knopf, 1948.

Rapley, J. "From Neo-Liberalism to the New Medievalism: Globalisation and Governance in the Pacific Islands". Keynote address presented at "Globalisation and Governance in the Pacific Islands" conference, Australian National University, Canberra, Australia, 2006. Available online: epress.anu.edu.au.

Rapley, J. "The New Middle Ages". *Foreign Affairs* 85.3 (2006): 95–103.

Ruggie, J.G. "Territoriality and Beyond: Problematizing Modernity in International Relations". *International Organization* 47.1 (1993): 139–174.

Schrodt, P.A. "Neomedievalism in the Twenty-first Century: Warlords, Gangs and Transnational Militarized Actors as a Challenge to Sovereign Preeminence". Paper presented at International Studies Association conference, New Orleans, Louisiana, February 17-20, 2010.

Simmons, C.A. "Medievalism: Its Linguistic History of Nineteenth Century Britain". *Defining Medievalism: Studies in Medievalism* 17.21 (2009): 21–35.

Strayer, J.R. *On the Medieval Origins of the Modern State*. Princeton: Princeton University Press, 1970.

Strayer J.R. and D.C. Munro, eds. *The Middle Ages, 395-1500*. New York: Appleton-Century-Crofts, 1959.

Vacca, R. *The Coming Dark Age*. Granada: Frogmore, 1974.

Van Creveld, M. *Technology and War: From 2000 B.C. to the Present*. New York: Touchstone, 2010.

Williams, P. "From the New Middle Ages to a New Dark Age: The Decline of the State and U.S. Strategy". Strategic Studies Institute, U.S. Army War College, 2008.

Wolfers, A. *Discord and Collaboration: Essays on International Politics*. Baltimore: Johns Hopkins University Press, 1962.

CHAPTER 3 — THE JOURNEYMAN'S GUIDE TO ANCHORITISM

Agamben, G. *Stanzas: Word and Phantasm in Western Culture*, trans. R.L. Martinez. Minneapolis: University of Minnesota Press, 1993.

Badmington, N. "Theorizing Posthumanism". *Cultural Critique* 53 (2003): 10–27.

Bennett, J. *The Enchantment of Modern Life: Attachments, Crossings, Ethics*. Princeton: Princeton University Press, 2001.

References

Bogost, I. *Alien Phenomenology, or What It's Like to Be a Thing*. Minneapolis: University of Minnesota Press, 2012.

Bourriaud, N. *The Radicant*. New York: Lukas & Sternberg, 2009.

Bryant, L. "Object-Oriented Ontology: A Manifesto," *Larval Subjects* [weblog], January 2, 2010: http://larvalsubjects.wordpress.com/2010/01/12/object-oriented-ontology-a-manifesto-part-i/.

Bryant, L. *The Democracy of Objects*. Ann Arbor: Open Humanities Press/MPublishing, 2011.

Bryant, L, G. Harman, and N. Srnicek. *The Speculative Turn: Continental Materialism and Realism*. Melbourne: re.press, 2011.

Bynum, C.W. "AHA Presidential Address: Wonder". January 13, 1996. Available online: http://www.historians.org/about-aha-and-membership/aha-history-and-archives/presidential-addresses/caroline-walker-bynum.

Cascio, J. "The Rise of the Participatory Panopticon". *World Changing*, 2005. Available online: http://www.worldchanging.com/archives/002651.html.

Cohen, J.J. "A Door Into Stone". *In the Middle* [weblog], February 27, 2013: http://www.inthemedievalmiddle.com/2013/02/a-door-into-stone.html.

de Certeau, M. *The Practice of Everyday Life*, trans. S. Rendall. Berkeley: University of California Press, 2011.

Deleuze, G. and F. Guattari. *What is Philosophy?*, trans. G. Burchell and H. Tomlinson. New York: Columbia University Press, 1994.

Deleuze, G. and F. Guattari. *A Thousand Plateaus: Capitalism and Schizophrenia*, trans. B. Massumi. New York: Continuum International Publishing Group, 2004.

Dionne, C. and E.A. Joy, eds.. *When Did We Become Post/Human?* [special issue] *postmedieval: a journal of medieval cultural studies* 1.1/2 (2010).

Gambini, A. *Journey to the West* [undated]. Project Guthenberg: http://www.gutenberg.org.

Gillick, L. "The Good of Work". In J. Aranda, B.K. Wood, A. Vidokle, eds., *Are You Working Too Much? Post-fordism, Precarity, and the Labor of Art*, 60–73. Berlin: Sternberg Press; 2011.

Grayson, J. "The Eschatological Adam's Kirtle". *Mystics Quarterly* 11.4 (1985): 153–160.

Guattari, F. *Chaosmosis: An Ethico-aesthetic Paradigm*. Bloomington: Indiana University Press, 1995.

Haraway, D.J. *Simians, Cyborgs, and Women: The Reinvention of Nature*. New York: Routledge, 1991.

Haraway, D.J. *When Species Meet*. Minneapolis: University of Minnesota Press; 2007.

Harman, G. "On Vicarious Causation". *Collapse* II (2007): 187–221.

Harman, G. "On the Horror of Phenomenology: Lovecraft and Husserl". *Collapse* IV (2008): 333–364.

Harvey, D. "The Art of Rent: Globalisation, Monopoly and the Commodification of Culture". *Socialist Register 2002: A World of Contradictions* 38.38 (2009): 93–110.

Hasenfratz, R. "Introduction". In *Ancrene Wisse*, ed. R. Hasenfratz. Kalamazoo, MI: Medieval Institute Publications, 2000.

Hayles, N.K. *How We Became Posthuman: Virtual Bodies in Cybernetics, Literature, and Informatics.* Chicago: University of Chicago Press, 1999.

Holsinger, B.N. *The Premodern Condition: Medievalism and the Making of Theory.* Chicago: University of Chicago Press, 2005.

Jones, C.A. "The Server/User Mode: The Art of Olafur Eliasson". ARTFORUM 46.2 (2007): 316–325.

Latour, B. *We Have Never Been Modern*, trans. C. Porter. Cambridge, MA: Harvard University Press, 1993.

Latour, B. *Politics of Nature: How to Bring the Sciences into Democracy*, trans. C. Porter. Cambridge, MA: Harvard University Press, 2004.

MacKendrick, K. "The Multipliable Body". *postmedieval: a journal of medieval cultural studies* 1.1/2 (2010: 108–114.

Meillassoux, Q. *After Finitude: An Essay on the Necessity of Contingency*, trans. R. Brassier. London: Continuum, 2008.

Morton, T. *Realist Magic: Objects, Ontology, Causality.* Ann Arbor: Open Humanities Press.MPublishing, 2013. Available online: openhumanitiespress.org/realist-magic.html.

O'Sullivan, S. *Art Encounters Deleuze and Guattari: Thought Beyond Representation.* Basingstoke: Palgrave Macmillan, 2008.

Petropunk Collective [E.A. Joy, A. Kłosowska, N. Masciandaro, and M. O'Rourke], eds. *Speculative Medievalisms: Discography.* Brooklyn, NY: punctum books, 2013.

Rancière, J. "Our Police Order: What Can Be Said, Seen, and Done." *Eurozine*, August 11, 2006: http://www.eurozine.com/articles/2006-08-11-lieranciere-en.html.

Rancière, J. *Aesthetics and Its Discontents*, trans. S. Corcoran. Cambridge, UK: Polity, 2009.

Raymond, E.S. *The Cathedral & the Bazaar: Musings on Linux and Open Source by an Accidental Revolutionary.* Rev. edn. Sebastopol, CA: O'Reilly Media, 2008.

Sauer, M.M. "Representing the Negative: Positing the Lesbian Void in Medieval English Anchoritism". *thirdspace: a journal of femi-*

nist theory & culture 3.2 (2008): http://www.thirdspace.ca/jour nal/article/view/sauer/178.

Seaman, M.J. "Becoming More (than) Human: Affective Posthumanisms, Past and Future". *Journal of Narrative Theory* 37.2 (2007): 246–275.

Serres, M. *The Parasite*, trans. L. Schehr. Minneapolis: University of Minnesota Press, 2007.

Soper, K. "The postmedieval Project: Promise and Paradox". *postmedieval: a journal of medieval cultural studies* 1.1/2 (2010): 256–261.

Steyerl, H. "A Thing Like You and Me". *e-flux journal* 15 (2010): http://www.e-flux.com/journal/a-thing-like-you-and-me.

Virilio, P. *Art and Fear*, trans. J. Rose. London: Continuum, 2003.

Virno, P. *A Grammar of the Multitude: For an Analysis of Contemporary Forms of Life*, trans. I. Bertoletti, J. Cascaito, and A. Casson. New York: Semiotext(e), 2004.

White, H. *Ancrene Wisse: Guide for Anchoresses*. London: Penguin Books, 1993.

Woodard, B. "Mad Speculation and Absolute Inhumanism: Lovecraft, Ligotti, and the Weirding of Philosophy". *continent.* 1.1 (2010): 3–13.

Yates, J. "It's (for) You, or, The Tele-t/r/opical Post-Human". postmedieval: a journal of medieval cultural studies 1.1/2 (2010): 223–234.

Zittrain, J.L. *The Future of the Internet: And How to Stop It*. New Haven: Yale University Press, 2009.

Chapter 4 — xyzzy: Contemporary Art Before and After Britain

Buskirk, M. *Creative Enterprise: Contemporary Art between Museum and Marketplace*. New York: Continuum, 2012.

Eco, U. *Travels in Hyperreality*, trans. W. Weaver. London: Picador; 1987.

Emery, E. "Medievalism and the Middle Ages". *Studies in Medievalism XVII: Defining Medievalism(s)* (2009): 77–91.

Fradenburg, L.O. "So That We May Speak of Them: Enjoying the Middle Ages". *New Literary History* 28.2 (1997): 205–230.

Gregory, A. "Does Anyone Here Speak Art and Tech?" *The New York Times*, April 3, 2013 (Fashion & Style): http://www.ny times.com/2013/04/04/fashion/art-and-techology-a-clash-of-cultures. html.

Helguera, P. *Art Scenes: The Social Scripts of the Artworld*. New York: Jorge Pinto Books, 2012.

Hills, M. *Fan Cultures*. London: Routledge, 2002.

Kaufman, A.S. "Medieval Unmoored: Through a (Cracked) Glass, Darkly". *Studies in Medievalism XIX: Defining Neomedievalism(s)* (2010): 1–11.

Larsen, L.B. "The Long Nineties". *frieze*, Issue 144 (January-February 2012): 92–95.

Leadbeater, C. and P. Miller. *The Pro-Am Revolution: How Enthusiasts are Changing our Economy and Society*. London: Demos, 2004.

Normand, T. *The Modern Scot: Modernism and Nationalism in Scottish Art, 1928–1955*. Aldershot: Ashgate, 2000.

Plastique Fantastique. *What is a Pre-Industrial Modern? The Gawkin Must be Made!*: www.plastiquefantastique.org/performance02.html.

Sennett, R. *The Craftsman*. London: Penguin, 2008.

Soper, K. "The postmedieval Project: Promise and Paradox". *postmedieval: a journal of medieval cultural studies* 1.1/2 (2010): 256–261.

Toswell, M.J. "The Simulacrum of Neomedievalism". *Studies in Medievalism XIX: Defining Neomedievalism(s)* (2010): 44–57.

Woodward, D. "Reality, Symbolism, Time and Space in Medieval World Maps". *Annuals of the Association of America's Geographers* 75.4 (1985): 501–521.

CHAPTER 5 — WHEN TRANSFIGURATION BECAME COMMONPLACE

Abu-Lughod, J.L. *Before European Hegemony : The World System A.D. 1250-1350*. Oxford: Oxford University Press; 1989.

Anderson, C. *Free: The Future of a Radical Price*. New York: Hyperion, 2009.

Boerner, L. and O. Volckart. "The Utility of a Common Coinage: Currency Unions and the Integration of Money Markets in Late Medieval Central Europe". *Explorations in Economic History* 48.1 (2011): 53–65.

Cahir, J. "The Withering Away of Property: The Rise of the Internet Information Commons". Oxford Journal of Legal Studies 24.4 (2004): 619–641.

Chislenko, A. and M. Ramakrishnan. "Hyper-Economy: Combining Price and Utility Communication in Multi-Agent Systems". Paper presented at "ISAS '98: Intelligent Systems and Semiotics", IEEE International Symposium on Intelligent Control/Computational Intelligence in Robotics and Automation/Intelligent Systems and Semiotics, Gaithersburg, Maryland, 1998.

Crowe, B.L. "The Tragedy of the Commons Revisited". *Science* 166.3909 (1969): 1103–1107.

Curta, F. "Merovingian and Carolingian Gift Giving". *Speculum* 81 (2006): 671–699.

Dietz, T., E. Ostrom, and P.C. Stern. "The Struggle to Govern the Commons". *Science* 302.5652 (2003): 1907–1912.

Friedrichs, J. "The Meaning of New Medievalism". *European Journal of International Relations* 7.4 (2001): 475–502.

Geary, P. "Sacred Commodities: The Circulation of Medieval Relics". In A. Appadurai, ed., *The Social Life of Things : Commodities in Cultural Perspective*, 169–191. Cambridge, UK: Cambridge University Press, 1986.

Gell, A. "The Technology of Enchantment and the Enchantment of Technology". In J. Coote and A. Shelton, eds., *Anthropology, Art and Aesthetics*, 40–66. Oxford: Clarendon, 1992.

Goldman, M. "*Customs in Common*: The Epistemic World of the Commons Scholars". *Theory and Society* 26.1 (1997): 1-37.

Graeber, D. "The Anthropology of Globalization (With Notes on Neomedievalism, and the End of the Chinese Model of the Nation-State)". *American Anthropologist* 104.4 (2002):1222–1227.

Hahn, C. "What Do Reliquaries Do for Relics?" *Numen* 57.3 (2010): 284–316.

Hardin, G. "The Tragedy of the Commons". *Science* 162.3859 (1968): 1243–1248.

Hayek, F. *Choice in Currency: A Way to Stop Inflation*. London: Institute of Economic Affairs, 1976.

Hicks, J. "Virtual Currency Exchange". *What MMORPG?* June 6, 2011: www.whatmmorpg.com/articles/virtual-currency-exchange.php.

Kurzweil, R. *The Singularity Is Near: When Humans Transcend Biology*. New York: Viking Penguin, 2005.

Micklethwait, J. and A. Wooldridge. *The Witch Doctors: What the Management Gurus are Saying, Why it Matters and How to Make Sense of It*. London: Mandarin, 1997.

Petrovsky, A. *Transfiguration is Commonplace*. Les Cours Mont-Royal: University of the Mall of America Online.

Pine, J. and J. Gilmore. *The Experience Economy*. Boston: Harvard Business School Press, 1999.

Richardson, G. "The Prudent Village: Risk Pooling Institutions in Medieval English Agriculture". *The Journal of Economic History* 65.2 (2005): 386–413.

Richardson, H.G. "The Commons and Medieval Politics". *Transactions of the Royal Historical Society* 28 (1946): 21–45.

Schmitt, J.-C. "Appropriating the Future". In J.A. Burrow and I.P. Wei, eds., *Medieval Futures: Attitudes to the Future in the Middle Ages*, 3–18. Woodbridge: Boydell Press, 2000.

Schulze, G. *Erlebnisgesellschaft: Kultursoziologie der Gegenwart.* Frankfurt: Campus Verlag, 1992.

Si-soo, P. "Ruling to Boost Sale of Cyber Money". *The Korea Times*, October 1, 2010.

Stern, E. "A Touch of Medieval: Narrative, Magic and Computer Technology in Massively Multiplayer Computer Role-Playing Games". In F. Mäyrä, ed., *Computer Games and Digital Cultures Conference Proceedings*. Tampere, Finland: Tampere University Press, 2002.

Toffler, A. *The Third Wave.* London: Collins, 1980.

VALVE. *Valve Handbook for New Employees.* Seattle, Washington: VALVE, 2012.

Verduin, K. "The Founding and the Founder: Medievalism and the Legacy of Leslie J. Workman". *Studies in Medievalism XVII: Defining Medievalism(s)* (2009): 1–27.

Wenger, E. *Communities of Practice: Learning, Meaning, and Identity.* Cambridge, UK: Cambridge University Press; 1998.

Sergeant-at-Law, Norman James Hogg is an artist, writer, and curator. He holds a BA in Sculpture and an MFA in Visual Culture from Edinburgh College of Art, plus an MA in Combined Media from Chelsea College of Art, London. He has been selected for both New Work UK (1999) and New Work Scotland (2010) and from 2008 to 2009 was a Director of the Embassy gallery in Edinburgh, Scotland. He is currently a PhD candidate at Concordia University in Montréal, Québec where he investigates ne-omedievalism with a particular focus on neomedieval aesthetics. In 2013 he was awarded a Joseph-Armand Bombardier CGS Doctoral Scholarship. His time is now spent entombed in his basement anchorhold in downtown Montréal, spilling strong wine over unreadable codexes while completing infinite power cycles on a Bowflex Revolution® Home Gym. (www.normanhogg.co.uk)

Keeper of the Wardrobe, Neil Mulholland writes about and produces contemporary art. He works collaboratively, using avatars that have interpretive flexibility. Currently, in addition to fulfilling his duties within the Confraternity of Neoflagellants, he is developing workshop models of artistic learning in participatory settings as Shift/Work. Neil is Professor of Contemporary Art Practice & Theory at The University of Edinburgh and Director of the MFA, Edinburgh College of Art, Scotland. His anchorhold is constructed from sandstone and has a bitumen floor and an ethernet port. (www.neilmulholland.co.uk)